BLACK MAGIC WOMEN:

TERRIFYING TALES BY SCARY SISTERS

MOCHA MEMOIRS PRESS

Offering New Flavors in Fiction

EDITED AND CURATED BY SUMIKO
SAULSON

MOCHA MEMOIRS
PRESS

Offering New Flavors in Fiction

Winston-Salem, North Carolina

Copyright Notice

Editor: Sumiko Saulson

Proofreader: Jessica Glanville

Cover Art: Sumiko Saulson

Published by Mocha Memoirs Press, LLC

OTHER MOCHA MEMOIRS PRESS TITLES CELEBRATING WOMEN IN HORROR MONTH®

Mocha's Dark Brew: Flash Fiction by Women in Horror

The Grotesquerie

TABLE OF CONTENTS

FOREWORD

SPEAKING WITH OUR OWN VOICES

A foreword to Black Magic Women
By Sumiko Saulson

"Saulson has collected magic in ways that hypnotize, entertain and make the reader shudder. In these stories desire and greed are answered with magical justice and getting what is wished for comes with ultimate, soul level prices. Walk with these women, through fables of magic, spells, werewolves, cursed days & nights and be prepared to be entertained and shook to your core."

—*Linda D. Addison, award-winning author of "How to Recognize a Demon Has Become Your Friend"*

I've been a horror fan as long as I can remember. I grew up in the seventies, before people decided it was important to protect children from skinned knees, bruised heads and horror movies. As a child, my parents took me and my brother to drive-in movies like *Its Alive*, *The Omen*, and *The Exorcist*. I still remember being five years old, playing on the slides and swings with my four year old brother, and watching cartoons like *Heckle and Jeckle* or *Woody Woodpecker*. We knew that once the cartoons were over, we were supposed to leave the playground and return to the car. We weren't afraid of being kidnapped, and we didn't know that some people thought *Heckle and Jeckle* were probably racist and based on minstrel stereotyped jive-talking crows in *Dumbo*.

We also didn't notice that none of the people in our favorite horror movies were black. See, the eighties trope where the black guy dies first hadn't started, and there were no black people to speak of in *Carrie*, *The Hills Have Eyes*, and *Jaws*. It wasn't until 1976's *Dawn of the Dead* that I saw a movie with a major black character in it. And he was the hero!

> *"In the 21th century there are very still few characters like us, and out of this small pool many are post-modern "Step-and Fetchit" stereotypes. This is why speculative fiction is so important. This genre helps us to see outside reality, to say: what if? It helps us to imagine and create spectacular, wondrous realms, step back and find the beauty and wisdom there, and then transform our own space."*
> — *Valjeanne Je￿ers, author of the short story* The Lost Ones.

Like Valjeanne, I have noticed a dearth of African Diaspora characters in fiction. Where they are present, they are relegated to support or background roles. I believe it is important for the self-esteem of a people to be able to envision ourselves as heroes. That means that we should be able to read stories and watch movies where there are heroes who look like we do. We shouldn't be brainwashed into viewing ourselves as less than central in our lives.

Nowadays, it's not as bad as it used to be. We see characters like Michonne on *The Walking Dead*, Bonnie Bennet on *The Vampire Diaries*, or Jenny and Abbie Mills on *Sleepy Hollow*, and feel encouraged that black people in general, and black women in particular, can be viewed as powerful, vital, and heroic. But the killing o☐ of first Abbie, then Jenny Mills, and subsequent cancellation of *Sleepy Hollow* tell a darker tale; people aren't ready for black women to be front and center. Even the creation of Richonne, the Rick and Michonne power couple on *The Walking Dead*, shows that people need a black woman to be clearly secondary to a white, male protagonist in order to be strong, or continue to live. Never mind the series of replaceable black men: T-Dog, Tyreese, Bob, Noah... and that other guy who was on there so briefly I almost didn't register that he wasn't T-Dog.

That's where projects like *Black Magic Women* come in.

"It's always an honor to be included in a project like Black Magic Women. Most of us are in our own corner, writing and promoting, so this project gives us a chance to catch up on each other."
— *Return to Me author Lori Titus.*

I was inspired by older anthologies like the *Dark Matter* series, edited by Sheree Renée Thomas. It debuted July 18, 2000 with *Dark Matter: A Century of Speculative Fiction from the African Diaspora*. When I put together a blog series on black women who write horror in honor of Black History Month and Women in Horror Month back in 2013, I had to do a lot of research to come up with my first three lists that year. The lists, and the interviews with black women in horror that were a part of that blog series, were eventually published in 2014 as the book *60 Black Women in Horror*.

When I first put together *60 Black Women in Horror*, a few

women asked if they could add stories to the end of the eBook. That's how I ended up with short stories by myself, Crystal Connor, Valjeanne Je[]ers and Annie Penn at the back of the eBook. They weren't in the print edition. So, when I started to work on *100 Black Women in Horror*, an update to the original book with over 100 biographies and more than 20 interviews, I decided that rather than toss a few stories in the reference guide, I should put together a separate anthology of horror stories written by women listed in the guide. I was thrilled when Nicole Kurtz from Mocha Memoirs Press expressed interest in the anthology, *Black Magic Women*.

> "*Black Woman Magic is the natural spiritual root for our ancestral legacy in life. It is protection, warrior work, praise/worship, love or it is root-work meant to hex those who harm, cause mischief or to even bring about life lessons and mores. Black Magic Woman is badassness others want.*"
> —*Kai Leakes, author of the short story Sisters.*

But this anthology doesn't only consist of badass women. It is a collection of horror tales where blackness is up front and center, and a black woman is always a significant player, even in stories like Delizhia Jenkins' *Dark Moon's Curse*, Valjeanne Je[]ers' *The Lost Ones* and Kenesha Williams *Sweet Justice, and* Cinsearae S's *Killer Queen,* where the protagonist is male. The women may be sensitive souls, like preteen title character in Kamika Aziza's zombie apocalyptic slice of life *Trisha and Peter*, thoughtful and introspective, like the witch in Lori Titus' *Return to Me*, or idealistic justice seekers like Kai Leakes' *Sisters* and the circle of friends in Dicey Grenor's *Black and Deadly*.

"In a world where Black Women are portrayed to either be mammies, angry, or sassy, I'm so happy for a project like Black Magic Women where we get to be the heroes and maybe even the villains. So many times, because of our lack of portrayal in the media, it seems as if all Black Women characters must be paragons of virtue lest we "shame the community". Embracing both sides of someone's humanity, the good and the bad, is to allow them to be fully human. We shouldn't have to be one end of the spectrum or the other, like all people, we are varying shades of gray and I think this anthology will show that."
—*Kenesha Williams, author of Sweet Justice.*

Of course, a well-rounded book of black women contains characters that are not necessarily good. Morally ambiguous creatures haunt stories like Mina Polina's *Appreciation*, Nuzo Onoh's *Death Lines*, Nicole Givens Kurtz's *Blood Magnolia*, Crystal Connor's *Bryannah and the Magic Negro* and my own *Tango of a Telltale Heart*. You have to read the whole story to figure out if they are heroes, villains, or something in between. In some cases, even after you're done you aren't entirely sure.

Some of these stories fit into the ancient and honorable horror tradition of the cautionary tale. What would it mean to have had a black scream queen in movies like *Halloween, Friday the 13th,* or *Nightmare on Elm Street*? The hopeless romantics, hapless nice girls, clueless ingénues, and ordinary janes in Tabitha Thompson's *Alternative™* , Alledria Hurt's *The Prizewinner*, R. J. Joseph's *Left Hand Torment*, Kenya Moss-Dyme's *Labor Pains,* and L.H, Moore's *Here, Kitty!* face extraordinary situations. Will they make it out alive?

"Black women have always been magical. It's our tradition, our heritage. It's in our blood. A part of that tradition is a belief in the

fantastic and supernatural. And yes, we do write and enjoy horror. Don't let anyone tell you otherwise."
    —LH Moore, author of *Here, Kitty!*

The first time I walked into a book store – Marcus Bookstore, a historical black bookstore in San Francisco – the proprietor expressed shock and awe at the idea of a black person writing horror. The closest thing she'd ever heard of was sci-fi writer Octavia Butler, and wanted to know if that's what my stories were like. So I started to research horror by black authors, to see where I fit in, in this wild world of unknown and potentially amazing stories by black women, on the edge of this new frontier.

Why have there been so few documented black women horror writers up until now? Part of it, I think, has to do with respectability politics. Black writers of any gender are told we should write literary fiction, be serious, and not involve ourselves in trash genres like horror. To this day, I am invited to speak at speculative fiction conventions and on panels where they start right out insulting my genre. They act like calling *Beloved* a ghost story is paramount to calling Toni Morrison a dirty name. That being the attitude of a lot of authors and academics many scribes are loath to admit to writing horror, even if they do.

The other factor is the tendency to view horror as a male thing. If a woman, say L.A. Banks, writes a series called *The Vampire Huntress Legends* about a bad ass slayer of demons and vampires, her hero, Damali, is in a paranormal romance. Conversely, if two white dudes, Sam and Dean Winchester do the same thing, they are in a horror series called *Supernatural*. This is not limited to black women: *Buffy and the Vampire Slayer*, *The Medium*, *Charmed*, and *The Ghost Whisperer* aren't really horror, because they center around girls and girly stuﬀ like marriage, children and romance. So people tend to categorize our stories as something other than horror; urban fiction, paranormal romance, supernatural, or even magical realism, because girls don't do horror, therefore it cannot be horror and must be something else.

That's why projects like *Black Magic Women* and *100 Black Women in Horror* are so important.

BRYANNAH AND THE MAGIC NEGRO

CRYSTAL CONNOR

The Gift

B☐☐☐☐☐☐☐ ☐☐☐☐ ☐☐☐ ☐☐ ☐☐☐ ☐☐☐☐☐☐ ☐☐ ☐☐☐ ☐☐☐☐ her grandmother had given her. The hunched over creature was wearing a red and white striped baseball cap, white pants, a white shirt, and a red vest. A yellow handkerchief was fashioned about his neck.

It was supposed to be a man, except...

He had extra black glossy skin, big white eyes with tiny black pupils. He had large red lips, a large flat gorilla nose, and nappy hair.

Most black people considered Jocko, the black lawn jockey, to be offensive. Bryannah was still too young to realize that all that it took for adults to judge and be suspicious of each other was simply the tone of a person's skin. But she was old enough to know that the doll she had been given was somehow wrong.

Bryannah had never seen a black person who looked like

this. She thought it was revolting, and she started to cry. She wasn't crying because of the monster she held in her small hands, but because she was afraid that her favorite grandmother, her Na-Na, had gone crazy.

"Now? Why you crying fo chile?" her grandmother asked her. "Jocko ain't nothin' to cry 'bout. This right here," Na-Na explained while tapping Jocko's forehead, "is a Magic Negro."

Well, that certainly stopped the tears.

"Magic?" she whispered. "What kind of magic?"

"Anykina magic you want."

Bryannah looked again at the figurine. It wasn't the standard size of jockey that one would expect see on display in the front yards of people's homes. Bryannah's jockey was just a few inches taller than a Barbie doll, but Jocko's clothes were unchangeable, and his limbs didn't move.

"Now listen to me *real* good gurl. You listenin'?" Bryannah nodded her head that she was. "You bes' be real careful, and I mean *real careful*, what it is you be wishin' fo now."

———

"Y□□□ □ □□ □ □□ □ □□□ □□□ □ □□□□□ D□□ □□□ □□□ that trilogy of terror doll she gave Bryannah?"

Derek was so caught o□ guard by Olivia's comment that he spit Scope all over the mirror. The bathroom was filled with laughter.

"I'm surprised that you held your cool when Bre started crying."

"Yeah, I'm pretty proud of myself, too. I so hate those vile, blackface minstrel show Aunt Jemima dolls. Why do people collect them? It just drives me mad."

"People collect them so that they can give them to their

six-year-old granddaughters for their birthdays." Olivia's laugh was boisterous. She shrugged her shoulder.

"I think I was okay with it because your mom didn't do anything wrong really. The only reason Bre started crying was because she was confused. She's not stupid; somewhere deep down she knew that doll was supposed to be a black man. I bet you anything the first man she compared that doll to was you, and then my brothers. It's a hurtful representation, of course she would cry. I thought your mom handled it well.

"Besides, it's better if her first exposures to such hatred and bigotry are introduced to her here at home, by the people she loves the most and who know firsthand what it's like. God, could you imagine if she had seen something like for the first time at school?"

"She didn't Liv, she saw it at home."

———

B□□□□□ □□ □□□ J□□□□ □□□□ □□ □□□ □□□□□□□ □□□ went into her bathroom to wash her face, brush her teeth, and change into her pajamas. When she came out of the bathroom she saw the doll standing on the dresser.

The little girl tilted her head in bewilderment. She walked to the dresser, picked him up, and spoke to him. "You have to follow the rules; its bedtime now. Well it's almost bedtime. I get to have a snack first, but then we have to go to sleep."

Bryannah laid the doll down on the dresser and covered him up so that he would be nice and warm. Once Jocko and the rest of her dolls were tucked in and settled down for bed, Bre put on her robe and skipped o□ to the kitchen for her snack.

When she got back to her bedroom, she saw the doll

standing on the dresser. With an indignant hu☐ Bryannah planted both her hands firmly on her hips. "What did I tell you?" She demanded of the Magic Negro. She wasn't answered.

Bryannah tried being reasonable. It was his first night in a new home with a bunch of other dolls he didn't know. Maybe he was just scared. Bryannah found a long shallow oblong box and lined it with little blankets and a tiny flu☐y pillow. She took two books from the large dollhouse and put them in the box so that he would have something to read before he fell asleep.

She gently placed him in bed and tucked him in. She put his bed on her nightstand so he would be close to her and would feel safe. As she climbed into bed, she began making mental plans for a tea party where formal introductions could be made. Bre was confident that by the end of the week her newest doll would feel right at home.

"Hey peanut, how's he doing?" her mom asked her as she sat on the edge of the bed. This was the first time that she had seen a doll "sleeping" on Bryannah's nightstand.

"He's a little scared 'cus he doesn't know anybody. I'm gonna have a tea party so he can make new friends."

"What a thoughtful idea," Olivia agreed as she made some adjustments to the tiny blankets. After a few more moments of idle chitchat, Olivia turned o☐ the bedside lamp and left the door cracked.

When Bryannah woke up the next morning, Jocko the Magic Negro was standing on the nightstand.

Fear

S☐☐ ☐☐☐☐☐ ☐☐ ☐☐☐☐☐☐☐☐ ☐☐☐ ☐☐☐☐ ☐☐☐ ☐☐ ☐☐☐☐ enlightened. There were some accounts that Jocko had heroic origins based on the life of a young boy named Jocko Graves.

Graves served with General George Washington, but the general felt the boy was too young to fight in the surprise attack against Trenton, New Jersey. So he left him on the Pennsylvania side to tend to the horses and keep a fire lit. That way the general and his troops would be able to find their way back home.

The story goes that Jocko was so faithful to his post he froze to death during the night with the raised lantern still clutched in his hand. The story also explained that the correct title for the original commissioned memorial statue of Jocko placed on the grounds of President George Washington's Mount Vernon estate was not "lawn jockey" but "The Faithful Groomsman."

Another tale stated that during the time of the Underground Railroad, Jocko helped guide fleeing Blacks to freedom. According to that legend, if there was a green ribbon wrapped around Jocko's arms the escapees knew that they would have temporary safe harbor. But if he clutched a red ribbon, the escaped would know to keep running.

Though these stories were a fascinating part of her own personal heritage, this was not the information that Bryannah sought.

As it turned out, her late Na-Na had been crazy after all. Jocko was indeed enchanted, and the magic he possessed was black.

At twelve Bryannah was highly intelligent, enjoying a private education, and had dreams of joining her fathers' alumni from North Carolina Central University. But because she was so distracted by math and this year's science fair project, she had yet to dine on the fine delicacies of global fiction. If she had, she might have known that the information she was so desperately looking for had been told in 1902 by an Englishman by the name of William Wymark Jacobs.

———

W☐☐☐ ☐☐☐ A☐☐☐ J☐☐☐☐☐☐☐☐ ☐☐☐☐☐ ☐☐☐ ☐☐☐ bedroom without knocking, Bryannah instantly flooded her mind with everything that was good in the world: red balloons, cupcakes, glitter, a hug from her mom, pancakes, butterflies, nail polish, lip gloss, bubble baths, kittens, raspberries, red Kool-Aid, her little brother...

She thought her aunt was the most hateful woman in the world, and she could barely stand the sight of her mother's sister. She pushed past the woman and left the room while thinking about ice cream, because Na-Na, God rest her soul, had warned her to be careful.

It took her awhile, but eventually Bre had come to realize why that advice had been given. Jocko was ill tempered, easily provoked, and *always* overreacted.

By the time she had realized what Jocko was truly capable of and remembered the warning issued by her Na-Na, things had already started to get out of control.

———

T☐☐ ☐☐☐☐☐☐ ☐☐☐☐☐ ☐☐☐ ☐ ☐☐☐☐ ☐☐☐☐☐ A☐☐☐ Margaret who spent more time competing in state pageants than at school. She thought she was better than everyone else because her daddy was rich, but that didn't make any sense to

Bryannah, because everyone's daddy was rich; otherwise they wouldn't have been attending this school.

Unfortunately, living in Alabama, Olivia was unable to shield her children from racial bigotry. Unfortunately for Anna Margaret, Bryannah had a sharp tongue, no impulse control, and ...a Magic Negro.

Bryannah had been sitting under the shade tree reading a book when Anna Margaret and her disciples approached. Anna Margaret had snatched away the book; Bryannah had bolted to her feet.

"Well, this looks entertaining. If you don't mind, I'll think I'll read it."

"No, actually you're going to give it *back* to me; you had no right to take it in the first place. And what are you doing here? Shouldn't you be in the bathroom putting on makeup? It's not like you know what to do with a book anyway. You're holding it upside down." Anna Margaret had begun to tremble as someone in her entourage giggled; the book was thrown to the ground. Anna Margaret would permit no one to speak to her in that manner.

"See, my daddy says that's the problem with you uppity niggers; you're always demanding your rights." Bryannah's sigh was exaggerated; she rolled her eyes and shook her head.

"Oh, Margaret," Bryannah started.

"Its *Anna* Margaret!"

"Margaret." The level of condescension in Bryannah's voice infuriated the pageant princess and, for a moment, it looked as if she'd forgotten how to breathe. "If it's your intention to insult someone, you might want to at least use the correct pronunciation.

"I hope the next time you say that word you choke to death on it."

Anna Margaret was so dismayed that Bryannah had actually walked away from her and turned her back to her, the veins in her neck turned blue.

"Where are you going, nigger, to call the ACLU?"

"If you take that book to Miss April in the library, I'm sure she could find an audio version for you. If you don't know where the library is, just ask one of your friends."

Bryannah didn't even give Anna Margaret the courtesy of a glance over her shoulder. She insulted her as she was walked away from her. Anna Margaret meant to throw the book at her adversary, but when she bent to seize the book from the ground a bumblebee flew into her mouth and got stuck in her throat.

Six weeks later at the funeral, family members were still struggling to come to terms with how a child who had been stung countless times before while picking flowers and fruit in her mother's champion garden could suddenly become fatally allergic to honeybees.

Bryannah hadn't been particularity upset over the death of Anna Margaret; she was, however, devastated by the other calamities that had been unintentionally caused by her brashness. Since the death of her schoolmate, Bryannah did what she could to watch her mouth.

Experimentation

A☐☐☐☐ ☐☐☐☐☐☐☐☐☐☐ ☐☐ ☐☐☐☐☐ ☐☐ ☐☐☐☐☐☐☐☐☐☐ the only logical conclusion for a twelve-year-old girl who possessed the power of the cosmos was to use that power for good.

Her father was under a great deal of stress as of late.

Despite the glaring evidence in their favor and the constitutional precedents, her father and his legal team feared a loss due to seditious judicial lawlessness.

Bryannah presented the problem to the talisman. The judge hearing her father's case suffered a heart attack that killed him. The adjudicator who replaced the dead justice upheld the law, and her father's case was won. "Well, that wasn't too bad," Bryannah told herself, justifying the death. "He was already old and most likely would have died soon anyway."

The next good deed that was performed was done for Caydon. Her little brother was competing for the lead pitcher position and hoping to become team captain. The other boy with the same aspirations fell from a tree, breaking his arm below the elbow. It was a clean break, and the doctor promised a speedy recovery and said that his baseball career wasn't in jeopardy. Now that was something Bryannah could live with.

What happened next was a complete disaster.

———

H██ ████ █████ B████ ███ (█ ███ ██ ███ █ ███ was a natural blonde), was the new Miss Junior Alabama. She was also a cheerleader, and not only that, a hopeful for the US Olympic gymnastics team. She called, ecstatic, to tell Bryannah that her team would be competing at cheerleading nationals … at Disneyland! In Florida! The excitement was contagious, and Bryannah ended the phone call with the encouraging term "break a leg." And in just two days, that's exactly what happened.

"You stupid fucking bastard!"

Bryannah threw the phone on the floor, and it shattered into six pieces as it slammed against the cool tile floor. She stormed upstairs and slammed her bedroom door; the chandelier in the sitting room gently swayed in response to the force.

Olivia left the ladies attending the luncheon to interrogate the housekeeper.

"Who was on the phone?" Poor Maria backed against the sink. She had no idea.

Unfortunately, Barbara Ann did know. She picked up her handbag and excused herself, explaining that her daughter had tripped in front of the ice cream parlor and broken her leg. Caroline called her firm and began barking orders in preparation for suing Debra's Frozen Treats ice cream parlor, or the city, possibly both. As valets retrieved cars, Olivia excused herself to check on her daughter.

A statement issued in a moment of unreasonable juvenile anger caused a death.

———

B▯▯▯▯▯▯▯ ▯▯▯ ▯▯▯ ▯▯▯▯▯▯ ▯▯▯▯▯ ▯▯▯ ▯▯▯ shopping in town and were leaving a boutique with arms full of bags, and a man who was checking email on his phone didn't see them. He crashed into Olivia, and as she fell to the ground, he told her that she should watch where she was going.

"It would be nice to watch you die."

"Bre!" Olivia's assistant helped her from the ground, and had to be stopped from charging after him. He picked up bags while glaring at the man, who was almost a block away. The man didn't hear what Bryannah had said, but Jocko the Magic

Negro, who was miles away standing on his mistresses' night-stand, had.

When the green minivan stopped at the light, the golden retriever leapt from the window and attacked. The assault lasted almost twenty minutes, ending only because the police shot the dog.

Bryannah cried for the same reason the pretty redheaded boy in the van was crying ...for the dog.

From that moment on, she did more than just try to watch her mouth; she mentally scrutinized everything she wanted to say before she said it, methodically constructing each sentence the way each of the forty-seven scholars must have done when commissioned by King James.

For months, Bryannah had controlled her temper and held her tongue. Those who had grown accustomed to the bombardment of venom-laced words began to miss them. Prefer them really, over the deadly looks that could kill, coupled with a secretive knowing smile.

For months everything was fine until Jocko the Magic Negro started cheating ... by reading Bryannah's mind.

Anger

B⬜⬜⬜⬜ ⬜⬜ ⬜⬜ ⬜⬜ ⬜⬜ ⬜⬜⬜ ⬜⬜⬜ ⬜⬜⬜⬜⬜⬜ ⬜⬜ ⬜⬜⬜ ⬜⬜ ⬜⬜⬜ that she hadn't been on in five years. This backyard jungle gym was now the dominion of her little brother and his friends. She smiled as the image of his big crooked smile and bright eyes floated up in her mind's eye. How happy Caydon had been when he was named team captain.

She closed her eyes and raised her ebony face to receive the full warmth of the summer sun. The first thing she saw when she opened her eyes was the state's fluttering mascot. The Eastern Tiger Swallowtail was large; the coloring of the butterfly, bright yellow with black stripes, marked it as male.

Bryannah stood from the swing as she pursued the flurrying swallowtail into the greenbelt. Engulfed in the serenity of the woodlands, Bryannah let her mind wander. Two weeks ago she had been in town with Caydon in tow. She had leaned against a brick building, texting, while waiting for her brother to come out with his newly purchased graphic novel. A stumbling, homeless woman had coughed up phlegm which sailed within inches of Bryannah's feet. She had glared at the vagrant in disgust.

"Nasty, mangy bitch!" was what the young girl had thought, and in a blink of an eye, the unfortunate woman had become just that. Bryannah had stared at the flea-infested dog through a blinding veil of rage.

"Change her back!" The outburst had gained the attention of a few pedestrians who briefly wondered what the girl was expecting the dog to do. "I said, change her back, now." Fury was intertwined with each word whispered, but her direct order was disobeyed.

———

T␢␢ M␢␢␢␢ N␢␢␢␢␢ ␢␢␢␢␢ ␢␢ ␢␢␢ ␢␢␢␢␢␢␢␢␢ ␢␢␢␢␢ act of aggression in Bre's opinion, sparked a war.

When Bryannah returned home she marched upstairs, snatched the doll from her dresser and stormed into the kitchen. The Magic Negro was drowned inside a Tupperware bowl that had been filled with water. Bryannah secured the lid and put the bowl in the freezer.

That was Saturday.

Tuesday morning she awoke to find the Magic Negro standing on her nightstand.

"I hate you." She hissed at the doll. She trapped Jocko within a ring of cornmeal (it had worked in a movie she had seen), said a prayer, and went to school, only to return from school to find him freed because the maid "swept up the mess." The cleaning lady was barred from her bedroom.

An internet search on How to Kill a Vodou Doll suggested that such a doll had to be buried with rum and gunpowder. Bryannah smuggled the rum from the liquor cabinet; Bethanie brought three shotgun shells, and together they dug a good sized hole deep within the woodlands. Unceremoniously, The Magic Negro was tossed inside. The entire bottle of rum along with contents of the shells were poured atop him. The disturbed earth was replaced, and, for good measure, the girls struggled to move a boulder over the grave site.

That was Thursday.

Wednesday morning she awoke to find the Magic Negro standing on her dresser. With a guttural cry, Bryannah threw her alarm clock at him. When she returned home from school, the Magic Negro was once again standing on her dresser.

She tried to appeased him with an o ering of Jolly Ranchers and bubblegum, but just hours later another thought was intercepted. Furious, Bryannah wrapped multiple layers of duct tape around the poppet's ears and mouth so that he couldn't "hear" her or "talk" all the while wishing the Magic Negro dead.

That was in June.

This morning, on the twelfth day of August, the Magic Negro finally freed himself from bondage.

Acceptance

S██ ████████ ███ ███ ████ █ ████ ███ █████ ███ brother calling her name. As she stepped out of the urban wilderness to walk across her manicured lawn, she watched her little brother run to her in tears.

"They're fighting again," Caydon reported. She knew who "they" were...her mother and her aunt. Bryannah's eyes narrowed as she hugged her brother. "Fine," she thought to herself. She would fix it; after all, she had a Magic Negro. That was the first time Bryannah smiled when she thought about Jocko the Magic Negro.

———

B██████ ███ C█████ █ ███ ███████████ waiting with their mother in the lobby of the medical center. Olivia had half a mind to take those damn iPads away from them. When she scanned the lobby, she noticed the quick glances people threw her children's way. Some with smiles, some with dismissive head shakes, and others ignored the children completely.

It was ba█ ing. At first the doctors thought it was a simple case of laryngitis, but after several months of silence they tested for an infection, a growth, or cancer. Nothing.

Jacqueline hated Olivia's career, her spoiled children, her wealthy husband, her sprawling home, the cars, the clothes, the jewelry, and the sta█. She attacked her sister at every opportunity, constantly demanded money, and blamed Olivia for all the wrongs in the world.

Bryannah rather enjoyed not hearing the sound of her wicked aunt's voice. When Jacqueline emerged with the doctor, Bryannah smiled. She already knew what the doctor would say. The loss of her voice caused the loss of her employment, which in turn made her lose her home. Her parents wanted to write a check, but with the help of the Magic Negro, Bryannah changed the course of Jacqueline's fate.

Her mute aunt was now living with them, surrounded by and reminded of all the things she so dearly hated in life ... Jacqueline was miserable.

Undisputed Dominance

T☐☐ ☐☐☐☐☐☐☐ ☐☐☐☐ ☐☐☐ ☐☐☐☐☐☐☐☐☐ ☐P☐☐☐☐☐ raise your right hand." Bryannah squeezed the hands of her mother and brother as her father did as he was told.

Bryannah did not consider herself to be a witch; however due to her personal academic discipline, others would beg her pardon.

"Do you swear that the testimony you are about to give before the committee to be the truth, the whole truth, and nothing but the truth, so help you God?"

"I do," her father said. In his opening statement during the first day of his confirmation hearing, he thanked his wife and family for their overwhelming support and sacrifice.

Because of all his hard work, her father, Derek Henderson, was the presidential nominee to the Supreme Court.

Because of Jocko, Bryannah's Magic Negro, his professional and political rivals had been eliminated.

Derek Henderson would be confirmed.

Bryannah's best friend Bethanie won this year's Miss America title, and her brother now played for the New York

Yankees. Her mother was the Doctor of the Year, sat on the State Board of Health, and hadn't aged in years. Father time had been equally as gracious to her father.

Live and let live was easy enough to do, as long as you didn't incur the wrath or rage of the Henderson's eldest child.

Many had died over the years, and because she was not yet twenty-five, many more would fall.

T⬚⬚ E⬚⬚

APPRECIATION

MINA POLINA

P☐☐☐☐☐ ☐☐☐ ☐ ☐☐☐☐☐ ☐☐ ☐☐☐☐☐ ☐☐

This was the perpetual thought of a party-goer standing in the corner, sipping on a mixed drink in a red cup. The atmosphere was mellow early in the evening but grew strident as more people arrived. Many came in singles and doubles and triples. Sometimes people came as a herd, carrying bags of food and bottles. One group brought a hefty metal cylinder with a spigot on the bottom, and soon the lights dimmed as someone cranked the music up to eleven. The beat pounded like two freight trains smashing against a cli☐-face on repeat; the bass was strong enough to give anybody a heart attack.

Even they felt a mild panic attack squirming from the base of their spine, through their belly, and up their esophagus.

Setting the drink down, they abandoned the safety of the corner. Hardly any of the party goers took note of their presence with the exception of their friend and hostess, a pretty little woman named Silvie who had invited them.

Everybody here was a co-worker they'd avoided since

getting hired, because these kinds of people preached good values by day but abandoned all inhibitions when parties were thrown by night.   The women attended with splotches of clothing taped and hung and bound to their bodies in the most avant-garde ways. They preferred the women's clothing. Guys wore jeans with dark shirts smeared in loud colors and kitschy designs.   Few wore normal clothing, and those few who did left early.

They, of course, wore a black dress with black heels. Their long, black hair was bound with a gold ribbon in a ponytail. Their black skin, the color of cherry wood with rich, red undertones, was painted with black eyeliner, gold eye shadow, and pale lipstick for the sake of contrast.

They enjoyed these parties, because here, people were their true selves.

They were halfway to the bathroom when Silvie showed up again, catching their arm with one well-manicured brown hand. "Where're you headed o□ to?"

Silvie was drunk; it was obvious.

"The bathroom."

"Oh. Gotta use the toilet, eh? Better hope it's not 'muy ocupado', if you know what I mean?" Silvie said with finger quotes before sputtering out a laugh.

Silvie was a golden beam of light dousing a gray street on a cloudy day. She was all curves and smiles with a head of rainbows and an open heart. Regardless of the brand of clothing or makeup, Silvie could make miracles out of any color or style with her russet-brown skin and thick, coiled hair. They longed to be like Silvie, but Silvie found what worked for her—and was on the hunt to help them find what could work for them. Hence, the party invitation. They needed to get out and sample the crowd—see what was attractive and in vogue. This style just wasn't doing it for them anymore.

"Yeah. Sure," they replied, unsure if their friend meant somebody could be shitting or fucking on the toilet. Either way, the door would be locked.

Silvie chortled, wrapping her limp arms around their form in an inebriated hug. "Come hang with me on the couch when you're done. I have people I want you to meet, and they keep asking about you. Don't worry, we'll get you assimilated as soon as possible. Like, not now, but *right* now. You betcha."

Their eyes plummeted to the floor as they nodded in response.

Silvie smudged her lipstick on their cheek, flipped around, grabbed the first warm body in motion, and struck up a conversation about fluoride in the water.

Down the hall and over the carpeted floor, already spotted with red and brown stains, they headed towards the bathroom through a sea of laughing, gyrating, and sometimes puking, strangers. Everybody here was a stranger. Nobody here had ever provided passionate conversation on any subject, by their standards, because most people never ventured far from their comfort zones. Most work conversations stumbled on for several agonizing minutes concerning mundane subjects, most of which only interested the initiator. One or two insisted they respond with more than just one word, so they would give three or four. None, though, induced a real conversation, except for Silvie.

They pushed through the cracked bathroom door but gasped when their forward motion continued and their midsection collided with the marble edge of the sink.

Somebody closed the door behind them and flipped on the

light. Turning around, there stood a familiar guy, probably from accounting or marketing. Aside from his flimsy dark button down and cheap slacks, his eyes gave away his intentions.

Drunk.

This pencil-pusher was drunker than on his usual week-nights when he ended up home alone with only his cable and internet to comfort him. They waited for him to say something, since he'd retreated from them, his back flush with the door and forehead mottled in sweat. He had to be in his late thirties given the sags in his pale skin and receding hair line.

"Excuse you?" they said, voice measured and arms folded against their stomach.

"Oh, fuck, yeah, hey. So, hey. Listen, I just, you know? And you were coming, like, on your way here, and I figured, hey, why not, right? Because I'm getting up there, so my friend the other day, he's like...he's always like, just fuck it, and I think that's fair. So I saw you coming here, and alone, of course, because who goes with someone else, and so I said why not and decided just fuck it," he replied, his thoughts as jumbled as his word soup explanation and as disjointed as his movements.

The poor guy didn't know whether to scratch his head, fold his hands together, shake their hand, or jam his hand neatly in his pockets. In a flourish of awkwardness, he performed every action. The result was an interpretive dance of pop-and-lock robotic motions accompanied by swooping limbs that pushed him forward before he yanked himself back against the door. The man was at once entranced and intimidated by their very presence.

"Fuck it? Am I it?"

"Whoa. Oh no no no-o-o-o-oo, please! No, I meant, like,

fuck it, like fuck waiting why not just let the universe guide me to where I want to be, and that's--"

"Inside me."

"NO. I mean, well, I'm trying to, like, I'm not gay so yeah, but I'm not, like, I don't want to hurt you, I'm just saying."

"Of course not," they replied with light sarcasm.

"Exactly! Or else I wouldn't have bothered, right? And you're just this beautiful, like, chocolate goddess, ha! Is that wrong? Can I say that? Cause you are, and I just really wanna get a drink with you sometime. Fuck, man, I actually asked. Tim's gonna be so proud of me!"

"Tim?"

"Yeah. Tim's my best friend from college."

"You pushed me."

"Shit, fuck...I lost my balance, and, I just..." The man looked down, pointing at the floor beside the door. "I slipped on the tile. I think I stepped in a spilled drink or something on the way over."

"Ah."

"I'm Mike, by the way."

"Hi, Mike."

"I'm also drunk. I'm really drunk. I could have never worked up the courage to ...umm...I mean..."

Mike stared in mounting disbelief as the person he flirted with began to disassemble one slice at a time. At first it was too miniscule to take any notice. Tiny flakes, like shavings, crusted up and slipped o□ their skin. Mike seemed uncon-cerned at first until the small shavings grew into what looked like long, hair-like strands curling up, detaching from their skin, and floating down to the bathroom floor. Mike paused, watching one skin-strand drift in smooth, peaceful strokes until it hit the bath mat at his feet. When his blue eyes glanced back up, it looked like somebody had taken the sharp edge of a knife and scraped it across the inside of their arm. The piece that curled up looked like chocolate--the strip had a thin, near-translucent middle and broken edges--until it detached and fell away. Beneath there was red, but it didn't drip or pour. It just lay there, glossy like Jell-O.

"Holy...fucking ..."

The entirety of their desiccated skin, from head to toe, shed from the blood and muscle beneath like this, as if an invisible attacker held them in place with sheer will power and flayed them in strips and slivers. Unable to look away, Mike stood, motionless, until all around his feet lay dried, beef jerky bands of bloodless skin. A layer of gelatinous blood black clothes clung to their muscles in the aftermath, until they used both hands to first shred the material from their body, then tear huge chunks of the jiggling blood from their muscles, pitching each handful to the floor until the bathroom looked like somebody had thrown around blobs of chilled jelly in a temper tantrum.

"What the fuck are you doing?" he asked.

"Resculpting," they said, before their tongue detached and tumbled to the floor.

The man turned to grab the doorknob, but the discarded body pieces congealed into a sticky substance that slithered up the wall and coated the handle. When he touched the viscous liquid, the substance sti[]ened like hard candy around his hand and tightened its grip on his skin until the soft flesh was trapped in a rigid shell.

When Mike whipped his head around, it appeared as though their muscles were dripping with sweat. He opened his mouth to say something, but was unsure of how to proceed. His mind told him he'd passed out in the bathroom, and this was nothing more than some ramped up nightmare due to mixing whiskey and tequila. What his eyes told wove a much darker tale where escape was not an option. Instead of speaking, he watched, drunk and dazed, as the muscle sweated from its body in long rivulets, mingling with the goopy blood, now sloshing around on the floor. Their organs, exposed to the cold air of the bathroom, seized up. The exposure caused them to wiggle at first, but then like a heart experiencing cardiac arrest, they tightened, held firm, then crumbled into a million grains of what looked like sand.

When only bones remained, Mike finally opened his mouth and cried like a hurt child. His intention was to let out a tumultuous scream to signal anybody outside the door for help, but the repulsive scene mixed with liquor created choking sobs he couldn't cease or swallow.

"Please," he cried, saliva dribbling from his mouth, "Let me go. Please let me go home."

In reply, the skeleton collapsed into shards. The hard shell that held his hand hostage warmed and became a syrupy concoction slipping over his skin and to the floor. The mound of bones shards drooped in the midst of the meat soup as if made of cloth. The once inflexible surfaces cracked and folded in on themselves as they melted into the swirling mass on the floor. Moving as an amorphous puddle, it slid back against the dark wood cabinet doors on the sink, leaving the floor in front of Mike spotless.

Wasting no time, Mike spun around and reached for the doorknob again. He had just wrapped his hand around its silver surface when he heard what sounded like water splashing in the sink behind him. Curiosity overtook his primal survival instinct. Mike craned his head around, finding the amalgamation sloshing around in the sink. It ebbed and slapped at the marble bowl, as if the moon outside the bathroom window urged the compound into high tide.

Mike's ragged mind couldn't stomach another second. He tried to turn away, but couldn't pry his eyes o⬚ the supernatural mishmash of blood, flesh and bone. As he convinced himself to pull the door open, the blob rose up, like a single arcing wave, blood frothing and foaming around its edges, and dove forward. The sudden dead weight of a human corpse knocked him against the door, shutting it tight as he collapsed, scrapping and clawing his fingertips against the tile floor. It was useless. Once the amorphous creature soaked into his clothes and clung to his skin, he couldn't move. The slurry grappled him into submission, then coated his skin and hardened into a chrysalis.

———

M⬚⬚ ⬚⬚⬚ ⬚⬚⬚⬚⬚⬚⬚⬚⬚ ⬚⬚⬚⬚⬚⬚⬚⬚ ⬚⬚ ⬚⬚⬚ putrefied viscera of what was once his o⬚ce crush. Just moments before he made the decision to approach the girl, he'd changed his mind. Mike had actually turned away from the girl as she entered the hallway, reconsidering his decision to follow Tim's advice from yesterday at work. It would have been easier to go home, bundle himself in blankets, and binge another show online after making a simple dinner of hotdogs and chili. In a split second, though, Mike's eyes has landed on the Millers, who came dressed in near matching leather outfits. Her pants had laces up the side, and his zippers. Her top was a corset, and his was a fancy vest. They kept plugs in their pierced holes at work, but wore them outside whenever the chance arose. Mike wanted to be like them. Mike wanted a love like that, and he couldn't stomach the thought of leaving this party alone.

Mike couldn't stomach the thought of what sort of creature encased its prey in its own flesh. So far, nothing strange had happened, at least he didn't think anything abnormal had occurred, as far as he could tell. His body was confined to a monstrous meat pod, but he could have been trapped in a slide at a park, or layered under comforters at home. His skin wasn't broken in any spots, nothing burned, his limbs were whole, and his mind ...

The chrysalis was so tight, Mike couldn't even move his lips to speak, nor open and shut his eyelids. So as tears began to stream, Mike tried to blink, but the inability made him so frustrated he tried to curse, but that proved impossible as well. Anger swelled in his chest, surged to his head, and rumbled in the pit of his stomach as he tried to roll back and forth in violent, swinging motions. Attempted screams bubbled and burned at his throat like indigestion, but nothing spumed past his vocal cords. His body did not move in rocking motions. Nothing happened. His chest couldn't even heave from hyperventilation, nor would breath exit his lungs. He knew the shell surrounded him, but it was like being suspended in the middle of a water tank or floating in space. It was as if he couldn't ...

No.

A thought deferred Mike's emotional outburst and physical attempts to break free from this cocoon. It wasn't a pleasant thought. The theory was so jarring he abandoned all struggles for physical movement. Distracted by the visual onslaught of the girl's transformation and attack, eager to break free, confused by everything he'd seen, and smashed on whiskey and tequila shots, Mike hadn't noticed why he couldn't break free or scream or cry or move or even breathe.

He couldn't *feel* anything.

In general, it took tactile sensations transferred between the surface of your skin and the world around you in order to perform kinetic actions. At least that was some of the going theory his woozy mind constructed. If he were correct, then this creature had e□ectively taken root in the pores of his skin and compromised his nervous system in a way that made moving ine□ective.

Of course, you can still move a sleeping limb, he thought. So more than just his nervous system was being a□ected here, he realized. There must have also been an attack on his motor skills, because something should have happened when he tried to roll. Nothing moved, though. He literally could not move. He couldn't even express his panic.

Resculpting. That's what she'd said, yes? She was resculpting...what? Her body? His body? Mike wondered if there was still skin on his body as he lay there trapped. He wondered if there were still muscles protecting his organs, or if he even had organs anymore. He lay there, on the bathroom floor, and wondered if his bones were being melted into a sloppy mixture of materials that made up the human body. A laugh, soft, yet present, formed in his mind. His body couldn't reproduce the action as it once could mere minutes ago, but he laughed. In his mind, it stretched, and grew, and widened, until he could almost feel the sting of tears at the corners of his eyes. It was like somebody had given him the wrong kind of brownies for his birthday.

His birthday.

Somebody once brought pot brownies to his birthday party back in college. He must have been in sophomore year at the time and finally crafting lasting friendships with the guys in his classes. One girl he'd befriended, Suzanne, suggested they throw this huge get together and just invite anybody from the dorms. What a dangerous night that was, he remembered. His body couldn't choose between the numbing feeling of the alcohol and the numbing feeling of the drugs coursing through his system, insisting that every word Suzanne spoke was the most hilarious joke ever told. He missed his old buddy, even though she had never returned his a ections. Suzanne, with her rich, green eyes and soft, olive skin.

Near the end of college, he met, Beth, his girlfriend of ten long years. Her sweet, honey-brown eyes told him she was the one from the first moment they met in Financial Markets class. They were Economics majors together, finding serenity in numbers and each other. After graduation they moved into a little apartment together with school debt, thrift store furniture, and their dreams of being together. She made the best homemade chicken and dumplings and always baked him a strawberry shortcake for his birthday.

Five years ago she broke o their engagement due to marriage fears. Those eyes, so big and beautiful, were almost the same color as his mother's, with the same kindness beneath their surface--until the end.

When was the last time he'd visited his mother, actually? Mike turned over the question in his mind, assuming it had to be on her birthday? With his father passed, it was imperative Mike visited her as often as possible. This was the same woman who, whenever he ran home from school crying about bullies, put on his father's old records and sang to him until he memorized the words and could sing along. The same woman who, when he was stressed out over grades, scooped a big bowl of ice cream for them both and watched action movies with him until he fell asleep. Unlike his father who worked too much, his mother was warm like tomato soup or the tangle of blankets on a cold, Saturday morning. He loved his father, but his mother, with her amber-gold eyes and brown curls, had always been his hero. Now she lived alone. No internet, no family left, and no son around to guide her. Mike didn't even think he had any pictures of her lying around.

Delilah.

I like that name.

Mike liked it, too.

It sounds like a nice person's name.

Mike had always thought his mother was the sweetest, most sociable person he'd ever known. She could work a crowd at any get together like a well-trained performer. She always knew how to phrase words just right to flatter the receiver or confuse a menace until they realized her insult much later that night in the shower.

She sounds smart.

Mike thought about furrowing his brow. Then he thought: "She is the best and brightest part of my childhood, I don't know why I don't visit. I'm an awful son."

You are.

The truth made Mike cringe in his mind. The truth hurt.

You don't deserve her. Give her to me.

"She's literally one of my strongest memories. Please."

Now that he thought about it, amber and honey-brown were pretty close in color.

I like the mother. She's the better of them.

"What are you going to do with her?"

Take her from you. I need her.

"For what?"

Hush now. I have what I need.

"I love my mom."

I'll do what you couldn't. You are relieved of your broken promises.

Please.

Please... what?

"I'll do anything. Anything you say, just please ..."

No.

Pain flourished through his veins and capillaries like raging water crashing through the floodgates of a dam. Everywhere the pain touched, he could feel his flesh mending together again, looping and interlocking and stitching itself back together in tiny pieces gathering to create the whole. It wove and wormed up from the soles of his feet, through his knees, and up his pelvis. The sheer torment crushed his mind with the thought of screams as his mind frayed from the edges to the center. Prickling, then throbbing pain dowsed the area where his lips reformed, then trickled down his throat to form his windpipe. His rib cage churned with primordial sludge until his heart thrummed, his stomach knotted and turned, and his kidneys bloomed beneath.

When Mike's lungs coalesced, and the shaft of his throat thickened into tissue and flesh, weak screams passed over his budding vocal chords. Cords of muscles, tendons, and ligaments stretched and retracted as Mike flexed with each new slash of bright, vibrant pain that suﬀused through his body. It burned through new nerves, coming in waves, until every inch of him was encompassed in the unrelenting spasms of what seemed like unending suﬀering.

He was born anew in the throes of agony, his limbs and core clenched as a deafening song of misery wailed from his lips.

———

M███ ████ ██ █ ██ ████ █████ T█ █ ████ █████ ███ scorched his pupils like a nuclear explosion. He was weak. He pushed up and was surprised when he could feel the sensation of his palm on the cold tiles. Mike sat there, holding his head and pushing the heels of his hands into his eyes, unable to shake the weariness from his mind.

"A bad dream?" The words fractured over Mike's tongue and fell into his lap in a coarse whisper. The sound was shriveled to his ringing ears. "No more drinking. Gotta get home," he said. Climbing to his feet, Mike staggered forward and kicked his phone against the door, hearing it bang against the wood with a thud. "Huh?" Mike knew it couldn't be his phone, because his was nestled in his back pocket. With shaky hands, he checked his back, then side pockets. No phone. He picked the sleek, black phone up from the floor and noticed the screen was on and unlocked. Had somebody been meandering through it while he was passed out on the bathroom floor? He scrolled through the messages, but since there were so few he was done within moments.

Without warning, Suzanne popped into his mind--his best friend from college. He wondered, for no reason, how she was doing. He thought about messaging her later, but god, he was pathetic now. Raised by his father from primary school to adulthood, Mike had never been good with women.

He might have been, he knew, if his mother had stuck around. Mike envied other people's relationships with their mothers. To him, mothers were supposed to be sweet women with short-cut hair and inviting smiles who always had a story to tell and a snack waiting after school. Instead, all he ever had was his father, who spent all his time working or with a new girlfriend.   Mike often turned over the thought of searching for the woman, but with his father long gone where would he even start?

––––––––

S⬚⬚⬚⬚ ⬚⬚⬚ ⬚⬚ ⬚ ⬚⬚⬚⬚⬚ ⬚⬚⬚⬚⬚⬚⬚ ⬚⬚⬚ ⬚⬚ ⬚⬚⬚ ⬚⬚⬚⬚ couch in her living room.   A woman wearing a flower-print dress with a white sweater over her black skin, stepped back into the living room.   She wore her hair short, brown curls bouncing at her shoulders with a white ribbon a⬚ xed to the top.   Amber-gold eyes scanned the room, visually inhaling the many friends and co-workers she saw during the week.

She smiled.

"Hey, over here!" Silvie beckoned, her hand waving the figure over.   The woman strolled over, her black heels gliding over the stains on the carpeted floor.   She took a seat between Silvie and a woman a mini skirt and frilly white shirt.

"Hey, there … umm …"

"Delilah."

Silvie's thin eyebrows raised as a smile spread over her red lips.   "Hey, there, Delilah.   What's up?"

"Oh, just scouting around and seeing who's here.   Silvie, you do throw some of the best parties," Delilah gushed, her smile radiant like afternoon sunlight.   "I hope you don't mind; I borrowed from your wardrobe.   Mike from Accounting spilled some wine on my clothes."

"Gods!   When will that man ever learn how to hold his liquor?"

"Among other things," Delilah teased with a devilish grin.

"Oh, yeah, guy's not doing too well.   I think he needs a girlfriend."

"Maybe. Maybe he needs to stop drinking and learn to appreciate the people he already has in his life. Not everybody does."

"Ha! Totally agreed! See? I knew you'd assimilate if you just came to the party," Silvie said with a wink. "Feeling better?"

"Oh," Delilah replied, her expression full of mirth, "Absolutely. I feel … I feel like I need a drink and gossip and to meet lots of new people and …"

"And?"

"And like I should visit some old friends this weekend. We have so much catching up to do."

T␣␣ E␣␣

DEATH LINES

NUZO ONOH

T⬜⬜ ⬜⬜⬜⬜⬜⬜⬜⬜⬜ ⬜⬜ ⬜⬜⬜ ⬜⬜ ⬜⬜⬜ ⬜⬜⬜⬜⬜⬜ ⬜⬜⬜⬜⬜⬜⬜ sticking his head out of his open window to hurl abuses at the other drivers blocking his exit from the service station. The midday sun was intense, and sweat poured from his face as if he had doused his head in a hot tub. His palm was hard on his horn while his foot on the accelerator revved up the engine, adding to the total air of impatient rage in the cab.

Behind him in the passenger seats, the pretty woman glanced wryly at her two young sons. She was used to their taxi driver's vile temperament. Ever since they got into the man's cab, she'd been forced to rebuke the driver for his excessive speeding. Each time, he apologized, slowed down a tad, then hit the accelerator again. She was getting tired of nagging him and wished she hadn't paid him upfront for the long trip to Abuja, Nigeria's a⬜uent capital city. Otherwise she would have abandoned his taxi and found other means to get herself and her sons to their destination in one piece.

"Idiot bush animal! Move your *yeye* rubbish car out of my

way before I turn it into a proper wreck for you," yelled the taxi driver through his open window. There was mania in both his eyes, including his crossed left eye, which twitched with his fury. He flexed his bulging muscles as if desperate to punch somebody.

"Driver, just calm down, you hear?" The young mother's voice was tinged with irritation as she leaned forward to tap the driver on his shoulder. "I've told you we're not in a hurry as long as we get to Abuja in one piece. Just be patient and let the tra c wardens do their job."

"Sorry madam." The man quickly glanced at her via the rear mirror and immediately poked his head out of the window again. "Where's that idiot warden by the way?" he shouted at no one and everyone. "If it's bribery they want, you'll see them loitering around like idiot flies. But tell them to do their jobs and the idiots just disappear." He made a hissing sound of disgust, kissing his teeth with his tongue. The woman passenger sank back wearily to her seat. The man was clearly deaf to reason. She glanced at her watch. Almost 2pm; less than an hour to the end of their journey in the lunatic's taxi. She smiled at her sons fondly, and the twins returned her smile, their identical faces filled with mischief.

"Don't!" she said, her twinkling eyes belying the sternness of her voice. She saw the toothpicks in their hands and knew her sons were up to some mischief, and she didn't want their driver more riled than he already was, though he deserved whatever the five-year old twins had in store for him. "Here, have some buns, and if you're good, I'll let you play some games on my mobile phone."

Soon they were on their way again with their taxi driver eating up the miles to make up for the delay at the service station. Again the woman admonished him for over-speeding and yet again he apologized and re-offended within minutes. Once again, she glanced at her watch; just 15 minutes to go before the end of their journey. At that instant, she heard a shout from their taxi driver, a scream that sent sudden chills to her heart. She glanced up and saw a great truck hurtling towards them, bearing down at them at an incredible speed as their driver fought to complete his rash overtaking at the bend.

Even as their car swerved violently to avoid the truck, everyone in the taxi knew it was over for them. A blind rage filled the mother's heart, a swift red fury at the reckless taxi-driver that had deprived her sons their future by his hot-headed folly. She felt hate as she'd never known it, a dark, blinding hate that was the last emotion she felt in her final seconds of life. The woman barely had time to wrap her screaming sons in her arms before the shattering impact and screeching sounds of crushed metal brought an abrupt end to the blind terror in the taxi, and everything went black.

Ada lifted her hands and stared at her open palms. In the small classroom filled with empty desks and poster-littered walls, she studied the pink planes of her palms. Yet again, as always, her heart sank to her stomach, bringing a painful knot to its core. Her right thumb traced the rigid curves of her left palm, imagining dark lines that stretched from finger to wrist, dark life-lines that were the gift of every living person, save for the few cursed by fate. *Like herself.*

She was four-years old the first time she discovered that she did not exist, that she was an aberration of nature whose existence was an impossibility. Her grandfather, *Nna-ochie* (Old Father), had told her to wash her hands before receiving a piece of goat meat from his soup dish.

She had done a thorough job of it before rushing back to

get her treat. She didn't want *Nna-ochie* to deny her the delicacy because of her filthy hands.

"Show me your hands; let's see if you washed them well," ordered *Nna-ochie* with an indulgent smile. Ada obeyed, proudly showing o[] her clean, pink palms. A sudden frown replaced *Nna-ochie's* smile. He grabbed her hands and peered intently into her palms. "What is this?" His voice was low, filled with shocked wonder.

Ada smiled a wide, proud smile. *She had shocked Nna-ochie with her clean hands, shown him she could wash them as clean as if an adult had washed them. Bet Nna-ochie hadn't expected her to be that clever.* "I washed them all by myself," she said with a proud smile, waiting for the praise from her grandfather and her reward.

Nna-ochie made a quick sign of the cross and looked into Ada's face. Something in his eyes made her shrink back, confusion sending the tears of disappointment to her eyes. *Nna-ochie* wasn't happy with her. She wasn't going to get her goat meat after all. She started sobbing, at first softly, and then into a full-blown howl when *Nna-ochie's* grip on her wrists tightened, hurting.

"It is well that you cry, child," said *Nna-ochie* with a voice filled with pity. The same pity was reflected in his deep, dark eyes, shielded by bushy, grey brows. Her mother had rushed into the veranda at the sound of her cries, her brows creased with worry. *Nna-ochie* had looked up at Mama.

"Woman, did you never notice that your daughter's palms are totally devoid of *Akala-Aka*, life-lines?" Her mother had looked down at her, grabbing her hands from *Nna-ochie* and staring into them. A furtive look of exposed shame replaced the earlier worry-lines on her face. Her mother's face killed Ada's wails, sending a di[]erent type of panic to her heart.

Mama was security, love, everything good. If Mama wasn't happy about something, then something was very wrong, badly wrong. "Mama....?" Her voice was hesitant, almost a whisper.

"Shh...it's alright child, you'll be just fine. Everything is alright." Mama hugged her close, wiping her tears with the edge of her cotton wrapper.

"Are you stupid, woman?" roared *Nna-ochie*, rising from his wooden chair, towering over Mama as he towered over everybody in the compound. "How can you tell the child that everything is alright when you can clearly see that she has no future? Here, look at my palms." *Nna-ochie* opened his hands wide. Ada stared goggle-eyed at the exposed palms which weren't as pink as her own. She'd never noticed how ugly *Nna-ochie*'s palms were with all those horrible black lines running across them. She looked down at her own smooth, pink palms, clear of lines, clean and nice.

"Show me your palms, woman." *Nna-ochie*'s voice brought Ada's attention back to her mother. Mama raised her palms, her actions slow, reluctant, as if she were being asked to part with her *Naira* bank notes.

"What do you see in your palms, eh?" *Nna-ochie* questioned. "What will you see in the palms of every member in this family and in fact, every member of humanity if you look? *Akala-Aka*, that's what. *Akala-Aka*, palm-lines, the life-lines of humanity which determines our destiny, whether we shall live long or die young, whether we shall be rich or poor, whether we shall live a healthy or sickly life. Each line has its own message, its own destiny for us.

Yet, this poor child has no lines; not a single life-line on her palms. She has no destiny, no future. We do not know where she has come from or where she will go...*when she will go.* Her life, as it is, hangs on a thread, a very thin thread which can snap at any second because she shouldn't be here in the first place. May the gods help her, for only the gods can help that which they have cursed."

Ada had stared in horror at her palms, palms which until then she had thought were beautiful and nice; palms which she now knew were cursed. Mama was weeping, a mixture of sadness and helpless fury. Unable to swear at the fearsome patriarch for the pain he had wrought in her little daughter, Mama had done the best she could. "There is nothing wrong with your palms, my child." Mama had repeated that mantra to Ada throughout her childhood, right up to the time she died from a virulent strain of malaria three years ago, when Ada turned twenty-six years.

But the damage had been done; the dark prophesy pronounced by *Nna-ochie* into her child's ears had left its mark in her soul, just like the invisible death lines running underneath her smooth palms. She felt the shadow of death hovering over her at every corner, waiting for the slightest error on her part, a slack in watchfulness, a weak chink in her armor to pounce on her and drag her into the unknown realms of her unknown ancestors.

But she had been careful, very careful. When her eyesight began to go and everything developed a distinct fuzziness in her teens, she had quickly obtained a pair of prescription glasses. *She would not tumble into her death because she did not see it coming.* When her mates all rushed into marriage in their late teens, she had spurned the advances of her suitors with ease. She dared not risk marriage and the attendant childbirth that accompanied it. *Did any day go by without hearing of yet another young mother that had died in childbirth?* So, she'd chosen a career working within the safety of the classroom with the very children she detested as much as she'd detested her late grandfather, children who had made her life a misery in the playground because of her cursed palms.

Ada sighed deeply and got up from her teacher's table, picking up her satchel before heading out of the classroom. Her head throbbed, and her eyes squinted in the intense after-noon sun as she waited at the main road for the bus to take her back to her bedsit at the other end of the city. Just then, a black Mercedes Benz cruised to a stop in front of her. The windows rolled down, and the driver smiled at her.

"Would you like a lift?" he asked, his voice deep and quiet. Ada looked at him, prepared to tell him to get lost, when her eyes met his and something jolted her chest, drying up her mouth. She stared at his thick grey hair, the deep grooves by his jawline, the sad depths of his dark eyes and something inside her opened up to him in a way it had never done with anybody since Mama.

"Thank you," Ada said, her voice rusty like one with a cough. "I'm going to Emene. It's a bit out of the way."

"No problems. Hop in," smiled the man, leaning over to open the front passenger door for her.

Ada got in and sank into the luxurious coolness of the air-conditioned car. "My name is Obi." The man stretched his arm for a handshake. Ada took his hand, careful to hide her palms as she had always done, so he wouldn't see the absence of *Akala-Aka*. His hand was cool, hard, just like his face. When she looked into his eyes though, they seemed to hold the sorrows of the entire universe in their dark depth.

Ada placed him in his sixties, old enough to be her father. She found him strangely attractive, yet she didn't feel towards him like a woman should feel towards a man she desired. She struggled to define what she felt for him and failed. Still, the conversation flowed easily between them inside the cool luxury of his Merc, and by the time he dropped her off at her street, she knew she had made a new and lasting friend.

Over the months, their friendship blossomed as if they had known each other for years despite the thirty-five years differ-ence between them. And when he asked her to marry him almost a year to the day after their first meeting, Ada did not hesitate to accept his proposal.

Her friends and family thought she was crazy. The man was a widower who had lost his wife and two young sons in a terrible car crash over thirty years gone, before Ada was even born. They said he had mourned their loss with an intensity that bordered on insanity. As an only son himself, the deaths of his twin sons meant that their family bloodline would be wiped out of existence should Obi die without children. Since the tragedy, he had married three times and each time, his wives had left him as they could not get pregnant by him. It was as if his sperm had died with his family, since all his ex-wives were now re-married with kids of their own. Why would Ada want to yoke herself to such an old man who wouldn't give her kids of her own?

"For that precise reason," Ada wanted to tell them but kept her peace. With Obi, she would fulfill society's expecta-tion of marriage with all the respectability that it conferred on a woman. She would equally escape the community's scorn for being childless in her marriage, since it was common knowledge that Obi was a man with soured seeds that could never impregnate a woman.

In fact, some people began to wonder if his dead sons had truly been his or if his late wife, Stella, a famous beauty, had played false by him. In the end, people decided Ada was nothing more than a heartless gold-digger, marrying Obi purely for his wealth. She left them to their thoughts, secure in her knowledge that her marriage to Obi would save her from the mortal dangers of childbirth and the curse of her *Akala-aka*.

She found out she was pregnant six months into her marriage. The shock of the pregnancy almost ruined both her sanity and her marriage. Obi's initial shock had turned into incredulous ecstasy when he found out that she was expecting twins. His unbridled bliss sent her resentment soaring, harvesting bitter thoughts in her mind. *How could he be happy when he knew her story, when he knew how terrified she was of dying in childbirth, how petrified she was of the doomed message of her Akala-Aka?*

When the dreams started in her seventh month of pregnancy, she kept them to herself. How could she tell Obi that she dreamt of his dead twin sons every night, boys she only knew by their smiling photos on the walls of his house yet were now an intimate part of her dream-life? How could she tell him that she was seeing endless streams of blood everywhere she looked, her blood, his dead sons' blood, the blood of her unborn twins, who in all likelihood would not survive the birthing ritual with her?

Ada knew her time was up. The dreams were the dark omens whose arrival she'd dreaded all her life; the secret message from the gods that her extended holiday amongst humanity was finally at an end. She didn't bother shopping for the babies in her womb. *What was the use when they were following her to her doom?*

Her water broke two weeks before her due date. Obi rushed her into the best hospital in the city. The twins were in breach position. She would die without an immediate Caesarean. As they wheeled her into the theatre, she took her final look at Obi, her pain-glazed eyes refuting the reassurance in his kind eyes. Within minutes, the anesthetist placed the mask over her mouth and nose and asked her to take a deep breath. She didn't want to obey. Now that death had finally come, she was desperate to cling to life, even a life she had no business living, a life she had stumbled into by some weird trick of fate. She shook her head, holding her breath till she could hold it no longer. With dark despair, she raised her palms for one final look at her accursed palms, opened her mouth and inhaled the gas. And everything went black.

V

He's in a white car, his special taxi he got with the large pay-out he received from that vile little girl's rich parents after she falsely accused him of molesting her and eﬀectively ended his teaching career. Even though he'd been found innocent, the stigma is still there and he has constant nightmares of being tried all over again in a special court run by toys and children with the words, "Guilty! Guilty!" shrilled into his ears by the gleeful little bastards.

Thankfully, he now works for himself, driving passengers across the country when not working out at the gym, bulging up his muscles. Best of all, he rarely has any contact with idiot kids, which suits him just fine. He smiles in happiness as he struts his way to the taxi booking oﬃce, flexing the bulging muscles of his arms with pride. They tell him a woman has paid to be transported to Abuja, Nigeria's aﬄuent capital city, as a private passenger. Big money! It means he can make a double trip in one day and earn more money. He pockets the fee and heads out to his white taxi to await his fare.

His fare turns up, together with two miserable kids. His heart sinks. No one said anything about idiot kids, just a private passenger. He wants to return the money but knows it would consign him to the back of the booking queue. He'll just have to deal with the idiot kids, stomach their high-pitched screeching. Whiney little beasts. He dumps their stu☐ into the boot and gets behind the wheel. They set o☐.

The boys start fighting, just as he's been dreading. Their shrill voices grate his nerves. He turns on the music, loud. The woman complains. He lowers the volume and presses harder on the accelerator. The sooner he gets rid of them the happier they'll all be. Again, the woman complains about his speeding. He should have known she would be a moaner the minute he saw her pretty face. Pretty women have a natural proclivity to moan and bitch about everything because they think the world owes them a living just for being beautiful. Shit!

A sudden vile smell fouls up his car. One of the disgusting little devils has farted, another thing he's been dreading. The little idiots just can't plug their stinking arseholes, dispensing their polluted air with gleeful pride, as if the world is waiting for a chance to inhale their noxious fumes.

And see the idiot woman smiling as she pretends to tell them o☐. He winds down his window and presses harder on the accelerator once again. His taxi is in desperate need of fresh air.

The idiot woman taps him on the shoulders and bitches on again about his speeding. He eases o☐ the pedal, grinding his teeth. Soon, he hears the little shit-machines telling their mother they need the toilet. He prays they don't do it in his cab. He hits his pedal. The quicker he gets them to a service station the quicker they can dump their shit and hopefully give him a stink-free ride for the rest of their journey. But is the woman grateful for his speeding to get her brats to a toilet?

Hell no! Instead, she taps him again on the shoulder and whines, "We're not in any rush you know. Just slow down and take it easy, ok?"

Again, he grinds his teeth and bites his tongue. Fucking passenger is always fucking right. His patience is at an all-time low when they decide to do some last-minute shopping at the service station after shitting, eating, shopping and then stuffing their faces all over again. At the rate they're going, he can't see himself squeezing in two trips as he's planned.

Fuck! The sun is bearing down on him, and the taxi feels like a hot funnel. He curses his bad luck for forgetting to top up his air-conditioning gas. It'd worked perfectly till they got to the service station. The woman hasn't stopped moaning about the fact that she paid for an air-conditioned taxi and now has to cope with the heat. He winds down the windows again and picks up speed to bring more air into the car to cool them all. Yet again, the Moaner-Lisa moans about his speeding, and the little brats join in, too. What's new? He mouths another apology and carries on with what he's doing. It's his fucking car after all, and he's the fucking driver.

He feels something prick his neck and winces. He glances back and sees a smirk on the faces of the boys. He frowns at them and swears under his breath. Their mother tells them to behave.

She doesn't sound as if she means it. In fact, she's smiling at them. His blood boils. Fuck them!

He'll drive as he likes and get them out of his taxi as quickly as he can. He honks his horn at the car in front, a slow car that's laboring under the weight of passenger overload. The car ignores him.

He cuts in to overtake.

That's when he sees the lorry hurtling down towards them. In an instant, everything flashes before his eyes…faces, places, dreams, and despair. They all crowd his mind's eye in those final fateful seconds. He hears her voice behind him. She's screaming, cursing him, telling him he'll pay for what he's done to them; she'll make him suffer, make him weep blood-tears for what he's done to her. He hears her voice drowning out the screech of the tires and the clash of metals.

Suddenly, there's a searing pain, swift, hot. And then, all is silent.

He's floating; looking down at the wreck of what was once his proud white taxi. Four bloodied and mangled bodies are trapped within its twisted metal, four still bodies.

Except, one of them is moving, the woman, breaking free from her crushed corpse, seeking him, finding him, screeching at him as she zooms towards his direction. Her shriek is a raging curse that strikes terror in his heart. "You will give back that which you took; you will give back that which you stole."

He screams and takes flight.

Then the pursuit begins. He feels arms around him, soft arms, yet strong, steely, relentless. They clasp him around the waist and will not let go. He tries to shrug them off, unclasp the metal bands around his midriff. But all he hears is her wild laughter, her mockery, and worst of all, her fury.

She will make him pay, she screams; make him give back her sons he stole. She becomes his dark shadow, glued to him in hate and fury. She follows him through countless reincarnations, aborted returns, leaving in their wake a litter of infant corpses and corpsed fetuses. For what baby can carry the weight of two raging souls, cursed to ride their joint destiny in eternal violent combat?

He asks her forgiveness, countless times; pleads with her to set him free. Without her forgiveness, he is denied entry into the realm of his ancestors for a rebirth into his own clan. But her hate is too dark, a black curse on him that rejects the light of mercy. She's happy to share his torture, his multiple and abortive reincarnations, as long as she's making him suffer. She does not care about the trail of dead infants they leave in their wake, the pain and the wrecked lives of countless grieving mothers. Her voice continues to screech her fury inside his ears, giving him no rest, no peace.

Then the incredible happens. One day...one night...he's not sure; time no longer means anything to him... he finds himself inside the body of a new fetus, who against all odds survives his return in its tiny body. There's a brief struggle as he fights and subdues its fledg-

ling soul. He nestles inside its chest and waits. He feels no metal arms around him, no screeching voice in his ears. After a while, he shuts his eyes and for the first time in forever, he sleeps.

And sleeps...and sleeps...free from his hunter, her fury, the black magic of her screeching curse.

Till the day she finds him in his warm, soft haven and brings her dead sons with her to complete his destruction. Her voice in his ears is the familiar, dreaded shriek – "You will give back that which you took; you will give back that which you stole."

Ada stumbled into consciousness to the sound of voices, happy and relieved voices. They drowned out the other shrill voice raging inside her head. They were telling her she had two healthy twins, two strong sons for her husband. Her eyes widened in terror. Remembrance rushed in, and her mouth opened in a blood-curdling scream, a soul-killing shriek that went on and on.

Pandemonium hit the room. A grey haired-man rushed up to her, tried to speak to her, to show her two tiny bundles, her twin babies. She saw their eyes, eyes she remembered seeing through the rear mirror of her taxi, two twin pairs of knowing gaze, un-baby-like, glittering with malevolence and mischief. They winked at her. She shut her eyes and screeched even louder, recoiling from the babies as one would a deadly viper.

The grey-haired man, the one the nurses called Chief Obi, was crying, shamelessly, uncaring of ruining his man-pride before the goggle-eyed nurses. "Ada...Ada..." His voice was a mixture of confusion and pain. He reached down to touch her face. She glared at him and punched his face.

W   A D I
like a fucking woman, you idiot man? Stay the fuck away from

me!" she screamed at him, her voice a deep, masculine rage that stunned everyone in the room. The nurses tried to calm her with soft admonitions. They told the grey-haired man she was reacting to the anesthesia. She fought them, her arms flailing, pushing.

Her eyes caught the pink flash of nail polish on her fingers, the smooth line-free curves of her palms. Suddenly, she went still. *Something was wrong, badly wrong.* A distant memory pushed its way through the dark fog of her mind, through the violent thoughts of another mind much stronger than her own. *Mama had tried to tell her it didn't matter, that her Akala-Aka wasn't cursed, that the absence of life-lines on her palms wouldn't make a di[]erence to her life.* Ada moaned softly as more thoughts, forgotten knowledge, flooded her mind's eye. *All this while, she'd thought Mama was wrong. But Mama had been right after all. The absence of her Akala-Aka didn't matter because it meant she didn't exist and that was the secret of life; not to exist. That way, you tricked death. Death can't take what doesn't exist.*

Ada began to giggle, softly, secretly. The giggle grew into a full-blown laugh, hurricane laughter. She threw o[] the sheet and stumbled out of the bed. The nurses and doctors tried to restrain her. She bit and kicked them, cursed them, demanded they let her go.

They held tight.

Suddenly, she felt her strength return, felt all her manly power surge in her blood. She flexed the bulging muscles of her arms and punched the idiots that tried to hold her back. There were screams everywhere.

"Shut up, you idiots!" she shouted at them, feeling the blood rush to her crossed left eye which twitched in her fury. She thundered past the crowd in the room, dashing towards the stairs. She was burning, slowly being devoured by the two warring minds inside her head fighting for possession of her soul. Ada pulled o☐ her cotton nightgown as she stumbled her way out of the crowded hospital, bumping into doors, into people, her vision a soft cotton wool.

People stared at the naked woman with the wild eyes. Some cursed her; others pointed and laughed at her. Ada laughed with them, at them. *Ha! Ha! Look, people; look at my palms. See my Akala-Aka; see how it makes me special, invisible, invincible. Bet you can't see me, bet I can just walk right into your faces, and you still won't see me. I'm invisible and invincible. I can never die! Death can't take what it can't see. Death can never take me because guess what? I don't exist! I DO NOT EXIST!*

(*Epilogue*)

There's a mad woman that haunts the streets of Enugu City when the days are bright and the nights are cool. She is a permanent fixture in the streets, known to all, including the police, who have long stopped arresting her for her foul language and nudity. Nobody knows where she came from or who she is. She appeared unexpectedly one sunny day in a filthy pair of men's trousers and a bright scarf, her exposed soft breasts jiggling against her chest.

On good days, she smiles at children as they come out of school and asks them if they have seen her twins, her beautiful sons. Her voice is sweet and sad. On other days, she hurls abuses at the kids, calling them idiot vermin and cockroaches. At those times, she sounds eerily like a man, her voice a deep manly baritone that defies logic. Nobody really minds when she's either a bad- tempered man or a kind-hearted motherly lunatic. People simply laugh at her and toss her bits of food and blame lady moon for creating lunar crazi-ness amongst the citizens in her infinite mischief.

The only time that people shrink away from the city's mad woman with unease is when she becomes the other one, the one that claims to be invisible, the one that doesn't really exist. For then, she raises her palms to prove her point and that's when they all see the clear, smooth planes of her palms, palms that should have the life-lines of all humans, *Akala-Aka* lines that define human existence and destiny, lines that are missing in the pink palms of the city's mad woman! For, then they wonder who...*what*... she really is.

T⬚⬚ E⬚⬚

THE LOST ONES

VALJEANNE JEFFERS

N⬚⬚ ⬚⬚ ⬚⬚⬚⬚⬚ ⬚⬚⬚⬚⬚⬚⬚ ⬚⬚⬚ ⬚⬚⬚⬚⬚⬚ ⬚⬚ ⬚⬚⬚ outskirts of Quincy, easily dodging the trees. *Running with the pack, there's nothing like it … smelling the wildness, the scent of future prey.*

But the werewolves were not hunting. They were running for the pure ecstasy of it, their streamlined bodies a synergy of human and wolf flesh.

Miles … his name sent desire coursing beneath her rich brown fur. But she hadn't seen him in weeks. *He'll be back. We are bound by love. He cannot escape this, and neither can I.*

It's getting late, and I have to work tomorrow…I'm heading back.

Me too, a slender wolf transmitted telepathically behind her. These thoughts were sent to the rest of the pack. The werewolves turned as one and headed back to town.

———

I⬚ ⬚ ⬚⬚ ⬚⬚⬚ ⬚⬚⬚⬚⬚ ⬚⬚ ⬚⬚⬚⬚ Q⬚⬚⬚ ⬚⬚ ⬚ ⬚⬚ ⬚⬚⬚⬚⬚⬚⬚

hot and muggy. Namia Johns, a mahogany-colored woman with golden-brown eyes, dressed in a short-sleeve blouse, bustier and knickers, descended the stairs to her shop entitled simply *The Spellcaster*.

It was 1970, and Namia ran a flourishing business selling charms, powders and *reading* her clients. Sorcery was completely legal in North America, unlike in True America.

No wonder they're always trying to sneak across the border. They can't do anything over there.

In 1955, after a series of bloody civil wars and the upsurge of the Red, Brown, and Black Power Movements, the United States was divided into *True America* and *North America*. In what became known as *The Grand Experiment,* politicians decided that the domestic wars were economically untenable.

Conservative states, newly joined and named *True America,* were allowed to secede from North America, keep their draconian racial and gender laws, and trouble the progressive states no more. Segregation went on in True America, with citizens living in racially divided communities and working at jobs designated by their race and sex.

Meanwhile, with sweeping, radical legislation termed *Restructuring,* North America outlawed all racial discrimination. Quincy City (where Namia lived), like most cities in North America, was a cornucopia of Native American, Black, White, Asian and Latino mixed-race boroughs.

Namia walked to the back of her shop, lit her gas stove and brewed a pot of cocoa. She walked back to the front and sat down at the round wooden table that centered the shop. She sipped the hot brew. Her first client would be there any minute.

A young woman dressed in a corseted blouse and skirt with petticoats opened the door, jingling the bells hanging on the frame. She had coconut-colored skin, and her wavy black hair brushed her shoulders. "Hello, Lydia," Namia greeted her, "I've been expecting you."

Lydia's green eyes widened. For a moment, she looked like she would turn and run back out the door. "You--you know my name?"

"And why you've come. Can I offer you some cocoa?"

"No, thank you." Lydia sat down at the table.

"You've come for a love spell," Namia said matter-of-factly.

Lydia chewed her bottom lip. "Yes, can you make my man love me...treat me right?"

Here we go. "I can," Namia said, "but only for a while."

"I want Jim to love me *forever!*" A tear slid down her cheek, and she angrily wiped it away. "They said you were the best!"

"I can't make him love you for an eternity," Namia replied. "No sorceress can. A heart cannot be compelled against its will. And Jim's heart is faithless and cold."

Lydia rummaged through her handbag. "I have currency! Lots of it! I can pay—I'll pay you whatever you ask!"

Namia reached across the table and touched Lydia's hand, her face sympathetic. "Lydia, this man cares only for himself. When the spell wears off, his love will fade, and he will return to pursuing other women." *She won't listen. They never listen.*

"How long?" Lydia whispered. "How long will it last?"

Namia sighed with resignation. "Six months."

"After that, you can sell me more!"

Namia shook her head. "I cannot. It would be dangerous."

There was a long, weighted silence. "Alright," Lydia said, "I'll take it."

Namia rose from the table and walked to the shelf on her right. She pulled a stoppered jar of blue powder off the shelf. Namia set the jar down in front of Lydia and closed her eyes, whispering words Lydia could not understand. She passed the jar to Lydia, and Lydia clasped it with a faraway look in her eyes, imagining no doubt the affection Jim would shower her with, once ensorcelled.

"Put a teaspoon of this in his food tonight; be sure to make love to him afterwards. Give him only one teaspoon a week...unless you want to drive him insane." Namia twisted her hands; she had to try again. "Dear one, this path leads to self-destruction. Leave this man; find one who will truly love you."

Lydia's full lips tightened into a stubborn line. "How much do I owe you?"

They never listen. "Two hundred even."

Lydia reached into her bag and pulled out a bag of coins. She counted the coins out and put the jar in her purse. "Thank you."

Namia watched her leave. *And in six months she'll be back, begging me for another charm.*

Moments later, the door of her shop was flung open, and a hefty dark man strode inside. He had a wide face, bulging reddish eyes, and he smelled like a brewery. He stood in the doorway, gazing at her with incoherent rage. "You sold my brother's wife poison!" he rumbled.

Namia returned his gaze calmly. She'd been expecting him. "Harry, I don't sell poisons. Only harmless spells."

At the sound of his name, Harry pulled up short. Emboldened by drink, he took another step toward her. "Lying *witch!*"

"Sally poisoned your brother with arsenic which she didn't get from me. Now, please leave my shop."

In two long strides he was standing over her. He glared down her. "I oughta wring your got—!"

Namia grabbed the man by the neck and lifted him from

the floor, growling low in her throat. "Listen to me, fool! Your sister-in-law is lying! Threaten me again, and I'll rip your throat out! Understand?"

He managed a nod. Namia let him down. "Get out!" she snarled. He turned and ran from the shop.

If he tries to repeat his lies, his voice will sound like a pig's oink. Chuckling to herself, Namia walked to the back of her shop to freshen up her cocoa. Another client was on the way.

————

Q CL M was sweltering. He'd raised both windows behind him but hadn't felt a breeze all evening. The bluish tint of the sky threatened rain; so far, it hadn't fulfilled its promise. Detective Miles Blakely, a big mahogany-colored man with a close-shaved haircut, beard and moustache and five unwanted pounds that he'd been trying for months to get rid of, sat at his desk sweating with his sleeves rolled up and his suspenders pushed down. The tie that he wore to look professional was folded on his desk.

"To hell with this," he muttered and stubbed his cigar out in the ashtray. He stood and shoved his tie in pocket.

At that moment, his glass-plated door swung open, and a young man stepped inside. He had a twentyish, baby face, smooth brown sugar skin, and close-cut wavy hair.

"Can I help you?" Miles said in his baritone voice.

"You the detective?" the young man asked, his voice tinged with a Spanish accent.

Miles smiled thinly, "That's what the sign says. Detective Miles Blakely here. What can I do for you?"

"I'm Constable Juan Rodriguez. I uh … I need to file a missing person's report."

"You a Constable?" The young man nodded. "Then what you coming to me for? File a report with your department."

The young man's eyes shifted away from Miles, his face twitching nervously. "I can't…because the man who's missing, he was *taken*."

Miles furrowed his brow in confusion. "Taken? You mean kidnapped."

Juan shook his head. "Naw, he … he disappeared right in front of me. And there was … *vete a la mierda*." He turned to go.

"Sit down!" Miles' voice was an inhuman thunderous command.

The young man whirled about, his eyes wide. He hurried over to the wooden chair facing the desk and sat down, his eyes still on the detective's face.

Miles sat back down. "Now, tell me what happened."

For a long moment Juan continued to gawk at him. "It's *true*," he said finally. "You ain't human."

Miles struck a match on his desk and lit his cigar. "I'm waiting."

"Last night, I was chasing this burglar on the West Side. We both ran past this building, a deserted warehouse—him running and me right behind him. We got to these cobblestones, and he stops. I figured he was getting ready to surrender, ya know? And then I heard this *music*, and he disappeared…Naw, that ain't right. He *dissolved*. His body just *melted*, right in front of me!" Juan shuddered with the memory. *"Fue horrible* … I woulda thought I was going crazy, but it's happened before in the same spot☐ people going missing, some of 'em children."

The detective pu□ed his cigar. *It's some kind of daemon and a powerful one at that.* Out loud he said. "And you want you want me to find out what's doing this and stop it, right?"

"*Sí.* My department has authorized me to hire you. Tonight. It's 250, right?"

Miles smiled humorlessly. "My fee is 500; that's if I don't have to travel. I'll take 250 now and the rest when I solve the case."

Juan reached in his vest and pulled out a cloth satchel. He counted out hand-printed notes and placed them on the desk.

Miles rifled briefly through the notes, then pushed them into his breast pocket. He got to his feet. "Well, let's go take a look.

———

C□□□□□□□ J□□□ R□□□□□□□ □□□□ □□□ □□□□□□ -□□□□ parked beside the tall wooden building. They took Miles' auto to the West Side. They parked alongside the warehouse, a yard away from spot. Miles got out first. He couldn't help but notice the warehouse's broken windows looked like jagged teeth.

"Stay behind me," he said over his shoulder.

"Yeah, sure," Juan said, only too happy to oblige.

Just ahead, there was an innocent-looking patch of cobblestones under a streetlight, but the stones looked unused, as if no one had ever walked over them. Then Miles heard it...a woman singing a wordless melody...sensuous and lilting. He took another step. Then another. One more and he would be standing right beneath the streetlamp...right on top of the stones.

Juan grabbed his arm. "What you *doin'* man?" The melody abruptly ended.

Miles whirled about, mad now—mad enough to slug the young man in the jaw. Juan drew back from the fury in his eyes. "Hey!"

In that instant, his rage vanished. Miles shook his head to clear it. "Sorry." Cautiously, he stretched out his hand under the light just above the cobblestones and snatched it back, holding it in front of his face. His hand was tingling, the hairs on it standing on end.

Behind him, Juan asked. "What is it?"

Miles turned to go. He'd seen enough. "I'm not sure. I gotta do some digging. But cordon this area o; do whatever you have to to keep people away, or more folks will come up missing." He hunkered down and turned the crank on his steam-auto. The motor sputtered to life. They got in, and Miles drove the young Constable back to his car.

"I'll be in touch by the end of the week," Miles said.

Juan got out and walked around to the driver's side of the auto. "I'm the lead detective on this case, with my unit that is." He reached into his vest pocket, pulled out a hand-cut card and handed it to Miles. "All my information is on there if you need to send me a post. You, ah, you think any of them folks are still alive?"

Miles held his gaze. "Hard to say. I wouldn't wanna speculate on it. But if they are, I'll get 'em back."

———

M story cottage. The mortgage was pricey, but he still managed to scrape it together every month. He couldn't stand apartment buildings. He couldn't stand the feeling of being cramped and boxed in. It was the wolf in him. He liked the trees that lined his cobblestone streets, liked having a front and a backyard. Most of all he liked not being able to hear his neighbors coughing, or farting, or flushing their toilet, or making love.

*Making love...*His thoughts turned to Namia. He couldn't dwell on them, or he'd go running o☐ to see her. Even now the memory of her lips, wet...wanting...seeking, her hands, her golden-brown eyes, her lithe body, made it hard to focus. He pushed these thoughts away by sheer force of will and made his way through the living area and down the hall to his den. It was dark in the house, but he could see in the darkness as well as any nocturnal beast.

Inside, there was a wooden desk with a quill, writing pad and oil lamp, a high-backed chair and two armchairs. Books lined the shelves against the wall. He took a match from the desk drawer, struck it on the wood, and lit the oil lamp. Holding the lamp, he walked past the desk and pushed the shelf facing him to the right, revealing his laboratory. A wooden table with candles and painted symbols atop it centered the dim room. The walls were lined with shelves stacked with powders, unguents and more books with well-worn pages. Volumes that he'd rather not expose to polite company...or to an enemy.

Miles chose a jar of red powder from the shelf on his left. He walked back to the table, set the oil lamp down and sprinkled the powder on the exposed hand. He lit a candle and held the flame over his hand for a moment. Miles studied his hand closely. His brown skin was glowing with fluorescent light.

I've been marked. And whoever, *whatever,* had marked him was coming for him.

Miles turned back to the shelves and thumbed through the books. Long after midnight, sleep finally claimed him.

———

H□ □□ □□□ □□ □□□ □□□□□ □□□□□□□ □□ □□□ □ □□□ song ethereal, seductive. Miles rose from his bed. Wearing only pajama bottoms, he left his bedroom and strode down the hallway, through his living area and out the front door...into the warm summer night. He stood on the cobblestones fronting his house.

"Miles, son of sorcerer and wolf." Her voice was a sensuous zephyr. *"Let me free you from your sorrow. Come, and I will take you."*

Miles transformed into a werewolf, hair growing rapidly over his body, his face lengthening, becoming lupine. Creatures appeared in the darkness. They skulked past him. Some with three bodies joined together, others without faces, and those with stooped backs, fangs and claws, hissing and glaring at him with glistening eyes. Creatures that humans could not see, that *he* could not see, until he became wolf.

"Not of this world, nor the other. Poor, lost child."

Miles was inundated with sudden emotions. Yearning, longing...the loneliness of being forever an outsider. Alone, *always alone.* Miles turned left and strode down the cobblestones, following the sound of her voice. Diaphanous spirits trailed him, flying through his chest and stomach. He roared, whirling about with fangs drawn to swipe glancing blows at them. A woman appeared before him, and the wraiths fled. A female werewolf with golden-brown eyes. Namia.

Except it wasn't her.

She sauntered toward him. *"Let go,"* her voice echoed along the street. *"Let go and be mine."*

Miles didn't resist as she pushed her body against his and threw an arm about his neck, pressing her warm lips to his lupine mouth...His member sti⬚ened. Breathing hard, he wrapped his hairy arms about her, pulling her even tighter against him. She flew them both upward, myriad lights swirling around them in the night sky, framing the moon.

I'm losing myself!

With an e⬚ort that was almost painful, he pushed her away. *"You're not her!"* he thundered. "You're *not* Namia!" Miles fell to the cobblestones with a thud and lay on his back shivering and bleeding. He healed quickly, the gift of his wolf blood, turned over on all fours, and loped with preternatural speed toward home.

Her song followed him.

———

W⬚⬚⬚ ⬚⬚ ⬚⬚⬚⬚⬚⬚ ⬚⬚ ⬚⬚⬚⬚⬚ M⬚⬚⬚ ⬚⬚⬚⬚⬚ ⬚⬚⬚ became human again. Inside, the epiphany he had sought all night blossomed in his mind like a black rose. *They're being taken, but they're being coaxed, too. They went willingly, for whatever she promised them. And their souls are being devoured.*

He rushed through the house, not even bothering to light a candle until he entered his lab. He held the flame against his body, examining his hands, chest and arms. "Come *on!*" he whispered fiercely.

She, *it*, had been careful, but he finally found what he sought on his right shoulder: a fluorescent ectoplasm clinging to his skin. Miles set the candle down and grabbed a pair of tweezers from his work table. He snared the squirming bit of ooze, ran to his shelf and picked up a glass jar. He went back to the table and managed to work the stopper o☐ with one hand. He thrust the ectoplasm inside the jar and quickly closed it. It glowed inside the glass.

But there was still much to be done.

———

O☐ ☐☐☐ E☐☐☐ ☐☐☐☐☐☐☐ ☐☐☐☐ ☐☐☐ ☐☐☐ ☐☐☐☐☐ ☐☐ ☐☐☐ apartments over Namia's shop. Miles reached the second story and stood before the door of her flat. He knocked and whispered, "I am a stranger in a strange land. Will you welcome me?" His face shifted under the light, for a moment revealing the beast beneath his human shape.

The door swung open, and he stepped inside. Beyond the doorway were spacious and opulently decorated rooms. Were-wolves, vampires and hybrid metahumans lounged about on couches and chairs. Namia, curvaceous and dark with golden-brown eyes, dressed in a corset and clinging pants, spotted him. His body warmed as it always did at the sight of her. She rose gracefully like a dancer, stepped over to him, and wound an arm around his neck.

Namia kissed him hungrily and lifted her mouth. "Where you been, lover? I missed you." Her voice was a husky contralto, a synergy of sandpaper and honey.

"I missed you too," Miles said. Oh, *how* he'd missed her!

"So, why'd you stay away so long?"

"It's only been two weeks," he stammered. *I can't think around you. My brain turns to mush.*

Unlike Miles, Namia was a full-blooded werewolf and seer. She spoke to his lupine spirit, and it answered to her scent, her touch, her taste. When he was with her, he forgot to be man and longed to spend his days and nights running through the streets and forests, taking whatever he wanted, taking *her*.

"I need your help."

"I'm listening," she said.

Miles told her about the ensorcelled cobblestones and the disappearances. Then he told her about what had happened to him the night before. When he'd finished, Namia asked, "Do you still have the ectoplasm?"

Miles nodded. "Yeah."

"We're going to need it."

They descended the steps together. "What you're up against is a kind of succubus," Namia said, "one that feeds on emotions ... fear, pain, desire, anger. It is what keeps the daemon strong, keeps her immortal. These things almost never cross over into our dimension. But when they do, they're looking for victims." She pushed the door open, and they stepped outside into the warm night.

Namia smiled up at him. "Run with me, Miles."

Looking down at her, into those golden-brown eyes, Miles suddenly found it hard to breath. "I...I brought my steam-auto."

Namia lifted her hand and ran one finger down his cheek. "You over-think things; you always have. Run with me now— for the sheer joy of it!"

She took off, and he raced behind her. In human or wolf form both were preternaturally fast and strong. The meta-humans blurred through the streets, reaching his house in a matter of minutes.

Inside, she followed him to his lab. Miles set the stoppered bottle of ectoplasm on the table. He placed his hands over the symbols on the table and spoke a mantra: *"Protect me as I seek the lost ones."* The symbols drew together to form a circle. He unstopped the jar and, with tweezers, placed the ectoplasm inside the circle.

Namia cast the second spell.

———

M□□□□ □□□□□□ □□ □□□□□-□□□□ □□ □□□ □□□□□ opened the door and got out. He walked to the cobblestones. Juan had been true to his word. Wooden slats had been placed around the stones, and a painted sign that said, "Danger! Keep away by order of the Constabulary!" was a□xed to the warehouse's wall fronting the stones.

His heart was beating fast, and he'd begun to sweat. Miles pushed the slats aside and stepped on the top of the cobblestones. For a long moment he stood there under the streetlamp. Nothing happened. Suddenly, he was swallowed in darkness. His faux lover appeared before him, dressed in clinging sheer garments. Miles knew it wasn't Namia; nevertheless, his body welcomed the sight of her.

"I knew you would come," she said. Her silken voice echoed in the darkness. She moved close to him, placing her hands on his chest. All at once she frowned and pulled back. *"You think to vanquish* me? *Foolish, foolish human! I will take everything that you are!"* The daemon threw back her head and shrieked in a banshee wail.

They appeared, spirit upon spirit, shapeless but deadly, and sprang upon him, Miles felt them gnawing at his flesh, biting o□ chunks of him. He became werewolf— throwing them o□ him two at a time. And still they came. The spell could not destroy so many daemons, only keep him alive.

And not indefinitely.

An entity sprang at him and sank razor sharp fangs into

his chest. Blood gushed from the wound. Weakened, Miles threw the monster o◻; another instantly took its place. He felt himself going under. Miles sank to his knees.

The daemoness stood over him. *"Now I will take what is mine."*

Suddenly, Namia and her pack were there, glowing with the same blue-green luminescence that protected Miles, driving the spirits back and circling him and the daemon. Miles stood and grabbed the daemoness by the throat.

Namia spoke the mantra that only she as *black woman* could speak.

The daemon howled in a long drawn-out cry, a sound bereft of any humanity. Miles watched as her human body melted away, until there was nothing left but a shapeless form with blazing eyes. Repulsed, he let go and watched the thing dissolve at his feet.

The darkness vanished.

He was once more standing beneath the streetlamp, this time surrounded by Namia's pack, his body already beginning to heal. *The perks of being a meta-human.* "Thank you," Miles said. The shape-shifters nodded and hurriedly took their leave, impatient to find their next adventure.

Namia lingered. "I almost bit it back there. I thought you weren't coming," Miles said.

"It took me awhile to round everybody up." She stroked his cheek with the back of her hand. "You owe me now. Meet me in an hour and we'll discuss your...payment."

Miles nodded; he didn't have to ask where. Namia kissed him and walked away. He watched her until she vanished in the night.

Minutes later, just as Miles had suspected, they began to return. Men, women, and three children, two boys and a girl.

All wore the dazed look of folks awakening from a long night-mare. He suspected, too, that this wasn't everyone who'd vanished, only those who'd managed to survive.

He ignored the adults; they could find their own way home. Miles wondered what the daemon had offered the chil-dren to entice them to follow her? *Whatever's going on at home, I hope their parents fix it. I may not be around next time.*

"Hey," Miles said to a small, brown girl. "You lost?"

She chewed her lips, her wide, scared eyes searching his face. She ran them over his bruises. In a few hours they'd be healed. But of course she didn't know that. He'd fought the creatures; that's all she could see. Deciding to trust him, she nodded. "Uh-huh."

"I'll take you to the Constabulary; they'll find your folks," Miles turned his eyes to the boys. "You too." The children followed him back to his steam-auto. *And while I'm there, I'll collect my fee. A man can't live on good deeds alone.*

———

T□□ □□□□□ □□□ □□□□□ □□ □□□ □□□□□ □□□□□□ □□□ for his mate, her scent in his nostrils. Suddenly she was there, loping alongside him. Namia and Miles ran to the edge of the dark waters and transformed into man and woman. Naked and as one, they rose, her arms wrapped about his neck as he lifted her from the soil by her buttocks ... her hot mouth on his ...

Bound by love. We are bound for an eternity.

T□□ E□□

DARK MOON'S CURSE

DELIZHIA JENKINS

Beware the beauty with the mysterious gaze
On the night when the moon goes dark
Her enchanting kiss and the call of her hips
Is enough to rip out your heart
Searching for a fool while her cauldron brews
While you are out chasing a good time
Her smile is her charm, her goal to disarm
So, you will take her home for the night
She will find her fool while her cauldron brews
Cursing you with the presence of the dark moon

T‍‍‍ ‍‍‍‍ I ‍‍‍‍‍ ‍‍‍‍‍‍ ‍‍‍‍‍ ‍‍ ‍‍‍‍‍‍‍‍ were that night, the more I realize I should have taken my horny ass to Bible study with my momma and her gossipy church friends instead of riding around with my boys looking for some ass. I could have gotten prayed over and baptized and still be walking this Earth as a regular guy and not some... nevermind.

Let's get to the story, shall we?

I couldn't have seen that shit coming wearing bifocals with a crystal ball sitting in front of me. I mean, damn! I've been fucked over by fly-ass females before. It is what it is. But the shit that just happened has me sitting on the edge of my bed, stumped.

I spent a great deal of my twenties learning every trick in the book on how to sex a woman so thoroughly she becomes addicted to the dick game. Dick so good, you don't even want to chance getting it from someone else. That's what I do! Unfortunately, I've encountered a few women who were immune to it and had their own tricks up their sleeve.

Whatever! Some women just don't recognize a good thing when they see it.

My name is Timothy, but everybody knows me as T. More accurately, they *knew* me as T. I don't know what the hell they are going to know me as now. I'm sure you're wondering what on Earth am I talking about. I'm going to get to that! I just want you to understand how *good* I had it before *she* came along and totally destroyed everything I worked for. Yes, *she*. Simone. Something told me not to step to that crazy chick seated in the VIP section, looking every bit as beautiful as the first ray of light in the morning. The closer I got to her the more my gut instinct screamed, "Run away and never look back." But did my stupid ass listen? Nope. I was being guided by something else--not this ten-inch rod I carry between my legs--but some otherworldly, mysterious force that I couldn't explain.

I was sitting in the VIP section of Club Vex, chillin' with my boys, Kirk and Steve, successful sports agents at the firm I worked for, Stein & Goldhammer. We were celebrating the recent acquisition of Anaheim Angels' All Star Jose Guzman, signing a multi-million dollar two-year deal with the kid we'd affectionately nicknamed Sonic. The kid was pure motion when he was gunning for those bases,

I worked in the legal department, but I had known he was going to require a bit of schmoozing to get him to sign with us. I knew Jose's sister and was able to work everything out through her. Jose is all about family and makes no decision without running it by his loved ones. It was easy for me to slide in and encourage Nadya to put in a good word after I laid some serious pipe game on her.

So I got to toast it up with two heavy hittin' sports agents and the possibility of a promotion. I'm a big guy, standing at 6'3", towering over just about everyone in the club. Plus, I work out a lot. I had my pick of the finest women in Los Angeles coming in and out of the VIP section, models, actresses, singers...you name it. They all was givin' ya boy the eye!

I took a sip of vodka and cranberry juice and surveyed the scene. Steve had his hands full, talking to this busty Latina chick whose tight-fitted, strapless, nude-colored dress clung to her like second skin. She tossed her hair back, offering Steve a casual smile, and he glanced back at me as I offered him two thumbs up. Steve is not exactly the smoothest, but the ladies dig him because the man can make a trash bag look like a Tom Ford suit just by wearing it. The man is successful, intelligent, and works for the most in-demand sports agency on the West Coast. He definitely wouldn't have any problems with her tonight.

Underneath the dim lights of the club, the DJ spun old school cuts, taking us back to the early 2000's--our high school years, when I was the star of the basketball team. Ladies flocked to the dance floor in small groups, giggling as they tiptoed in six-inch heels, luring a number of men in pursuit. I took another sip, smoothing my hand over my fresh fade. I was careful not to spill even a drop of my chosen poison on my white blazer. Swallowing thickly, I embraced the burn of the liquor as it chased away the week's stress and awakened me to what was taking place in the club.

She came in like a bolt of lightning: brilliantly bright, blindingly beautiful, and terrifyingly seductive. All eyes were definitely on shorty as she sashayed her way into the VIP section. She walked as if she owned the place, but the actual owner hadn't figured it out yet. She strutted across the crimson floor, her six-inch gold Giuseppe's creating their own rhythm to match the sway of her hips. This chick was baaaaad. Raven dark hair flowing like black silk to the base of her spine, dark brown skin perfected by the blessed rays of the sun. Slanted dark eyes greeted the bartender who damn near fell flat on his face the moment she asked for a Sex on the Beach.

All I could think about was sex on the beach...with her. Sex on the beach, sex in my car, sex on the hood of my car, sex in the kitchen... raw and uninhibited. I wanted her like an alcoholic craved that last drop of liquor in the bottle, and I was going to make it my mission to have her.

Looking back, the moment she entered my section was the moment I should have ran out of the club, hopped into my car, and raced home without looking back. Then covered each entryway to my home with the sea salt my crazy ass Aunt Lucille gave me years ago after sharing one of her visions about death and destruction coming my way.

It was not until much later that I would wake up regretting

DARK MOON'S CURSE   71

the very moment I spat my best game to her. Pretty faces are guaranteed grave plots. Trust me.

The shorty took a seat, two patrons to the left of me, and I played it cool, casually sipping my liquor, enjoying the scenery. Two young players approached her, vying for her attention, and I peeped from the corner of my eye to see what she was about to do. I needed to know if she'd already made her decision for the night. I secretly hoped that none of the cats in here had a chance with her.

She was mine. I had claimed her. But, if she'd opted to go in a different direction, then I would have sucked it up and moved on. However, it was not long before both of her potential suitors were sent away with their tails between their legs, running off to different corners of the club. I watched her calmly toss her hair over her shoulder, my eyes following every curve of that glittery tight-fitted dress she wore hugging her body to perfection. She caught me watching her, and she offered a warm smile, flashing white teeth so unrealistically perfect, I forget every single detail of thought. I was lost. Her dark eyes found me.

I had no idea I was staring death in the face.

Next thing I knew, I was out of my seat, abandoning my empty glass on the counter and every ounce of common sense I had left. I smiled as I slowly approached, feeling every bit like a predator without knowing that I was actually the prey. I could smell her perfume, and whatever she was wearing had me hypnotized--nothing existed in the world but this beautiful creature and me.

"Excuse me?" I drawled, hoping my voice had the same seductive pull that her presence had.

"Yes?" The melodious tone of her voice reminded me of wind chimes.

"I simply wanted to introduce myself to a beautiful woman," I told her.

"I'm flattered," she said, licking her lips. "What is your name?"

"Timothy," I said confidently, offering her my hand, which she graciously accepted. Her hands felt like satin. All I could think about was how badly I wanted those buttery soft hands all over my body.

"Timothy," she breathed. "They call me Simone." She flashed a picture-perfect grin, exposing pearly white teeth.

"What do you mean *they* call you Simone?" I asked. All sorts of red flags and warnings were flashing throughout my nervous system. At first, I wasn't sure what to make of Miss Simone, but being the man that I was, I was more concerned about how quickly I could get my face between her legs than my own safety. Simone was fine as wine. The way she had me damn near about to cum all over myself from just a few words in conversation.

She shrugged, and took a sip from the martini the bartender had slid in her direction. "I have many names, and Simone is easier on the tongue to pronounce."

"Well, Simone," I said, sliding into the empty bar stool next to her. "Are you here waiting for someone?"

Taking another sip of her martini, she casually replied, "Yes."

I felt my shoulders slump and mentally kicked my own ass for assuming that a woman that fine would be out solo.

"You," she continued. "I was waiting for you."

My mouth went dry, and all of the blood in my body flooded to one location. Clearing my throat, I shifted around in my seat, fighting back intense erotic images that flooded my vision. In all my thirty years of existence, with all of the women I'd been with, not one had ever had me on edge like this. I should have known something was up. I felt like-- without consciously being aware--I'd signed a deal with the devil. It wouldn't be for another couple of weeks that I would come to realize that I had...and her name was Simone.

We chatted for a good while until the club began to empty out. Steve and Kirk were long gone with their choice selections for the night. I offered to walk her to her car, but as luck would have it, she came alone, via taxi--or so she said. Being the opportunistic horn dog that I was, I opened the door to my red two-door Porsche, asked her which direction I should head in, and when her response was, "My house," hit the 101 freeway like a NASCAR driver on the Indy Speed 100.

Simone's pad was a two-story town house in the suburban area of Glendale. It was well after three in the morning, and we barely made it out the car and into her living room before I had her panties pulled to the side, balls deep and delirious from pleasure. She came instantly, her walls milking me until I thought I was ejaculating dust. I honestly could not tell you when we finally passed out.

I woke up the next morning face down on her queen-sized bed, buck ass naked, Simone nowhere to be found. Usually after a good night of sex, I wake up feeling energized and ready to start my day. When I awoke that morning, I felt like I had the worse hangover in the history of hangovers even though I didn't drink that much the night before.

I'm not sure how I even made it home that day. I just know every bone in my body ached as though individually broken by a sledgehammer. Nauseated. Dizzy. Slipping into the jeans I wore from the club was a painful experience. Like I said, I don't even know how I made it home.

I do recall leaving my number on a piece of paper I found

on her dining table before I let myself out. I had no idea where she'd gone, but once I stepped outside, I hauled ass to the car because the exposed areas of my skin could not tolerate the heat. Hours later I made it to my apartment and crashed for some time. I took a look in the mirror and the side of my face and back of my neck had a purplish red tinge to it from the sun burn.

I did not hear from Simone for the rest of the weekend and I didn't think about her either because my ass was still recovering from the one-night fuck session. At one point, it was impossible to keep food down. Sunday night came; when I should have been preparing myself to get ready for work the next day, I was wrapped up underneath the covers, shivering, having broken out in a cold sweat. I had no idea what could have been done to me.

Monday I called in sick to work because I had to. I couldn't get out the bed. Between the fever, the night sweats, and the instability taking place in my stomach, there was no way I could make it in to work. I called my mother to bring me some Pepto Bismol and Tums. She came by immediately after the church meeting to do what mothers do, bring over some of her famous homemade chicken noodle soup. She even brought one of her church sisters with her, Sister Gloria, to pray for me.

My mother is an overbearing, smother-you-until-your-last-breath type of woman. I'm the last of her sons. Both my brothers were killed on the streets the year I was away at college. All that is left are my sisters Tanya and Tina and me. My father died when I was young, of cancer, and my mother did everything she could to raise us on her own. If she could, she would lock us all away in a bubble and never let us out of her sight.

People say I look like her. We share the same dark chocolate skin, slanted hazel eyes, and dimpled grins. In her hey-
day, my mom had men lined up around the corner, but it was
my dad who stole her heart. She and my dad had that forever
type of love. She never remarried.. He was the one for her, and
that was it. So, when any one of us is sick or not doing well
emotionally, my mother is there to baby us. She reminds us,
despite of the ugliness in the world, we still have a beacon of
light to look to. I always told myself that whenever I decided
to deactivate my player card, it would be with a woman just as
a ectionate and doting as my mother, Katherine. But the way
that my life is going at this point...nah, I'm good.

She spent the day praying for me with Sister Gloria,
burning sage from room to room.

Sister Gloria was one of those older, hat-wearing church
women with so much wisdom flowing through her veins, it's
scary. The woman had to be in her eighties, having raised
eight children with almost twenty-six grand-kids that came in
and out of her house on a monthly basis. Not one wrinkle
lined this woman's face, proof that black doesn't crack.

Sister Gloria was quiet for the larger part of the day, until
they got ready to leave. She waited for my mother to kiss me
on the forehead and head for the door before she turned to
me and whispered, "You've been kissed by *death*, son. You
better start praying. Whatever demon you done laid down
with, if I were you I would come by the church this evening
for prayer. I prayed over your house, so this creature can't
come in unless you invite it in. From the looks of thangs, this
is the root work of a female. Listen to this old crone when I
say this, come get prayed over tonight. I will be waiting for
you." She patted me on my head and left behind my mother
without another word.

I should have gone to church that night, but like a dumb ass determined to head straight to hell, I stayed at home in the bed, feeling sorry for myself.

I felt much better the next morning, well enough to clock in for work. The day went by smoothly. Kirk and Steve teased me off and on, claiming that I wasn't old enough to handle my liquor. I brushed it off as usual. I was still waiting on my promotion. I hoped they were shooting jokes to pass the time while waiting to tell me the good news.

Six o'clock rolled around, and I headed to the underground parking structure where I heard the sweet sound of an all too familiar voice. Like a bloodhound on a mission, I followed the sound of wind chimes to the third level, and lo and behold, there was Simone, engaged in a deep conversation with one of the partners that owns the firm. She had on this tight black dress which highlighted all of my favorite parts of her body and was leaned against the associate's 2017 Mercedes. His back was turned to me, but her eyes met mine, and she offered a sly grin, tossing her long dark hair over her shoulder as if I was about as important as the junk mail that eventually gets tossed in the trash.

I started to approach her, but I didn't. She didn't belong to me. And not once did she mention anything about having a husband or a boyfriend, so she was not my problem. I spun on my heels and left. During the drive home, I hit the streets like a mad man. I was so pissed off that that bitch had played me I didn't know what to do! She didn't even have the decency to call me to see if I made it home, how I was doing—nothing! I at least call the women I bone after the fact just out of cour- tesy. She didn't even know I spent the rest of my three-day weekend sick as a dog, and judging by the way she was eyeing Mr. Goldhammer, she would not have cared if I told her.

This is exactly why I am not ever getting married.

I make it back to the house after stopping at KFC for one of their eight-piece specials just in time to watch the Lakers face o☐ with the Clippers. Full from the chicken and mentally exhausted from work, I dozed o☐ on my leather couch, peaceful as hell. That is when the dreams began. At first, seeing Simone's fine ass in my sleep was cool. Fucking her in my dreams brought back memories of that one night together, and I woke up sticky from own orgasms, but functional. I could get up the next morning, head to work and that was that. As a matter of fact, I didn't even think about Simone during the daylight hours. It was always at night when her beautiful face and curvaceous body would invade my subconscious mind.

It was not until the fourth night things really started to get creepy. I woke up in the middle of the bed, buck naked, the scent of sex tainting the air, and my body felt like it'd been hit by a dump truck. I called in sick the next day and spent another three days recovering. The next week, same thing, but this time each night, around two in the morning, I awoke not only to the scent of sex, but the sensation there was a dark presence lurking about in my apartment watching me.

I thought of Sister Gloria and her words, *"You've been kissed by death, son. You better start praying and whatever demon you done laid down with, if I were you I would come by the church this evening for prayer..."* Naturally, I freaked out and called my mother and begged her to call Sister Gloria to come down and visit me. She reluctantly agreed, overall concerned about my mental health. At this time, *I* was concerned about my own mental health. I knew that none of what I was experiencing belonged in the realm of the natural. There was no way I was about to go back to sleep with a new wave of nausea creeping up on me and the terror plaguing my spirit at what was happening to me.

I decided to take an early vacation from work before the firm started to catch on. I had accrued enough hours to last for a little over a week. I was doubled over on the side of the bed retching into the waste basket, when my mother came in with Sister Gloria. Both women were visibly concerned. I looked like I had lost twenty pounds in a few days due to these night time episodes. Dark circles had formed underneath my eyes. I was forced to seal o☐ all access to sunlight because I ended up with what looked like a third degree burn on my shoulder from the ray of light that came in through the window.

Sister Gloria didn't bite her tongue. As soon as she saw me she said, "Boy, I told you to come down to church, boy," she scolded, eyeing me suspiciously through her thick bifocals. "But you was jus' like yo daddy and didn't listen."

"Whatchu' mean just like my daddy?" I asked through a dry heave.

I could feel my mother's discomfort at the mention of my father but was too consumed with vomiting to make an inquiry.

"Don't, Sister Gloria," my mother whispered. "Please."

"No, Katherine, it's about time you told the boy," Sister Gloria insisted. "I told you son, you've been *kissed by death*. The same thing happened to your father and your brothers. Yo' family is cursed. I don't know what your great ancestor did to piss this she-demon o☐, but I told you to come to church and get prayed for. She don't like prayer and the energy that surrounds the person she is hunting. Now, I don't know if you can be helped."

My mother burst into tears in front of me and dashed out

of my room and into the bathroom. Her sobs echoed in the hallway.

"What are you talking about?" I demanded, finally collapsing on the bed.

"I told your mother to invite you down to church with us two weeks ago because I knew it was coming. You Watson men all have a problem when it comes to women, and chile as much as yo' daddy loved your mother, he just could not confine that love to her alone. He was like you, chasing tail and anything with two legs and just like you, he was out on the night of a Black Moon--something witches and demons look to for a power boost--and got himself caught up in her web. The Curse of the Dark Moon is what killed yo' daddy and yo' brothers, son."

"Ain't no such thing as curses Sister Gloria," I said with a frown. "No disrespect, but you are crazy if you think I'm gon' believe something like that."

"Ok son," she said calmly. "Tell me why are you losing sleep? Explain to me why you are experiencing flu-like symptoms and intolerance to sunlight? I see that third- degree burn. You can't tell me you got that from cooking because you don't cook. You've lost blood son, and you don't even know it. I bet you can't even close your eyes without seeing that she-demon's face. She chose you as her mate son, and she is waiting for the transition to take place. Your daddy and your brothers weren't strong enough to survive the change which meant your poor mother had to bury them all. Now she is about to lose you, too."

At the mere mention of Simone, the image of her beautiful face replaced that of Sister Gloria's. Her haunting dark eyes and sexy grin substituted Sister Gloria's bifocals and grim expression. But when her smile shifted to an exposed row of razor sharp teeth, I screamed.

I didn't realize my screams had sparked the neighbors to call the police. It was not until I was apprehended and dragged out of my apartment I realized my life had taken a drastic turn for the worse. When they strapped me onto the stretcher for the ambulance driver to tote o□ to the nearest hospital, I heard in the back of mind the haunting wind chime of a voice whisper to me,

"Come to me my love…as soon as it is finished, come to me…"

I spent three long days undergoing a psychiatric evaluation before I was released into the custody of my mother and Sister Gloria, who watched me like a hawk. During my stay in the hospital, I did not experience any late night sex episodes.

Upon release, I was told that I was under tremendous amounts of stress and should refrain from working for another couple of weeks.. They didn't release me from the hospital until late that evening. There was no way of knowing if I was still intolerant to sunlight. I felt fine when I made it back to my apartment. Both women refused to leave once I was settled in. Seeing my mother's red-rimmed eyes was too much for me. She made me feel like I was a walking dead man. I told them that I needed space to think and clear my head so they left.

Sister Gloria waited until my mother was out of sight before she handed me a .38 caliber, and said, "Inside is one silver bullet. Put it in your head or your heart. If the burn in your throat cannot be quenched through conventional methods, like juice and water, do us a favor, and put an end to yourself. I don't want to have send nobody after you. Your mother's heart has already been broken three times, and unfortunately, I'm going to have to watch it break again. But don't make me come after you. Please." She left without a word and her head held high.

I don't know who the hell this lady thinks she is, but she ain't coming after shit!

I was finally alone with my thoughts and decided to pass the time with some television. I turned it on the news just in time for the newscaster to report a total of six missing persons the police were searching for in the same week in Los Angeles. Dread creeped into my psyche, and I thought to myself, this *has* to be a coincidence. Then I turned to Animal Planet and dozed off to the sound of the ocean and the narrator's voice discussing the dangers of sea life.

I awoke a few hours later; my throat was on fire. It was like I'd swallowed an entire gallon of Tabasco. When I say nothing worked, I mean absolutely nothing. I drunk everything I had stored in my refrigerator, from Sunny Delight to vanilla flavored coffee creamer. All of it just intensified the burn. Clutching my throat, I dry heaved into the sink. I became dizzy. The blood flowing through my veins felt like battery acid, pumping what little oxygen I could inhale to my heart. My last thought was of my mother, smiling as she pushed me and my sisters on the swings at the park after church. It's funny how important things you never knew were important seep into your awareness as your body begins to expire. If I'd known that there was an entity out there responsible for the deaths of the men in my family I would have done things differently. Some lessons are learned a little too late, and I was one of the unlucky bastards that wound up a day late and a dollar short.

———

A☐ I ☐☐☐ ☐☐ ☐☐☐ ☐☐☐☐☐ ☐☐ ☐☐☐ ☐☐☐☐☐☐☐☐☐☐☐☐☐ ☐☐☐ my night out on the town, I could sense Simone out there somewhere, hunting, luring men to an untimely demise. She chose me as her mate, her blood source. Vampire. That is what we are. We sustain ourselves on the blood of mortals. In order to maintain eternal youth, she needed a strong mate to feed from, and now I will eternally be tied to her unless she dies. Then I will have to find my own mate. And when I do, it will be a female that is willing to accept me for all that I am. If she can accept my fangs, she's wife material. Period.

Looking out the window of Simone's town home, the sun had completely disappeared beneath the horizon. I realized it'd been days since I'd last visited my mother. This was going to be hard for her. The last time I saw her, I knew she could rest well at night knowing that her son was still alive, still surviving. Perhaps through prayer I could be redeemed. I somehow doubted it. She would find it unforgivably unsettling if she found out that Simone and I had gorged ourselves on the blood of a couple of police o☐cers and a doctor. Speaking of my mother, there was one other person I owed a visit to...

Sister Gloria.

I needed to know how capable that old woman was of making good on her threat of coming after me. As a matter of fact, I was sure she was expecting me. I took one last look at myself in the mirror. The black Tom Ford suit looked great on me, and I wondered if it would be acceptable to wear to a funeral. I disappeared into the night and reappeared on Sister Gloria's one-story duplex. I materialized into solid form and rang the doorbell and did not respond to her inquiries as I listened to her shu☐e to answer the door. The door swung open, and her expression was priceless as she eyed me standing at her doorstep, a hint of fang gleaming underneath the moonless sky.

"Good evening Sister Gloria," I said with a smile. "May I come in?"

Sister Gloria stared back at me and smiled. The hair on the back of my neck stood at attention, and my enhanced senses told me that this eighty-something-year-old woman who had raised damn near half of the people in the community she lived in had more up her sleeve than my vampire ass could have bargained for. She carefully removed her bifocals, her eyes never leaving mine. She studied me with a razor focus I would have never suspected she possessed.

Instinct told me to step away from her doorstep. Off in the distance I heard the panicked cries of Simone, pleading with me to come back. The presence of a threat greater than I flooded my senses, and Sister Gloria's smile widened.

"I told you about the Curse of the Dark Moon, you foolish boy," she gritted through her teeth. "But I never told you about the Moon's Guardian..." Her whiskey brown eyes instantly turned to silver. In her hand, a long sword materialized. "You are a curse upon humanity, and I am here to send you and that bitch Simone back to hell where the likes of you belong!"

I managed to miss her hard strike with the sword, barely escaped its sharp tip piercing the center of my chest. Simone's cries invaded my mental space, drowning out Sister Gloria's curses. I spun around to take flight into the night, but instantly discovered a magnetic energy holding me in place. I struggled, using every ounce of strength at my disposal, but I was unsuccessful. Sister Gloria circled me, dragging the tip of her long blade on her front porch.

"I have been fighting your kind for centuries," she whispered just loud enough for only me to hear. "But I have been tracking Simone for the last fifty years. You are the last of her reign. Without you, she will be easier for me to kill."

I swallowed thickly, regretting not only having appeared at this woman's house tonight, but all of my adult transgressions--the main one breaking my mother's heart. Her strike was swift and dead on, and the last thing I remembered before my soul returned to my body for the last time and what was left of me became ash, was the ancient Kemetic symbol: an Ankh, wrapped around Sister Gloria's neck.

I never noticed it until now.

If you ever see a fly ass female with raven dark hair and even darker skin, run.

And if you ever see an older woman, sitting at the front of the church with big red bifocals but with the gait and walk of a warrior, do not underestimate her. That is Sister Gloria, Vampire Hunter...oh, and more thing: if you do happen to run into Simone, tell her that Sister Gloria is looking for her.

T☐☐ E☐☐

TANGO OF A TELLTALE HEART

SUMIKO SAULSON

T⬚⬚ ⬚⬚⬚ ⬚⬚⬚⬚⬚⬚ ⬚⬚⬚⬚ ⬚⬚⬚⬚⬚ ⬚⬚⬚ ⬚⬚⬚⬚⬚⬚⬚ ⬚⬚⬚⬚ shocks of scarlet, tangerine and crimson over the surface of Stow Lake. One leg of my woolen tights had been shredded. Blood oozed out of the gash in my calf and spread over the hem of my cotton Arawak African Print dress. A floret of blood spread over my knee. I winced as I dragged my injured leg behind me.

Blood... it runs through our veins telling a story more nuanced than any report or record Ancestry.com can provide. Inheritance... what we relay in our oral histories doesn't include all of those skeletons hiding in dank corners of the musty closet we call our family tree. Mine? Almost every African American descended from a slave is also the progeny of a slave-owner. My family is no exception.

My blood, strongly scented of iron and fear, might attract the leashed dogs that belonged to the Stow Lake Killer if I didn't focus. Five girls disappeared before me... three of them in the past month. The news said he was escalating. Only one girl escaped so far. I hoped the second one would be me.

My breath grew labored from panic and walking. Afraid I'd wear myself out; I found shelter against the mossy trunk of a low-slung, widespread tree. A leather strap held a drum in place over my shoulder. I lifted it over my neck and set it down for a pillow.

My drum is part of my family inheritance. The drumhead is made of untreated rawhide bound with thongs to the red-brown hardwood body. As a child my tiny, calloused hands learned to pound out rhythm on it. My grandfather left it to me when he died.

I could barely hear the soft stir of katydids over my pounding heart. In the distance I heard the barking of his dogs, the steady whistle of the breeze against the branches, and the thrashing of his feet in the under bush. All of these sounds created intersecting rhythm.

What can I say about rhythm?

Back in high school, I went to a presentation by the Maranatha Christian Youth Group. Maranatha was an Aramaic word that appeared in the New Testament exactly once, meaning 'our Lord has come' or some such thing. I have no idea why they chose that particular name, but we used to call them the Merry Nazis because they claimed that African drum beats in rock and roll music made it the devil's music. Allegedly, these beats were used for the worship of ancient gods. The entire rhythm section was in cahoots with the Antichrist. Four-four rhythm was based on the human heart beat, but these African rhythms focused on the downbeat, which was contrary to nature. I rolled my eyes at their discourse upon the unnatural rhythms of my black body.

They'd decided there was some impurity in my blood, a

summoning from deep within my body that called me to the drubbing beat on the dancefloor. But how could it be unnatural, when Africa was our mother? Every race found its genetic heritage in Africa - that was science fact, not fantasy. Theirs was the fantasy, that there was something evil in the very genetic makeup of me. If there was anything evil in me, I assure you it didn't come from Africa. It came from the blood of the oppressors – the plantation lords – that ran through me. How did any African American ever come to terms with the blood of the rapist white slave owning sperm donors that ran though our veins along with that of our African mothers?

Anything evil that came from me was part of white Christendom, not alien to it at all.

"Come out of the bushes, whore!" the killer yelled, still out there searching for me. "I'll find you! My dog can smell the stink of your sex!"

I cowered below the tree, applying wet leaves to my leg to mask the scent of blood. When I was done, I began to softly scratch at the head of my drum. The sound echoed o☐ the walls of the base, making comforting sounds in my ears to mask his evil voice. He hadn't gotten to me yet, and if I had anything to do with it, he wouldn't.

"Come protect me, ancestors from every side..." I whispered, caressing the drum with my fingers. "Come protect me ancestral spirits, from far and wide..."

The Stow Lake Killer didn't know what I knew. The drum was possessed of dark magic, magic that wasn't African in the least, and the kind of mysticism one would be well warned away from. Indeed, the ancestral spirit warned me against using the spells carved into the wooden kettle drum by Lacey Evans, an angry young slave girl.

Delwyn Evans, Lacey's plantation lord father, was unaware

of the lessons Lacey learned at the hands of her half-sister, Brynn. Perhaps if the man hadn't been evil to all of his daughters – slave and free alike – the young Welsh witch wouldn't have taught these arcane runes to her black half-sister. Then, the taint wouldn't have come upon the drum. And the temptation wouldn't be upon me. The temptation to invoke what should never be called upon.

But extreme times called for extreme measures.

The Stow Lake Killer was a predator, but so was the spirit that lived in my drum.

How did the drum grow in power? It depends on who you ask. Those who vilify you sometimes have the power to focus their wicked minds on everyday objects. How many generations had it taken to curse the drum? The drum in question was a small Djembe, a type of kettle drum from West Africa. Rumor has it that it arrived with my ancestor when they dragged him here in chains from Mali two hundred years ago.

My grandfather didn't think the curse comes from our African blood. He said it came from the Welsh plantation owners who danced in and out of our bloodline every time they forced one of our mothers to lie with them. He said it came from the jealous wives who beat senselessly slave girls who were sometimes their cousins or half-sisters. The curse was born of blood begetting blood and kin betraying kin. It was from fathers flaying the flesh from the backs of daughters and sons who were born into slavery.

That's why the drum hated men like the Stow Lake Killer in particular.

He preyed on girls like me. Nubile, young college girls who hung around the drum circle smoking marijuana with the good folks who made music there. Girls like us gathered around in the drum circle at Golden Gate Park on the week-ends. Hippie hill had a coed, multicultural vibe and was a definite all-ages sort of gathering.

Some of the girls around the circle are homeless. Not me. I attend the University of California San Francisco, where I learned to pound out rhythm of the flesh in my dorm room two years ago. A free-spirit with a dust cloud of tightly curled dark hair running wild and ungreased and untamed most days. Today I wore afro puffs with a jewel-encrusted turquoise butterfly hairclip off to one side. I wore flowing gowns of African kinte cloth or Jamaican colors, proudly attesting to my heritage. But my loose-fitting dresses were knee length, and I wore them over tights and knit stockings with oxblood Doc Martins.

I lifted the drum and carefully placed it between my shoes. One leather clad foot cradled either side of it. There was always a price for invoking the spirit that lived within, but I felt I had no choice. My desperate situation fortified my resolve. Without hesitation, I pounded on the rough skin of the Djembe. My voice rose over the beat, a soft moan crying out to my ancestors. I heard a baying in the distance. The man's dog cried out in kind.

Slowly, my head began to turn, neck wringing of its own accord. He sat beside me, dark as pitch, not enclosed in but composed of shadow. My hands moved in time with an earthly beat, counter to the rhythm of my heart. Sound rose in pulsing intensity as the shadow beast solidified. The drum beat rose to a crescendo beneath my furious hands. The dark hound began to howl. Red eyes pierced the gray mist of dusk. He was Cŵn Annwn, Welsh hound of the hunt.

Christians called them hellhounds. I believed that their superstitions were what cast the hounds of the hunt as villainous. What did they know? It seemed the Maranatha and their ilk feel as certain of my Welsh blood's demonic taint as they were of the African. Perhaps this is why I am no Christian. The palms of my hands began to ache, but I continued, pressing forward with the kinetic sound of the dance.

A gray, hooded figure appeared in the mist beside the hound. She stepped forward and lowered her hood so I could see her face. It was my friend, Marigold. She'd been dead for two weeks now. She winked, closing one of her glinting ruby eyes. Then she grinned, her teeth long and sharp as the tines of an iron fork.

"You are the one who will be found!" I bellowed at the man. "Cn Annwn will find you, or perhaps you will find me, but it won't help you." I pounded into the Djembe until his brothers appeared... more hounds of the hunt. With each new dog appeared a woman... one of those cut short in her life by the Stow Lake Killer. The dogs were escorts of the dead, but tonight they appeared as vengeful spirits.

When I looked down at the drum, my hands were bleeding. I winced when I looked at it. Blood fed the instrument. My blood and the blood of many of my ancestors soaked into the rawhide head. Once all of the women had arrived, he appeared... an Azawakh. Pale beige, long and thin as a greyhound or a whippet. He was an African hunting dog. The Azawakh always appeared last.

He sat directly across from me, fixing me with a sad stare. "How can you betray your ancestors?" he seemed to say. The Azawakh was dismayed by my decision to use the white man's magic against him. But I was Welsh and the dogs that ran with Herne would protect me.

It was like my grandfather told me when I was a girl. Back in 1814, Delwyn Evans had no idea that the blood that ran through his illegitimate daughter's veins carried magic. When he set out to rape her, as he had raped her slave mother Sally, and her sister, Brynn... Lacey called upon the old spirits to protect her and avenge her mother's death at her father's abusive hands. She called them with this drum. The same drum I played on Hippie Hill.

My name isn't Lacey. It's Matilda. On nights like this, it seems to matter more.

"You aren't scaring nobody with your drum, girl!" the man yelled, running towards me. I heard him crash through the underbrush. Branches snapped under his feet, drawing closer. My eyes began to roll into the back of my head. Mallt-y-Nos began to take over. They call her Matilda of the Night. She controls the beasts known as C□n Mamau, the hounds of hell.

What is it like to be possessed, you ask? Her pale blue fingers sliding under my brown skin, keeping time with the omnipresent drum beat. She was here to drive the dead women to Annwn, the Otherworld. It was madness to play with faerie folk, my father would have said. He was a minister, true to Christian world that abhors such things. There was always a price to pay. But what were a few wandering souls? Who is to say that Annwn is worse than whatever afterlife they were headed to? My father, a minister, would have said I was damning them. I saw it di□erently. I was giving them the opportunity for vengeance.

My great, great grandfather shook his head once more. He sat beside his familiar, The Azawakh. "You are deceived, child," he cautioned. "It isn't just the Christians that abhor the wickedness you do. Let those girls' spirits go free! Don't bow to the spirit possessing you. You're worse than the man what murdered them right now."

"Not now, old man!" I rebuked him, relaxing my body to allow the invading spirit to take me over completely. Only

Matilda of the Night could help them. Matilda Sarah Evans was useless! Sacrifices had to be made. I gave myself over to the spirit.

My fingers went cold as Mallt-y-Nos took over completely. I felt as if it were someone else, tormenting the drum with bleeding fingers and stress-fractured nails.

"I do not fear you! I howled with Mallt-y-Nos, giving myself over fully to the possessing entity, "You will fear me!" I screeched and tittered, cheering the dogs on in their mission. Annihilation would come for the man first, next the apparitions avenged and in the end, possibly me. But what was any of that to me, at this point? I was beyond caring.

My father and grandfather alike warned me that playing with the spirit put me at risk. One day she would take me over entirely, and consuming my flesh, and leave nothing but a dried husk. My spirit would be bound to her forever.

"You're the one who's scared!" the Stow Lake Killer screamed, pulling up in front of the bushes. He yanked a tree branch to one side and slapped me hard, knocking me away from my drums. My eyes were white, irises folded back under my lids first, then deeper in my head... where they go in trances. I could see him through other means. I grinned, my skull flashing pale blue through my dark skin. The edges of my lips were covered in wild frothing foam like a rabid dog. With a hoarse whisper I commanded, "See them... see!"

"What the hell?" the killer yelped, finally able to view the hounds and the lost women.

"You killed me," Mary accused, pointing one finger at him. Her tongue lolled to one side of her torn mouth. Needle-sharp teeth completed her sardonic smile. She stroked the drooling hellhound who heeled at her side.

Janet, another of the dead, followed suit. "Murderer!" she

hissed, lifting an accusing digit. Each of the other women in turn, accused him. Afterwards, Mary gave a swift swat to the haunches of the dog beside her. Each of the other women did the same. The hounds of hell went sailing at the rapist, ravening teeth tearing into his calves as he fled.

"You belong to the fae now," Mallt-y-Nos cackled, causing me to rise and lumber forth towards my friend. The drum fell down into the moist grass below. The Azawakh ran over to its side and curled around the Djembe, whimpering. Through the back of my head I could see his dejected eyes observing in shame as I opened my mouth.

Mary stepped back. "What are you doing, Mathilda?"

"The hounds do my bidding," Mallt-y-Nos screamed. "Mathilda has naught to do with their power. Yet she struck a deal for you. Vengeance is sweet, is it not?"

"I don't need revenge..." Mary whispered, slipping backward with her ghostly feet until the tree behind her interceded.

She turned to one side, ready to sprint... but it was too late. My dislocated jaw stretched out like a snake's. Sharp, thorny teeth erupted from aching gums. My strained mouth distended further until it covered the face of my deceased friend Mary. I swallowed her head whole. The other women, frozen, trembled in fear as they waited to be devoured.

Behind me, the Azawakh began his transformation. Mallt-y-Nos paused between bits of spectral flesh to eye him suspiciously. As for me, I could not speak. The African dog transmuted until I saw the image of a man who greatly resembled my grandfather behind me. As with every previous time, I must await his verdict.

"I told you not to do this, girl," the ancestral spirit chided. "You owe a debt every time. Your debt is growing too great."

"You nag and chide like my old maiden aunt," I said. "I know you mean well, but you have no idea how bad things have gotten around here!"

"Not as bad as they will get if you tamper with that old Welsh magic," he said, shaking his head. "Every African spirit attached to the drum couldn't cleanse the curse that Lacey Evans carved into the side of it with her daddy's blood and her dirty little bone knife. All we do is hold the wickedness in check. But how can your ancestral spirits protect you, willful one? When all you do is fight us!"

In the distance, I heard the Stow Lake Killer scream as a hellhound snapped into his thigh. I could see everything now at once... what Mallt-y-Nos saw, what the Azawakh saw, and what the C☐n Annwn saw. I grinned in spite of myself as the hounds tore into the buttocks of the fallen rapist. I could taste his blood on my tongue. Warm, his flesh in the mouths of the hungry dogs. Teeth tore into muscle, shredding tendons with ease. The lead dog dug into the meat of his eye with hungry jaws. The maw of Janet's dog was covered in gore. The piteous cries of the dying man bought no sympathy or thought of remorse in the dogs or myself.

"I did what was right," I told the ancient one. "I sought justice for these women."

"You condemned their souls," he rebutted. "I have rescued you from your fate every time thus far, but this is growing too easy for you, Mathilda."

"You don't know where their souls go," I argued. "They may be safer with the faerie folk than to wherever you might relegate them."

"You see it for yourself, then," he spoke with grave finality. "You are not the only one who can use the drum, child." His hands began to pound at the drum. Sound rose in roiling waves of thunder, passing under my skin, mingling with my blood sound, altering the pace of my beating heart.

Over his shoulder, a shadowy cloaked figure appeared. This was a man I'd never seen before, but I knew him instantly. He was Arawn, King of Annwn.

"It is time to go, Mathilda," he said calmly. Your ancestors can't save you now."

"It was inevitable, I fear," the Azawakh told the wizened African elder at his side. "Her grandfather shouldn't have let her touch that drum."

I was about to refute him when a ghost appeared at my side. Tattered and bloodied by his recent encounter with the hellhounds, it was the Stow Lake Killer. A chill came over me. Could what I have done possibly have been so bad that I must accompany this man to the afterlife?

Arawn waved his hands and the sky before him began to crumble. Cool sweat dried against my naked arms. A frozen grin stuck on my shock-worn face. Dimensions collapsed upon each other, and in a moment, Mallt-y-Nos separated from me. Her mouth stretched over the Stow Lake Killer, and she engulfed him as a snake would a feeder rat. I stood immobile, waiting to be devoured.

"A moment, please..." a new voice spoke from behind the Azawakh. She was a young black woman in a wide-brimmed russet bonnet, a cream-colored apron over her simple brown frock. I recognized her from an ancient sienna photograph my grandfather used to carry.

"Lacey..." Arawn hissed. "Don't you think it's a bit of a late hour for your sudden arrival?"

"Don't you mean our arrival?" Lacey countered, gesturing towards the blank space beside her. I looked down, suddenly. Twin footprints were visible in the damp grass. A ghostly apparition formed in the fog. As she slowly solidified, I began to notice a striking resemblance between the flaxen-haired, peaches-and-cream complexioned young woman standing beside her in a light green cotton Victorian school teacher's dress.

"Brynn…" Arawn moaned, holding his head as though it were suddenly throbbing with a migraine headache. "Haven't you caused enough trouble?"

Brynn looked at her sister and shook her head. Neither of them spoke a word to him. Instead, they ran behind me and grabbed me, each pinning one of my arms to her side, while they walloped me across the back with incredible strength.

"I'm afraid you've eaten something that doesn't agree with you," Lacey snarled, hitting me over and over again between my shoulder blades until I began to cough. Brynn joined her, smashing the flat of her palm into either of my sides until I began to vomit. The sisters beat my body until I crumbled to the ground.

It was difficult to breathe. The taste of cold swampy water tore at my throat. A puddle of moist ectoplasm and fetid lake water piled on the ground in front of me. Slowly, the last of the girls, Janet, appeared in a damp pile at my feet. Her hair, dark and slimy, was clotted with bits of vomit and congealing fat. They all poured out, one by one, until at last, my friend Mary emerged as baby through the birth canal – my distended jaw and torn throat creating the birth passage, my torn stomach a womb.

My ancestors stood there, with each of the newly rebirthed women between them, raw and covered in spectral substance the way a newborn is covered in amniotic fluid.

Angry, Lacey snatched the drum from my hands and

tossed it at Arawn. "They aren't yours! Leave!" she screamed. "Take your wicked spells with you, demon!"

"Take your accursed drum and be gone!" Brynn joined in, hissing at the god.

"How can you rebuke a god?" I howled, clutching my torn fingers over my aching belly as I fell into the putrid pile of fluid at my feet. Mary and Janet stood over me, casting down accusatory glares.

"Silly girl..." Lacey mumbled. Sending out a low whistle, she called the Azawakh to her side. "I've sent my ancestor and my familiar to guide you, but it's been a waste of time. You never listen."

"I warned her," the Azawakh complained as Lacey stroked him between the ears.

"Tell your god to take his curse o□ my drum," the elder ordered Brynn, his voice soft and calm. "You know you put it there, not your sister."

Brynn's bright blue eyes widened. "I did it to *help* her!" she protested.

"It is no help," the old man replied. "You can't have the drum I made, Arawn. You can't have this wayward child. You can't rope her into your hunt. Take your foul curse o□ my beautiful drum."

Arawn shook his head. "You can't unhex what is hexed! Best you teach your children not to play with cursed objects next time, old fool!" He screamed, his raw voice soon joined by the screech and chatter of Mallt-y-Nos, and the howling of the angry C□n Annwn.

"Then, go!" Lacey ordered. "Leave this place."

Arawn looked at the drum briefly then dropped it on the floor where he stood. "Better one soul than none," he said. "Come along, Mallt-y-Nos!" Turning around, he crossed over the veil into Annwn, the hounds of hell following at his heel, Mallt-y-Nos beside him, with the tortured soul of the Stow Lake Killer imprisoned in her gullet.

"I didn't expect Arawn himself to show up this time!" I panted in excitement from where I lay in a pool of filth on the ground.

"You're lucky you aren't in Annwn now," Brynn chided.

"Fool…" the elder hissed, looking away.

"I subdued the Stow Lake Killer," I defended. "Because of me, he won't take another life. Yet you vilify me. Hypocrites."

"You're not a hero!" Janet spat. "You're just some asshole on a power trip."

"You ate me!" Mary screamed hysterically. "You fucking bitch, you ate me! You ate me!" She ran round in a circle, agitated and temporarily unaware of her death.

Lacey Evans rolled her eyes. "Don't bother talking to her. She won't listen," she said. "Grab the drum, won't you, Brynn?"

I lay on the ground immobile as Lacey and Brynn Evans sat on the ground, carving Arawn only knew what on the drum. It was freezing outside, and the dew was setting upon my frozen shoulders and vomit-dampened clothing. I was sure I was catching a cold.

"Here you go," Lacey mumbled, throwing the drum down at my feet. "You take that and you go on now. It won't perform any magic tricks for you anymore."

"Don't call me. I won't call you," Mary said, following Brynn and the ancient one into the darkness. Janet saved her breath, and flipped me the bird instead. I suppose I can't blame them for thinking the worst of me.

Lacey and the Azawakh sat and stared at me, back facing the others as they walked away. An hour had passed since

Brynn and the others had faded away into the mist, but Lacey and the Azawakh remained, staring.

"Once, I was as stubborn as you are now," Lacey finally spoke. She waved her hand over me, releasing me from the suspended animation that held me for so long. "It bought me nothing but pain. I hope one day, you'll do better."

"Does your ancestor know?" I asked her, carefully sitting up.

"That I asked Brynn to enchant the drum?" Lacey whispered. "That I am as much to blame for the taint on his drum as my white sister? He doesn't know because he doesn't want to know. He doesn't want to know what we've become."

"Like them," I agreed. "We've become like them."

"If you know that much, you should take your lesson to heart. Don't show up here wasting my time again!" Lacey screamed. Then she stomped o[] into the fog and disappeared behind her sister. She seemed as much a child as I did, the ancient wise woman, with her wise words, repeated so many times they became empty.

The Stow Lake Killer's body was found the day after. Within days, the police matched his fingerprints with those found on the corpses of Mary Wharton and Janet Goldman. They found him in the database, a petty thug with a history of domestic violence and a college rape accusation named Robert Jones, of all innocuous and non-descript things. The papers said he was killed by an unidentified victim. They begged her to come to the police and turn herself in. You and I both know I never did.

They talked for years about how his own dogs tore apart his body. The dogs were never found, they say. They probably wandered o[] into the park somewhere. They might be dangerous. The girl who killed him, she might be dangerous.

I might be dangerous, but I've never killed another man.

It's been twenty years since that day in the park. I can't say if I've become the wiser. I'm older, certainly. I spit out platitudes with the best of them... live by the sword, die by the sword. Violence begets violence. I sit in the drum circle and pound on an instrument that has been bound specifically to prevent be from doing any magic with it. From time to time, I reflect upon the writing and think about the night my ancestors showed up to save my immortal soul.

Over the past twenty years, many men like Robert Jones have emerged. Every time one does. I wonder what I might do if I still have the drum? Then Janet Goldman's final words come to me once more.

"You're not a hero. You're just some asshole on a power trip."

I've decided by now that she was probably right.

T☐☐ E☐☐

HERE KITTY!

LH MOORE

J░░░░ ░░░░░░ ░░ ░░░ ░░░░░░ ░░░░-░░░░░░ ░░░░░░ every day as she walked to and from her home to the bus stop. It didn't stand out that much and wasn't striking at all. There wasn't really a reason that it needed to be. It was just a two-story place with green shutters and a porch. Run of the mill. Average. Like most of the little houses in her neighborhood.

Sometimes its owner, an elderly woman named Mrs. Mills, would sit outside on her porch in a plastic chair, a slightly warped, cheap, white one with a leg that buckled as she shifted around in it. She seemed friendly enough, and was one of those persons who liked to keep an eye on the community. Nothing missed her watchful gaze.

Ever present in her striped cotton housedress, knee-high stockings and black shoes, she would chide the kids and teens one moment, then ask them about school and tell them to "Do good!" the next. If she was out, she'd greet you as you passed. If the weather wasn't so great, she would sit in her front window instead. It was just what she did, and she had become a fixture, in a way, because of it.

One crisp, early autumn day, Josie was walking home from the bus stop, as usual. Her day at work had been long. *Anyone who thinks being an administrative assistant is easy is crazy*, she thought, shaking her head. Her phone started to ring, and she stopped on the sidewalk in front of Mrs. Mills house to dig through her large handbag to find it. By the time that she did, it had stopped ringing. She noted that the battery was almost dead, and sighed as she hoisted her bag back up onto her shoulder.

Just as she started to walk away, Josie heard the creak of a screen door opening, and Mrs. Mills leaned out, waving a dark brown hand at her.

"Hello! Hello there, young lady!" she called out.

"Hello!" Josie said with a wave back as she resumed her walk home.

"Wait, wait!" Mrs. Mills said, stepping out onto the porch. "Young lady, do you mind helping me out for a moment, please?"

Josie turned, facing the metal chain-link fence around the woman's small front yard. There were a few scraggly flower bushes in need of a trim, and a little statue tucked among them. *Probably a garden gnome or some knick-knack like that,* Josie thought as she came closer to the gate.

"How may I help you?" Josie asked with a smile. The older woman's face was elated.

"It is my cat, Kiki. I can't find her. She's here in the house, and I'm afraid that she might be stuck somewhere and can't get herself out. Can you help me find her?"

"I can try," Josie said as she made her way up the wooden steps onto the porch.

Mrs. Mills' warm brown eyes lit up. "Oh, thank you, young lady! Thank you so much! That is so kind of you. Come on in! What is your name dear?"

She smiled back as she stepped through the doorway into the house. "Josie, ma'am. I'm Josie."

———

L☐☐ ☐☐☐ ☐☐☐☐☐☐☐☐ ☐☐☐ ☐☐☐☐ ☐☐ ☐☐☐ ☐☐☐☐☐ ☐☐☐ simple. Mrs. Mills led her to a small front living room. A slightly worn, dark red, tufted couch took up most of it, a multicolored crocheted afghan blanket carefully folded along its back. There was a wooden co☐ee table and end table. There were a few photos of Mrs. Mills when she was younger. Family members. Her with a man that Josie assumed was Mr. Mills. In one photo, they were dressed up for a fancy event of some sort.

"You can put your bags down in that chair over there," the older woman said as she pointed to one that matched the dark red fabric of the couch. As Josie walked over to it, she noticed that there were small cat figurines, all black. Some porcelain. Some wood. All di☐erent shapes and sizes and variations on the black cat theme. Mrs. Mills saw her looking at them.

"Kiki is black," she said wistfully as she lightly touched one of them. "So I buy ones that remind me of her. And sometimes people give 'em to me. Black cats are so sleek and mysterious. I love them. Don't you?"

"They are alright, I suppose." Josie said with a smile.

Mrs. Mills led her through a small dining room, its table

set with china and a centerpiece, and they walked through an arched doorway to the kitchen. "May I offer you something? Make you some tea first? I find that tea really calms me."

"Oh no, ma'am. Don't go through any trouble for me, please."

"It really isn't any trouble at all, honey. It's the least that I could do for your helping me out." Mrs. Mills opened her refrigerator and pulled out a plastic bottle of water. "How about some water? Would you like that instead? I also have some juice…"

Josie smiled. "Alright then. I would like some water, please." Mrs. Mills handed her the bottle and walked over to a cabinet to get her a glass. "Oh, no need," Josie said, holding up the bottle. "I'm fine with drinking it out of the bottle."

Mrs. Mills smiled and gestured for her to take a seat in one of the high-backed kitchen chairs. As Josie sat down, Mrs. Mills did as well, her hands folded in her lap. Her gray hair was well-coiffed in a roller set, not a curl out of place. She pushed her dark-rimmed glasses back up on her nose.

"I have lived here for a long time now," she said. "It has been quiet for some time now. The neighborhood has changed a lot. It used to be rougher. Really rough. A tough time for us all here who remembered when it was a good place. There were drug dealers and crack addicts and all of the drama that went along with that. I'm glad those times have ended here."

Josie nodded. "A lot of communities had that happen. Sadly, some still have it happening. It seems to be a nice neighborhood here now though. I like that it is quiet."

"Well, it's quiet because things got really cleaned up. Young people like you are moving here and making it different too. There used to be a whole lot of random deaths. Girl, there were just bodies turning up left and right. They said some of them were even mutilated. Some were just...pieces left. Cops never figured out who was doing all of *that* kind of mess. Never found 'em and no one ever admitted to it. For all we know they're still out there, you know?"

Josie looked alarmed. "That's horrible! I am so glad that it's gotten better, that's for certain." She sipped from the bottle and finished the last of the water. She set the bottle down on the table.

"One thing about it being quiet is that it is definitely a lot harder to get away with things around here now. There are way more eyes. Way more persons paying attention to what's going on."

"I could see that." Josie said as she nodded again. Mrs. Mills smiled at her. "But given everything that had happened in the community, that's a good thing though, isn't it?"

"Oh, you have no idea."

Josie looked outside the kitchen window and frowned. "The sun is starting to go down, so I'd like to try and help you find her as soon as possible, in case I need to look outside, too." She stood up.

"I don't think that you will need to go outside. She's very much a house cat. I'd *never* let her out there. She wouldn't be out there. That would be a bad idea." She shook her head emphatically.

Josie shrugged. "Alright then. Let's go and find Kiki."

———

M☐☐ M☐☐☐ ☐☐☐ ☐☐☐ ☐☐☐☐☐☐☐ ☐☐☐ ☐☐☐☐☐☐ T☐☐ started in the kitchen, looking everywhere. They opened the small pantry filled with canned goods and little containers, its single light bulb overhead. Josie opened wooden cabinets and peeked into boxes. She checked under the metal-legged table with its plastic tablecloth covered in a red rose design.

"Well, she is not in here," Mrs. Mills said as Josie closed the last of the bottom cabinet doors. Josie nodded in agreement. They checked the back room thoroughly. Nothing but a washer, dryer and utility sink. No Kiki. She shook her head. "No, not in here either."

They walked back towards the front door and stopped at the bottom of the stairs to the second floor. Josie waited patiently as Mrs. Mills took her time carefully going up the steps, sometimes pausing to catch her breath as she used her cane for leverage.

"Ooof..." she grunted as she planted the cane down solidly on the step ahead. "My knees just ain't what they used to be, you know?"

"When was the last time you saw Kiki?" Josie asked as they slowly made their way upstairs.

"Hmm... last night? The last time that I saw her was last night. I think that she has to be really hungry by now." She steadied herself with the railing as she went up the last step. "I have to take care of her. She is really something special. She's all that I have left now."

There was a small bathroom at the top of the stairs. Josie took a peek inside, just to make sure Kiki wasn't napping in the tub or in the cabinet under the sink. No. She wasn't in any of those places either. She sighed a little bit. "Are you sure that there is not any way that she could've gotten outside?"

"Oh no. She really is an indoor cat now, remember? She's not allowed outdoors *at all*. Who knows what kind of trouble she would get into out there, you know? All sorts of bad things could happen."

They went into the smaller of the two bedrooms. It had a plain bed with a dark wooden headboard. The bed was neatly made up with a cream-colored bedspread. A braided rug was on the floor beneath. A wooden dresser was against one wall, a white lace doily spread across its top. There were framed pictures of beautiful geometric designs. *So pretty! How artsy of her,* Josie thought.

More black cat figurines were arranged on top of the dresser. *It's a bit much, but I guess she really, really loves this cat,* Josie thought to herself with a smile. *She does seem to have a touch of cat lady to her. Honestly, I'm surprised that she only has one of them.*

Mrs. Mills stood in the doorway watching as Josie lifted the bedspread and peeked under the bed, Then she opened a musty-smelling closet of old clothes. Her hand brushed against some dark velvet fabric with gold embroidery. A cape or cloak of some sort. *That must have been beautiful to wear out to somewhere nice,* Josie thought as she closed the door.

"Doesn't seem to be in here Mrs. Mills. This is crazy. I'm really wondering where she is."

"On to the next room then, Josie. I hope we find her. I hate to think that she could be stuck or something's wrong. I have to watch out for her. She can be a very tricky one to deal with sometimes."

Josie laughed. "Cats can certainly be like that."

"Do you have any pets?"

"No ma'am. Unfortunately, the place that I am renting doesn't let me have any pets. I had some dogs growing up, but no cats. They creeped my father out. He said he always hated the way they seemed to sneak up on you."

"My late husband was the same way as your father. He really did not like Kiki at all. Didn't understand why I kept her. Until his end, he absolutely detested her and wanted nothing to do with her. He even tried to get rid of her once…" Her voice trailed off. "Well, how about you Miss Josie? Do you like cats?"

"I like them just fine as far as pets go, but have never had any myself."

"Oh, a shame. They are so special." Mrs. Mills said as they walked down the hall to the master bedroom.

Josie always found being in someone else's bedroom—particularly a stranger's—for the first time to be a weird feeling. Their most private place. It felt almost intrusive, but Mrs. Mills didn't seem to mind at all. She sat down on a wooden chair in the corner as Josie searched around under the bed and into the closet again. Like the second bedroom, the master bedroom had a frugal simplicity to it. A plain bedspread as well as a colorful quilt was upon the bed. A nightstand had a small clock and a container for her dental work to soak overnight. There was a photo of a younger Mrs. Mills with a group of women sitting next to the clock. They were all standing together with serious looks on their faces. Mrs. Mills noticed her eyeing it.

"Those were my…sorority sisters."

"A sorority? Which one? Deltas? AKAs? Zetas? I was never in one. They seemed fun, but I wasn't much of a joiner."

Mrs. Mills laughed.

"Sorry," Josie said. "Were you all close?"

"Yes, indeed. We were quite close. I trusted all of them with my life. We had some interesting times together."

"Are you still friends with them?" Josie asked.

Mrs. Mills looked sad. "I am the last one left."

"Oh no. I am so sorry to hear that. That must have been really hard, to lose all of them like that."

Mrs. Mills shrugged. "We all got older. It happens. One by one, we pass away." She quickly changed the subject. "Do you have any family or friends in the area?"

"I moved here for work not too long ago. I have more acquaintances than friends right now, you know?" Mrs. Mills nodded in understanding. "My only best friend—we had been friends since we were very little—died in an accident about two months ago. I was an only child and both my parents are gone now too. So no, I don't really have anyone right now."

"Not even a handsome beau?" Mrs. Mills said with a wink, smiling at her. "Or a pretty lady?"

Josie laughed. "There's this one person that I really like, but it's not seri..." She started to say more and then suddenly clammed up. She laughed again. "I feel like I've been rambling. I seem to have a tendency to do that."

As she passed the photo again, Josie stopped to look at it a little more closely. They were all dressed in the same dark velvet robes, like the one she'd brushed up against. "You're dressed alike. I know how much sorority sisters like to wear matching things. Was this for a theme party or special occasion?"

Mrs. Mills looked at her and a strange expression crossed her face. "You could say that," she said as she waited in the doorway. Josie felt a chill, and quickly said "Well, she's not in here either. Is there somewhere else that we can look? I've got to get going soon."

Mrs. Mills sighed. "I have kept you for quite a while. It has been so nice having you help me out like this, dear heart. Well, I suppose we had better check the cellar."

Josie grimaced as Mrs. Mills walked ahead and started to

make her way down the steps. She hated going down into cellars. They were always the stu□ of horror movies and nightmares: dark, dusty, and filled with unused, unwanted, forgotten things.

Mrs. Mills opened the door and flipped a switch. The light bulb overhead came on with a buzzing sound and the cellar was exactly as she expected: a dark, dusty nightmare.

The wooden steps creaked and felt unsteady under their weight as they went down. "Kiki? Kiiii-kiiii? Are you down here?" Mrs. Mills called out. Josie held onto the railing for dear life going down. The last thing that she wanted to do was trip and fall.

Even with the lights on, the cellar seemed dark. *Ugh, I hate basements so much,* Josie thought as she followed Mrs. Mills and the tap of her cane on the concrete floor. Light filtered in through a narrow, bar-covered window, yet it still seemed dim and gray. Old chairs were stacked up in a corner. There were stacks of books and papers everywhere. A workbench covered with jars was in another corner. *Who knows what is in those jars?* Josie thought, shaking her head as they wound their way through the cellar. It wasn't large, but the stacks and piles were like obstacles as they made their way through.

"You know, I would think that we would have heard her mewing or something before now though, especially if she was stuck."

Mrs. Mills stopped for a moment as if to think. "That is a very good point! I haven't heard her meow or anything since this morning, either. That is rather strange. That is also pretty worrying as well. I am definitely worried that something's happened to her now!"

A film of dust seemed to cover everything, making Josie

sneeze loudly. She stopped for a moment. Thinking that she heard something in response to her sneeze. Josie looked around the piles and stacks as best as she could. "I think that could be her! Maybe she really is down here. I would not be surprised!"

Mrs. Mills exclaimed "That would be wonderful!" and began calling the cat's name too. Josie joined Mrs. Mills and called out to the cat as well. "Kiki! Kiki! C'mon out girl, c'mon!" she said, imploring it to come out of its hiding place to them.

After a few minutes of calling out to it to no avail, Josie turned to Mrs. Mills. "You know, I really could've sworn that I heard something move around down here. Maybe I didn't?"

"Well, let's keep looking then?" Mrs. Mills said, walking ahead until they reached a door towards the back of the cellar. It was locked. Josie stood and waited as Mrs. Mills unlocked it. The older woman pulled on the door latch and found it hard to open. "Mmph!" she grunted. "This door sticks a little. Could you give it a try?"

Josie shrugged and said "Sure, I'll try." She stepped forward and easily opened it. The room beyond was dark, so dark she couldn't quite see anything at all. She thought she saw movement on the far right of the room.

"Kiki?" she called out, thinking that the cat had somehow gotten herself locked up in there at some point. She heard shu ing sounds from the other end again. "C'mon girl. C'mon out."

In the dimness of the room, a dark shadow raised itself up at the other end in the direction from which she had seen the movement. *What the...?!* she thought, her eyes becoming wide. *This can't be happening. What IS that??* Josie thought that her mind had to be playing tricks on her in the dark. Then, two very large yellow glowing eyes opened, looking directly at her in the darkness. This was no kitty. She didn't know what this thing was, but this was not a cat *at all*.

It was then let out a long, low growl. She screamed and jumped at the sound of it, everything in her knowing that she needed to leave. *Now.* She backed away from it towards the door, her eyes still on whatever that creature was that was in there with her.

It was then that Josie felt hands on her back, shoving her forward into the room with surprising force. She fell down onto her hands and knees, shocked and rattled as she scraped them against the hard ground.

She staggered to her feet, struggling to try to comprehend what had just happened to her. Then she heard the door quickly shut, and the click of its lock behind her.

Wait...WHAT?!

Josie whirled around and started banging on the door with both fists over and over again, screaming in panic. "Mrs. Mills! Mrs. Mills! *Please!* What are you doing?! *What is going on?!* Let me out! Please! Oh my God, open up and *please* let me out!"

She kept banging on the door, and then the realization that it wasn't going to be opened truly sank in. Josie started to shriek as the beast advanced in the darkness, its glowing yellow eyes getting closer and closer.

She could hear Mrs. Mills' voice from the other side of the door. "Oh honey... thank you! You have found my Kiki! Now you know why I just couldn't possibly let her outdoors. Way more eyes now. So much trouble she could get into." She paused for a moment. Josie could hear Mrs. Mills' footsteps and voice getting fainter as she walked away.

"You really should've gone ahead and accepted some of my tea though, dear. It would've made everything hurt a lot, *lot* less."

T□□ E□□

LABOR PAINS

KENYA MOSS-DYME KENYA MOSS-DYME

G☐☐☐☐☐ W☐☐☐☐☐☐☐☐ ☐ ☐☐☐ ☐☐ ☐ ☐☐☐☐ ☐☐☐☐☐ ☐ ☐☐☐☐ but one thing he knew he could do was deliver babies.

He'd read books on pregnancy and childbirth, and watched countless YouTube videos of women giving birth, but securing the janitor's position at the hospital provided him with unlimited access to medical supplies. Completely under the radar, George smuggled drugs and surgical instruments out of the hospital in his lunchbox and often, under his jacket, and none were the wiser.

In his small cottage-styled home on a quiet suburban street, he had been using his internet education and the stolen tools to deliver babies in secret for several years. The birth of Angel presented him with the first opportunity to put his skills to the test, and he delivered her safely and without issue, however, Brittany's high risk delivery was challenging and almost made him doubt his abilities. By the time the twins Charlie and Danyelle came screaming into the world, his self-confidence was restored once he hugged their warm slippery bodies to his chest.

But each successful delivery pushed him closer and closer to the brink of madness.

"Don't push until I tell you to," George ordered, wiping the sweat from his brow as he spoke soothingly to the woman laboring on the bed. "It's going beautifully; you're doing great, honey."

She groaned through her teeth and gripped the bed rails so tightly that her fingernails cut in her palms and drew blood. "Please, please, please, I need to push!" The pain from the contractions subsided as the baby's head squeezed into her lower section. After 14 long hours in labor, the urge to push had become overwhelming but she chewed on her bottom lip and suppressed her cries.

"Okay, I can see the head now – that's a lot of hair," he joked. "We're almost there, sweetheart!"

They had done this many times before, so she trusted him to safely guide her through; she pushed at his command and expelled the baby from her body with relative ease. Collapsing on her back so she could catch her breath, she kept her ear trained in his direction so she could gauge his reaction. In the moments that followed, her brief excitement at the delivery was replaced by dread and fear of the silence that hung thick in the air while George examined the newborn.

"George?

She could hear the baby softly whimpering but George's silence was deafening. Eventually, he uttered an anguished moan and she heard the rubber soles of his boots strike the floor as he stepped away from her. Tears welled up in her eyes as she squeezed them shut and opened her mouth and wailed.

The baby sputtered and coughed as George wrapped it

tightly in a flannel receiving blanket and turned to leave the basement, holding it in the crook of his arm like a quarterback on his way to score the winning touchdown.

"Wait, please – can I see her first?" The woman begged weakly, searching for a hint of compassion in his stern face. He deliberately looked in the opposite direction as he passed, holding the baby away from her, ignoring her pleas. He mounted the basement stairs and slipped out the side door, heading to the shed behind the house.

———

T☐☐ ☐☐☐☐ ☐ ☐☐☐☐ ☐☐☐ ☐ ☐☐☐ ☐☐☐☐ ☐☐ ☐☐☐ ☐☐☐☐☐☐ place; retrieving from beneath the cabinet a roll of hazardous waste bags and medical tape; the slow drawing of water into the tub - it was a ritual with which he was all too familiar. Placing the baby on the table next to the tub, he reached into the overhead cabinet and withdrew the small rubber plugs for his ears, heavy duty leather gloves that reached to his elbows. After draping himself in the thick plastic vest, he pushed the plugs into his ears and donned the gloves before opening the blanket. He scooped the baby with both hands and laid her, naked and wiggling, into the cold plastic tub.

His rough hands smoothed the infant's silky black hair as he examined her. Her face was tiny, round, with creamy terra cotta skin still adjusting its tone to the air and light. He tried not to show revulsion at her deformity; he didn't want such an expression to be the last image she saw, as if it really mattered in the grand scheme of things. She stared back at him with wide trusting eyes and he kept his lips pressed together in a tight half smile, avoiding her gaze. Her little feet kicked harmlessly against his stomach and made tiny squeaking sounds as they brushed against the protective covering.

"You're the sixth, so I'm going to call you Farrah," He whispered, using his fingers to drizzle water across her cheeks. Baby Farrah squealed as the wet droplets rolled down her cheeks into the opening of her ear.

Her tiny fingers found his wrist and she grasped wildly at his arms for balance as he lowered her into the tub. As the water rose around her head and covered her ears, the one-inch wide slit in the center of her forehead popped open and the eye glared at him accusingly. Her mouth gaped and emitted a high pitched wail that filled the tiny shed and pierced George's eardrums.

George snatched one hand away from her grasp and su□ered a deep cut on the back of his hand as her claws cut into his flesh. The third eye blinked at him furiously as Baby Farrah whipped her head from side to side and tried to nip at his hand with her tiny mouth. She caught the edge of his finger and he could feel a row of sharp fangs bear down on the glove before he snatched away.

He pressed her head to the bottom of the tub and held her still, looking away until she gave up the struggle. Her mu□ ed underwater screams created bubbles that rose to the surface and obscured her monstrous face.

Baby Farrah was going to haunt his dreams for a long time; much longer than the others. Each baby's transformation was more demonic and terrifying than the previous; and the subsequent nightmares grew darker and more hopeless as time passed. Each time George made the walk to the shed, he feared that it might be him that wouldn't emerge.

"George, we have to try again. As soon as she heals."

His wife Leolah sat calmly in the kitchen at the top of the

basement stairs. She normally stayed far away during the deliveries and waited instead for George to walk down the hallway to their bedroom where she waited nervously for him to present her with a perfectly, healthy baby. A human baby.

But Leolah was getting restless and impatient, and all of the failures were wearing on her soul. She stood in the kitchen this time, listening to the soft cries of the child and cringing at the sound of George's boots on the basement stairs. Her breath caught in her throat as she anticipated which way he would turn when he reached the top. Her heart sank when she heard him pull open the door to leave the house because then she knew.

She'd sat quietly and watched him exit the side door with the bundle beneath his arms; there was no need for questioning things for which she already knew the answers. She glared at him with a mixture of sadness and disgust, and picked up a pack of cigarettes from the table. Holding the cigarette between her lips, she leaned slightly forward, waiting for George to obediently pick up the lighter and set fire to the end of the cigarette.

"But after that, she has to go. Time to replace and refresh!" She said flippantly, as if she were instructing him to purchase new bathroom towels.

"Yes, honey," George agreed, staring down at his calloused fingers; the light from the kitchen window gave his mocha-colored hands a tint of copper, like sparks of magic in contrast to the horrible act he had just been forced to perform.

"I'm going to do another spell on her, while her womb is open. Gather my items and then bring her to me, said Leolah, dismissing him with a nod of her head.

George shuⓍed down the hallway into the bedroom and retrieved the doll from the drawer. With one arm, he held it stiy against his chest as he rushed about the room, collecting the additional items he knew she would request next. He grabbed the three partially melted tapered candles and holders and a Ziploc bag of dried oak leaves, clutching them tightly between his fingers as he pinched the red wax marker from the bottom of the dresser drawer.

He headed to the living room and dutifully began the ritual which he knew by heart: arranging the candles in their holders in the shape of a triangle and lighting each one; then he stacked the leaves into a pile at her feet and set fire to the edges with his lighter. A tightly rolled yoga mat leaned against the coee table; George grabbed it and snapped it open, spreading it on the floor at Leolah's feet. She pulled up the front of her muumuu and squatted, resting her hands on her bent knees. Her eyes were closed, head tilted to the ceiling, and her braids spilled down her back, giving her a regal appearance that reminded George of why he was so smitten with her when they met. She began breathing deeply, settling into her meditation pose, and George almost lost himself in his thoughts of how beautiful she was to him in that moment.

She rocked gently back and forth as she cradled the doll to her breasts, whispering wildly into the molded rubber ears on the side of the doll's head.

George laid the marker next to the pile of leaves and backed up until he ran into the wall on the far side of the room, where he stood and watched silently. He knew to stay far out of the way while she worked her spells, as it was often unpredictable, messy and even dangerous. But George assisted her with whatever she required because he knew that the black veil over their lives was because of him; it was punishment not only for their union but for that horrible thing he'd done several years earlier on that quiet Sunday morning, before the curse had been placed upon them.

The way he remembered, it seemed to have been someone else whose hand lingered a bit too long on the back of Baby George's head, pressing his face deep into the crib mattress. In his mind, he was floating above the room, watching it take place, and even though he screamed at the man in the room to stop, the figure ignored him and continued firmly patting and pressing, until Baby George struggled no more.

Now, all Leolah wanted was another baby, but in his own selfishness, all George wanted was her.

"Get her. NOW!" She barked impatiently, interrupting his thoughts. "The leaves burn quickly, there's no time to waste!"

Her name was Lily.

Six years earlier, he'd found her at the truck stop over by the highway. She was cold, hungry and willing to do anything to avoid returning to an abusive pimp. George had something she could do. Suddenly he had the answer to his and Leolah's problem sitting in the passenger seat of his car. Lily was very similar to Leolah with her petite frame, tawny beige skin and full lips, so George saw their meeting as a sign. To Lily, the stranger's offer seemed like a no-brainer at the time, but she had no idea of the real horror she was agreeing to in exchange for housing.

It didn't take much to sell the idea to Leolah, after all, she wanted another baby more than anything in the world, even more than she wanted him. But they had been cursed and could produce nothing together, at least, nothing that could be considered a child.

———

H⬚ ⬚⬚⬚ L⬚⬚⬚ ⬚⬚ ⬚⬚ ⬚⬚⬚ ⬚⬚⬚⬚ ⬚ ⬚⬚⬚⬚⬚ ⬚⬚ ⬚ ⬚⬚⬚ ⬚⬚⬚ cross-legged in the floor. The pile of oak leaves smoldered on the floor in front of her, and the three candles still burned in a triangle at her back. A faint stream of white smoke rose to the ceiling and Leolah waved her hand through the line to spread it into the air.

"Hurry up, lay her down on the mat!" Leolah barked, carefully placing the doll on the floor at her thigh.

Lily held on to George's arm and dutifully lowered herself to the rubber mat, carefully, grimacing at the pain between her legs from giving birth just hours earlier. Leolah pushed up the girl's t-shirt up to expose her stomach, and without another word, she used the red marker to scrawl tiny words on Lily's stomach.

"Sow in my womb a child as tall and healthy as the mighty oak."

She sat back and gazed at her handiwork before reaching behind for one of the tapered candles. Lily closed her eyes tightly and balled her fists, steeling herself for the pain to come.

Leolah read the phrase aloud three times while tilting the candle slightly to allow drops of wax to spill onto the girl's body.

She repeated the action with the two remaining candles, then scooped a handful of the burned leaves and scattered them through her fingers across Lily's belly.

Lily arched her back and accepted the dusting of the ashes; it felt somewhat soothing on top of the wax and it also signaled the end of Leolah's twisted ceremony. She knew she would soon return to the basement and await George's arrival in a few weeks to *seed* her, as Leolah liked to refer to it. But she'd have a welcomed break from him until that time came.

"I'm finished, take her back," Leolah picked up the doll and scooted around until her back was facing George and Lily.

———

G□□□□□ □□□ □□□ □□ □ □□□□□□ □□□□ □□□ □□□ □□□□□□ □ the words he would say when he faced Leolah. He had made that miserable trip up the stairs so many times with the same result, yet he still wasn't sure what he would say when their fortunes changed.

His hands were shaking when he reached out and gripped the bannister to help steady his climb. He knew that once he reached the top of the stairs, their lives were about to change and not necessarily for the better. He imagined presenting Leolah with the baby and having to watch her melt down into an emotional mess once she realized that the curse was gone and her dream had finally come true. After which she would become obsessed over the child's every whimper, sni□ e and sigh, and her entire existence would become entwined with her baby. She would spend night after night sitting next to his crib and staring at him under the moonlight shining through the window, stroking his fat cheeks with her fingers, leaning over to feel his breath on her cheek.

He remembered wryly how it was before. Leolah loved that baby so much that she didn't even know George was alive. All he could do was watch from afar; dare he even attempt to touch, soothe or pacify the child – HIS child – she would shriek and swoop down upon them as if she thought George was going to cause harm.

He reached the last step and his knees buckled, causing him to almost pitch forward and lose his grip on the child in his arms. He paused before turning the corner into the kitchen, listening for the sound of Leolah rocking back and forth in her chair in the bedroom, but he couldn't hear a sound and the silence caused him to panic. He took a deep breath and scaled the last big step, landing in the center of the doorway.

He was surprised to find that Leolah was missing from her usual spot at the kitchen table. The small round ashtray held a single cigarette that burned unattended. He could then hear her moving around and slamming drawers in their bedroom down the hall. It was a clear sign that he needed to seize upon that moment to make his move. He turned quickly on his heel and rushed out the side door and down the pathway toward the shed. His heart was pulsing in his ears as he feared Leolah would suddenly rush through the house and jump on his back as he moved further and further away from the house, gripping the baby between both of his hands. He made it to the shed and pushed inside, then slammed the door and locked it behind him.

"What should I call you, little guy?" George held the baby boy under the lamp on the bench and stared into his perfect face. The boy blinked – his two perfect eyes blinked and George smiled. He used his fingers to examine the baby's head and along the spine for horn-like formations. He cautiously pressed a fingertip against the forehead, seeking an opening but relieved when the skin failed to pop open and reveal an angry eye like each of the others. The baby opened his mouth to utter cries, newborn cries, not the screeches of a wounded mythical animal – and George noted with satisfaction the healthy pink gums, no sign of sharp fangs breaking through the tissue.

"I will call you...Geno. Baby Geno, nice to meet you," he said before lowering perfect Geno into the tub of water.

———

W░ ░░ ░░░░░░░░ ░░ ░░░ ░░░░░░L░░░░░ ░░░ sitting at the kitchen table, dragging deeply on a cigarette as she watched him with suspicious eyes. She waved a hand toward a hot cup of tea sitting at the empty chair, signaling him to take a seat.

He pulled the chair away from the table and sank his tired body into the seat. Nervousness caused his hands to tremble but he avoided Leolah's eyes and drank until the cup was empty. Heat flowed through his body and he felt instantly relaxed; he leaned his back against the chair and raised his heavy head to look at his wife.

"It wasn't me," Leolah said, narrowing her eyes as the smoke from her cigarette crossed her face.

"What?"

"It wasn't me. She didn't curse my womb. We had it all wrong. She cursed *you*," Leolah mimicked the voice of George's ex-wife. *"All of your babies will carry the scars of your betrayal and you will shake with fear when you gaze upon their faces."*

George shuddered and recalled the last time he'd seen his ex-wife and their children. The day that he packed his belongings while Leolah and newborn Baby George waited for him in the car; his kids were clinging to each other in tears, while his wife stood in the doorway, chanting and screaming threats at George and Leolah as they drove away to begin anew.

His eyelids wanted to close, he was so hot and tired, but he struggled to focus on Leolah's face and the words coming out of her mouth.

"I should have known, *sweet Judayo*, what was I thinking all of this time!" Leolah closed her eyes and shook her head slowly, side to side. "One priestess cannot curse another priestess, it doesn't work, it protects us from our own emotions."

"Wait...wha? Whaddya mean?" George stuttered, his arms felt like weights and they fell from the table to dangle on each side of the chair. His body felt inflamed as the heat rushed from the top of his head down through his groin, and the surface of his skin glowed a blazing red from the intensity.

"We've been doing it all wrong. I know that now."

George gasped for air and struggled to remain in the chair but he had lost all feeling in his limbs and he began to slide toward the floor. Leolah's face floated before his eyes and he felt as if he were being sucked into a fiery furnace, but he couldn't even raise his hands in defense.

"Time to replace and refresh," Leolah said, taking another drag from her cigarette as she watched her husband's lifeless body crumple to the floor and burst into flames.

T□□ E□□

RETURN TO ME

LORI TITUS

M□□ □ □□□□□□ □□ □□□ □□ □ □□□□□□ □□ □□□ □□□□□□ right at the edge of Chrysalis, an unincorporated part of town. The roads stopped a mile short of us, and were left unpaved to save the state a handful of pocket change. It was a nice place to live. Quiet, and everything so green: the sky, the water. All summer there was the buzzing of living things in the air. The mosquitoes, the bees and of course the quiet whispers of dead things too, their voices twined together in the trees, like the echoes of an old record stuck inside one groove.

I don't really know how my mother got that house, or the land, some thirty acres of wilderness, really, other than to say it was a plot that nobody else wanted. Maybe, she told me one day, it was a place wild enough for people like us, who savored the elements, the vibrations that moved through the land and the air. There weren't too many that knew how to harness such power, and those that didn't feared it.

People will tell you God's spirit is heavy there. I would

ask, which God? Not the one that allowed us to be bartered up and down rivers and sold across seas. Maybe not the ancestors that knew us before we left the mother continent, who had traveled in chains to the New World with us. Which one do you think cares for us?

Mama had a simpler explanation. All things that had life had power. It was a matter of knowing how to use it. I don't believe she ever subscribed to calling upon any particular gods. She believed in the use of life force: from animals, people, from the elements. She said that was really all one needed to know, and that she'd never bothered to think about it beyond that.

At least that was the way mama raised us. I was the youngest of three daughters. To be honest, I don't remember my older sister Ruby from my childhood, but from time we spent together later as women. She is fourteen years older than I am, the only child from Mama's first marriage. Ruby left town and got married herself when I was about five years old. We heard from her sporadically after she moved to the city. Now my younger sister Cherise, is a different story. We are only two years apart, and grew up thick as thieves, always in some kind of minor trouble: going down to the lake when we were supposed to be finishing our chores, stealing sweets from Mama's pantry when she wasn't looking. Those little things built trust between us. I knew she could keep a secret.

When Cherise turned nineteen, she got married and left home. She moved with him out west, first Washington State, and then California.

At seventeen I was the only one left alone with Mama, and by then the secret Cherise kept for me I could no longer hide. Mama caught me staring out into nothingness and she called me out of it. That's when I realized she knew her baby could see the nonliving. I never told her, but now I had to tell her the voices were getting louder and it was getting harder to ignore them. Once we had the house alone we had a long talk about it. I knew what people would think. How could I have explained that I saw standing out in the garden at night, wearing a full suit, white with a fedora? Or the woman by the lake, wearing a plain yellow dress and barefoot? Over time they whispered their stories to me: how she died on the lake, and how the man was killed in an accident on the road, right at the juncture where our house stands. Those were not tales for reasonable, respectable folk. Not that we knew many. Those that did accept the idea of ghosts most likely would not appreciate the idea of voices telling me these things.

Mama sat me down in the kitchen with her one evening and we had a talk about it over tea. She was casual about it as if we talked about the latest music or town gossip. Watching her sit, legs crossed, one arm over the back of her chair, I realized that she had thought about how to approach me with this for a long time. She was comfortable with the things she was telling me.

"I don't know how long you think that you could fool me, but I have known about your gift for the last forever. You had it since you were a little thing. Always knew that you would carry on for me. Ruby was too headstrong and quite honestly, she never believed in anything she couldn't see and hold in her own hand. Cherise showed no interest. She could have nurtured the gift when she was younger if she hadn't been too afraid to wield it. You come by it naturally, without having to pour your concentration into it. In that way you're more like me than any of the girls. Why do you think you were always the one brought into the room to watch me give readings?"

Mama taught me the simple tools of the trade early: I

could read tea leaves and tarots by the time I was thirteen. She told fortunes for people, and gave them whatever they asked for, whether they came for love potions or revenge spells. Sometimes what they needed was a simple as home brewed poison. Other times they asked for things that she simply couldn't or wouldn't give. That happened infrequently. Mama said that there were some things she knew better to grant, and it was better to tell those people that she couldn't do it rather than be drawn into their mess.

She took her clients in the den, which was always cleaned and polished up to look nice; lace doilies on the couch and a fresh tea service, no matter the time of day. The table always smelled of lemon cleaner, and a bookcase held carefully displayed porcelain pieces, all sorts of figurines, everything from ballerinas to jumping fish. Most of those belonged to my grandmother, but Mama kept them well. When we were kids, Cherise and I never played in that room. Breaking one of those little figurines and facing Mama's wrath over it was perhaps one of our biggest fears.

Though I was with her when Mama did readings, I never spoke to the customers. She told me that she wanted me to hear exactly what it was people requested, and what her reaction was to each kind of problem that was posed to her. I knew that this was her way of teaching me the business, even though I couldn't quite conceive that one day I would be the person that they would ask for.

After a time I learned the rhythm to the requests, the body language with which each was employed. Those searching or spells to bring lovers to them never met your eyes directly, but if you caught their gaze, you sensed the tenseness in their fingers as they shook or clasped and unclasped themselves. They would bite their lips. Those who wanted to kill looked directly at you while they asked for their poison or inquired to the likelihood of an 'accident,' because they wanted one to realize that they were quite serious. When seeking the healing of illness, people often clenched their fists, or bit the inside of their jaw. Pain, and people fighting the signs of it, were the most obvious tells that I learned.

On evenings when the weather was warm enough for it, Mama and I would go and sit by the lake, our feet at the edge of the water. If you looked up at the sky, there were so few clouds that you could count them all on one hand. As the heavens darkened to a deep velvety blue, the fireflies would come out, and if I called to them, they would surround us, lighting the way through the darkness. As it grew later, the voices of the dead ones in my ears grew more distinct, a gentle buzz of background noise. Over time I learned to ignore them.

"What did you think of that woman that asked for her husband back?" Mama asked quietly.

"Doesn't matter what I think," I told her. "I see that you turned her away."

She smiled at me. "Mya. You have an opinion and I am asking you for it."

"Well, honestly, I was wondering why you turned her away. It sounds easy enough. A return spell is one of the easier ones. And it wouldn't bring harm on him."

Mama shook her head. "That woman was not telling me the whole story. You know, when a woman's husband is a cheater, she's usually very quick to tell you, because people are quick to blame the wife when her man runs off. I know that's foolish, but it's the way people talk. If a woman comes to you and she says she wants her man back but won't give you the details of why he's gone, that's better left alone. Some people do better without you helping them."

"If you say so," I told her. Put in that woman's position, I would want someone to help me. Losing a husband was no small thing, likely to bring down the rest of a woman's fortune. Not everyone was like Mama, twice a widow and able to make money on her own. In fact I didn't know any other woman in our town that did.

"I feel sorry for her," I admitted.

Mama nodded. "I know," she said. "Just make sure that feeling bad for folks doesn't make you do things that you shouldn't. Especially not when those things have got to do with magic. Half the time, people don't know what's best for them anyway."

———

T⬚⬚ ⬚⬚⬚⬚ ⬚⬚⬚⬚⬚M⬚⬚ ⬚ ⬚⬚⬚⬚⬚

I came to wake her up one morning. She appeared to be sleeping peacefully, a little smile on her face, her right hand on her stomach; the classic posture of repose. I didn't realize at first, and was talking to her just like normal about how bright the day was and that the birds seemed out earlier than usual. What caught my eye was that she was too still. I touched her forehead and jumped backwards. The cold of death is like no other chill. I screamed.

Mama had su⬚ered from a little cold the week before. She barely coughed. I knew she was more tired than usual the night before but she didn't complain. She'd taken a cup of hot tea with lemon to bed. The town doctor theorized that her heart gave out. It may have been that what she called a cold was really walking pneumonia and it was too much on her.

One of her brothers had died young from a weak heart but he was the only one who did. The rest of the family had lived to be old, cantankerous people. We would never have guessed she would be the one to share her brother's fate.

It happened peacefully and suddenly in her sleep. I couldn't have asked for a better end for her because it came without pain. I wasn't ready for it. No one is ready for such things, and youthful as she was, one easily forgot her true age. I said my final goodbye to her by making her ready for her wake. I brushed her hair and made sure she wore her favorite black dress. I kissed her cheek one last time and then broke into tears. I remembered well what she told me when we lost our grandmother. "Don't cry for the dead, they have gone back to the oneness that birthed them," she'd said. "We are never really gone, just absent from the vessel which carried us."

People came from long distances to say final goodbyes, including both my sisters, their husbands, and the growing brood of children in tow. Cherise was pregnant, so round and plump in her little face that I barely recognized her, except for those big precious eyes of hers. Ruby was looking well, and this was my first time meeting her children, my two nieces and nephew, who were only eight and nine years younger than I was. We all teased her because the kids looked more like our side of the family than her husband's. For a time they filled the house with talk and gentle laughter. There was food around, brought in by neighbors: cakes and casseroles, pot roasts. I was genuinely surprised by the outpouring, but then again she had helped many people. Even some of her customers came by to give their sympathies. Those were awkward, because I didn't know the older ones, and a few of them confused me for one of my sisters.

Ruby told me that I shouldn't stay here. She suggested that I move to the city. There would be more possibilities for me to meet someone, she said, and at nineteen I was getting just old enough that people would wonder why I wasn't at least engaged. I'd no intention of going anywhere, and though I tried to be nice about it, I made myself clear. The last thing I was worried about was marriage and babies. She said that I shouldn't want to be alone for half my life like Mama was. Ruby always thinks she knows everything.

People crowded into our small chapel for the funeral. There were hymns, prayers, and weeping. Afterwards Mama was buried in the Negro cemetery, beside her parents and her older sister who had proceeded her into death only a few years earlier. I knew very little about my mother's family. I couldn't say if her magic was passed down from them, or if it was something that they wouldn't have approved of. It had never occurred to me until then that as much as she taught me, Mama kept many secrets.

On the Monday morning after the funeral both my sisters and their families returned to their lives.

Finally I was left alone in the house. I had mixed feelings about being there. In one way, the reminders of Mama were comforting. I wasn't sure if I could ever part from it, but I had not decided it this was a good thing or not. It was very cold that winter, and I kept the fireplace and the heater going, for what good they would do me. There had always been little drafts around the house, but that year brought snow, a rare event for our town. Each leak of cold air felt like a personal affront, an attempt to harm me.

As alone as I felt, I was not alone as I liked. The barefoot girl in the summer dress and the man in the suit who stood beneath the trees were no longer alone. They were joined by other voices, other images. There were so many that sometimes they rushed altogether, a twittering behind my own thoughts and the sounds of the outside world. I would stay in my room with the curtains drawn and the comforter over my head, trying to hold onto what warmth I could. I wondered what would happen if I just faded away, became one of those voices as well. I didn't want to do anything to cause my own end, but I couldn't shake my fascination with death. I wondered if my pain would be ended if I died, or if it would only be prolonged into eternity.

I never heard the voice of my dead mother. I decided that there must be some rule against it. Perhaps it was just that she had passed all her wisdom on to me in life, and there was no need for her to speak anymore, or at least not to me. Maybe the dead didn't really talk to those that they belonged to, seeking instead the comfort of strangers who had never known them. I hoped that she was resting peacefully. Though the voices were always with me, I hoped that one day I would rest without them.

————

T☐☐ ☐☐☐☐☐☐ ☐☐ ☐ ☐☐☐☐☐ ☐ ☐☐☐☐☐☐☐☐ ☐☐☐☐☐☐ ☐☐☐☐ ☐☐☐ cold and a release from the deepest hold of my grief. I made myself go out again, even tried to look presentable in public. I had to go into town to get supplies to replace all the things that had been used up over the winter. People were surprised to see me. I was thinner and my hair was longer. There were questions about how I was getting along by myself, and I told everybody I was fine. They didn't need to know that I was barely functioning, and that until a week before they saw me,

I staying in bed most days and hiding from the voices every night. It wasn't their business.

When it got warm I went back down to the lake and just sat by the water in the evenings, remembering all the things Mama and I used to talk about. I didn't see the new ghosts, but their voices were clear as bells. It was hard not to be distracted when someone always seemed to be whispering in my ear. Sometimes they stood at the edge of the tree line. I would have the instinct that I was being watched, and then start when I realized they stood behind me. When they did talk it could be all matter of things. Usually they wanted to when they were going home, or if they were indeed locked to this Earth forever. Questions I couldn't answer.

One day, I was out back in my garden, turning soil and pulling up weeds. It was late afternoon but the sun was still high, with the breeze o the water blowing in. I saw a yellow hem from the corner of my eye, and looked up. I was startled whenever I saw dead that I had not encountered before. This little spirit I knew well. She was at least as familiar as any of the neighbors who occasionally crossed my path.

The girl in the sundress stood beside me, looking as much a solid thing as you or I ever did. Wind blowing against her hair played havoc a few loose strands not caught by her pony-tail. She had never been this close to me, and I saw the freckles that stood out against her skin, the most vibrant of deep brown, was smooth and sun kissed. How old had this poor child been when she died? I wondered if she had told me before and I failed to listen properly. Sometimes I tried not to learn the details even when they told me. It seemed too easy think about them as being real if I connected names and stories to their images and voices.

"You've got company, ma'am," she said softly.

I stood up, putting down my trowel. Someone indeed was knocking on my front door. When I turned to look at the girl, she was gone.

T☐☐☐ ☐☐☐☐☐☐ ☐☐☐☐☐☐ ☐☐ ☐☐ ☐☐☐☐ ☐☐☐ ☐☐☐☐☐ ☐☐ the customers that came calling. Word had gotten around that I had resurfaced, and all of Mama's customers came back, and some new ones who had never come to us for readings. There were some who had not been around for a time and still came looking for my mother. In recent weeks there were a couple who had cried when I gave her the news. I accepted all who came. I needed the income after all. I took my mother's place as the town's fortune teller, healer, and kitchen witch. She always said that I would do that for her, and I slipped into the role with minimum e☐ort.

———

O☐☐ ☐☐☐☐☐☐☐ ☐☐☐ ☐☐ ☐☐☐☐ ☐ ☐☐ ☐☐ ☐☐☐☐☐S☐☐ ☐☐☐ changed so much that I scarcely remembered her face. As she crossed the threshold into my front room, she grasped my hands. She looked older than I remembered. The black dress she wore high boots made her seem thinner and taller, her body erect in the most severe manner.

"Mya it's so good to see you again. I was sorry to hear of your mother's passing, she was a good woman."

"Thank you," I said with a smile. Good was not a word often used to describe my mother. Generous, often kind, but most people were very hesitant to associate the things that she did with any kind of good. The hardest of the Christians in this town said she was in league with the Devil. This woman would impress me to be a Christian herself. Many of them come for their fortunes even though they are quick to say it's ungodly and against their beliefs; when He doesn't o☐er them the quick and easy comfort they seek, they show up on my doorstep anyway.

"I appreciate you saying so. It's been a few years. Your name is Evie, isn't it?"

Evie nodded, her curly hair bouncing about her face. She was a brown woman of medium complexion, with small features and a button shaped mouth.

"Come into the kitchen, and we'll have tea. Tell me about all the things that have happened since the last time you were here."

———

I ☐☐☐☐☐ ☐☐ ☐☐ ☐☐ ☐ ☐☐☐ ☐☐ ☐☐☐ ☐☐☐☐☐☐☐☐I☐ ☐ ☐☐ ☐ much bigger space than Mama's cramped den, and I found that conversation flowed more freely there. Evie and I drank tea, and while I placed the leaves in a saucer, she reminded me of why she had come to Mama for help.

"My husband was cheating on me with this woman in town," she began. "Melanie. Or Melody. One of those names. Some little high yellow woman from Louisiana. I heard about it from friends at first. Someone saw them one afternoon having lunch when I was sure he was supposed to be at work. I didn't really believe the rumor when I heard it the first time. Then I just started to notice little changes in him. You know, he wasn't paying attention so much as usual. Started coming home late, and without explanation.

"By the time I heard the second rumor, I was finding

lipstick stains on his collar and smelling perfume on his coat that isn't mine. I believed it then."

Evie paused, taking a sip of her tea. I looked down at the leaves, and continued to listen. "My mother used to tell me you can't expect men to be faithful, especially when some years have passed. I don't know about that. I can tell you we hadn't been married more than two years, and I hadn't expected things to go cold between us that fast. You'd have never guessed how he chased me before we were married. He came every week and begged to see me when I didn't even want to court him. And once we started together..."

Evie's voice drifted. I noticed that her gaze shifted. She looked towards the open kitchen window, out towards the garden. There was a little gray cat who sat upon the sill. The cat meowed, and then started to purr. Evie frowned, as if something disturbed her. I have felt that emotion myself many times before: the gentle tingling of her fingertips, the fine hairs on the back of her neck raising. It's the subtle change in temperature, a dryness of the mouth. I've encountered those feelings before when the dead have crossed my path.

Evie couldn't see was the little ghost in the yellow dress, petting the cat. Though Evie could not see her, I could sense that she felt her there. It always interests me, how most feel the dead, but can't make out their form. If their minds were more open to what their bodies told them, perhaps their eyes would be allowed to *see*.

"Well," Evie said, turning her gaze back to me. "I guess that part of it doesn't matter. This went on in silence for a few months – I was not saying anything to him at all hardly, just hello, goodbye. I remember asking him one morning if he wanted his eggs over easy and that somehow turned into an argument. But that fight was the most we'd spoken in weeks. That day, he went to work, and he didn't come home."

"I see," I sighed. I kept rearranging the tea leaves, and they continued to say the same thing, no matter how I cast them. In situations like this, I had sometimes seen my mother do a reading with the cards to see if the results were the same and if the cards pointed to a different result, she would take that as the final word. Something inside me knew that it was no use reaching for the cards. They would tell me the same thing.

"Evie, I don't like to give bad news, especially of this kind. But I believe that your husband is dead."

She didn't speak. Her eyes began to tear up. She shivered.

"No one has heard news of him since he left. I figured maybe he'd ran off with that girl, left town…"

"Evie, didn't you ask my mother for a spell to return him to you?" I asked. "I believe she told you the answer was no."

"She didn't say my husband was dead."

"No, I was in the room, and she didn't say that," I affirmed. "That was years ago. I can't say when or how it happened, but I can tell you that he did die. It could be that he was still alive back then, when you came to see us that first time." I added this bit of information, though it wasn't entirely true. I wanted to soften the blow. I could see now why Mama hadn't really confronted her about it. All this time and Evie still loved her husband. Perhaps she loved her hope for what they could have been to each other more than she'd ever loved the man himself.

"No," Evie shook her head, tears flowing. "He ran away with that woman, but he can be made to come back to me. Do the spell! Please. I will pay you what you want. If you're right, and he's dead, he won't come back. Then I will know for sure that you're right. But give me a chance to know for certain, and then I'll be done with it."

I knew then that Evie was so deeply hurt that she was going to keep at this until I said yes. I could imagine her coming to see me every day until she got her way. Despite the feeling I had in the pit of my stomach, it was getting late and I wanted her to be on her way.

"Alright then."

I told her to go out to the front porch while I pulled together the herbs that I needed for a potion. I presented her with the potion in a Mason jar, and told her that she was to drink a little of it every night, for the next three nights. I told her that if her husband was indeed alive, he would show up at the end of the fourth night. If not, nothing would happen at all.

She hugged me, planted a kiss on my cheek. "Thank you."

"It's nothing, Evie," I told her. "Since you came and saw Mama before, this is free. If your husband doesn't return, come see me, and I'll give you something to draw new love to you. He was stepping out on you, there's no reason you can't find someone else to be with."

She thanked me again when I handed her the potion. I stood on the porch and watched her walk down the road, the Mason jar pressed against her breast. I felt sad for her because I knew that she would not find what she was looking for. Soon, she would figure out there was no way to go but forward.

———

F□□□ □□□□ □□□□□□ □ □□□□□□ □□□ □ □□□ □□□□ E□□□□
I hadn't expected any. It occurred to me that maybe she was

embarrassed that nothing had come of her hopes to reconcile with her husband. I took this as confirmation that I was right all long about the man being dead. It wasn't unusual that when things ended in a way that was not what a customer wanted, they didn't get in contact again.

The days passed peacefully for me. I worked in the daytime, growing herbs, harvesting the ones that were mature enough, and making notes of some of my mother's spells. She had made many brews from memory, and though I had followed her lead, I decided it would be good to have it written down. It wasn't like I could ask her or anyone else, so better to have notes to refer to.

The voices settled to a gentle murmur. I wasn't sure why that was but knew to be grateful and not question too much. My little ghost followed me around the garden, and some-times to the lake. She did not mean any harm, and her presence did not bother me. I could only gather the little spirit was curious, and perhaps lonely. I grew to expect her odd form of companionship.

Five nights after I gave her the potion, Evie showed up on my doorstep.

Evie came in the door shivering, on a night that was still warm out. The moon was high, and I could see that she had been crying. I took her to the kitchen and she sat down. I gave her a glass of water to drink. It wasn't until then that I real-ized that she was barefoot. She had walked over the unpaved roads to reach me, through mud and dirt, across stones and pebbles. Her feet bled.

"What happened?"

"On the fourth night. He came back to me," Evie said, eyes wide. "I heard his footsteps. Slow. Him coming towards me. He came to the door and knocked. When I opened it I told him to come in, and he sat with me in the front room, but he asked that I keep the lights low.

But I insisted, and turned on the lights.

"At first, I just looked at him. His face was... swollen and sunken at the same time. There were patches of flesh just falling o a and his eyes.... they drooped around the edges. And the smell. Mya. I never smelled death before but I knew it, everything in my body did. He begged me to listen to him. He confessed about his a air with that woman. The morning we argued, he went to her and told her that he wanted to leave town with her. They got in the car, and started on their way back to her home in Louisiana. He had second thoughts. About a week into their road trip, he told her that he'd changed his mind and wanted to come back home.

"That's when he died?" I asked.

"That was when she shot him. She had her brothers come and help her bury his body."

"Where is he now?" I said, touching her shoulder. I didn't like the idea that she had drawn this dead thing to my door. There were enough ghosts wandering this place without a dead thing with flesh roaming the place. Ghosts were one thing but a walking, resurrected corpse was surely another.

"You won't have to worry," Evie said. "I killed him again. Bashed in his head with a skillet. The killing him wasn't so bad," she said. "It was the digging of the grave, and the *smell*. It took me a whole day, all the while, afraid someone might see me with that thing out in my back yard. I covered him in a blanket. And then I took his shovel out from the shed and dug until I was so tired I couldn't dig anymore."

I poured both of us a glass of whiskey, full to the rim. We drank in silence for a time, both trying to take this in. Evie looked down at her hands with glazed eyes. Under the harsh glare of the kitchen's light I could see smudges of dirt on her face and clothes.

"Did you know this would happen?" Evie asked. "That he'd come back dead or alive, one way or another."

"No. Evie, that potion I gave you was harmless, because as I told you, I already knew he was dead. It wasn't a potion to make him return to you, it was a spell to make you open to new love. Whatever dark magic that was, it came from your desire. And your belief."

"Fine, blame it on me," Evie spat. "I just wanted my husband back."

"Yes you did," I told her. "It wasn't *how* you wanted, but it was exactly what you asked for."

I knew from that day forward. It really is like Mama told me, some people are better off without help. Of all the spells I have practiced over the years, I never put that one to use again.

T⬜⬜ E⬜⬜

SISTERS

KAI LEAKES

☐I ☐☐☐☐☐☐ ☐☐☐☐☐H☐☐ ☐☐ ☐☐☐☐☐☐ ☐☐☐ ☐☐ ☐☐☐ ☐☐☐☐ don't you understand?" My pulse quickened. A sheen of moisture dotted my temples, made the nape of my neck slick from the kick of heat in my body. Anxiety made me look around, darting my eyes at the shadows.

A loud bang made me jump.

"Candance." That was my little sister Alisha. "This puts you at risk and you know it."

"I don't care if it does." I retorted. "And you know this."

Fear darkened her golden eyes to a smoky brown while her gaunt face and the dark shadows under her eyes, gave her a haunting appearance under the *'I ain't bothered'* sweater hoodie she wore. My little sister's small hand gripped my arm in a painful clasp. Her sharp nails cut into the fabric of my jacket and I did my best not to react. If she wasn't careful, blood would be drawn, and it would only add to the danger that hunted us.

"Breathe sis," I urged, feeling my body shudder.

I was scared. The wave of icy nausea which gripped my stomach disappeared. The tremor in my hands dissipated. Each digit of my fingers was tinted in red. My head throbbed with my sharp hearing and only added to my anxiousness at the falling liquid from my nails and lips.

In the vast skyline backdrop behind us was the grand St. Louis Arch. Alisha and I had taken shelter, no, more like hid for safety in the large storage hanger somewhere downtown. The bright radiance of the Arch was once hope for the city. Now it was a symbol of the threat that was running rampant in the bodies of the people of the city.

The Demented were coming bringing with them their contagion. We needed to leave A.S.A.P, but... Exhaling, my body shook. My mouth was dry. What I took earlier had me looking like I had played paintball in blood, was helping me feel full. But that aching need to taste Demented essence was strong and overriding my logic.

It made my skin and scalp tingle. Made my fingers flex while my throat was left with a sensation of bliss like I just drunk freezing water during a summer heatwave. Only thing was, I wasn't cooled o. I was fired up.

"Sis!" I heard Alisha say. "I'm shaking too, but you said we can't stay here, so we gotta go, yeah?"

I hated when my body took over like this. That feel-good sensation was so intense that it had me ready to rock back and forth just to feel some balance. I was on alert, but I wasn't. My senses on height, that I could smell the enemy coming.

"Oh, my gosh, I hate this craving," I said looking around as I swiped at my nose. We didn't have long to hide. What I had done was a risk I had to take in protecting my little sister and myself. But ultimately it left us open for attack.

With a quick glance at the huge windows in the compound, Candance and I ran to hide again. This time, further in the storage building. Jarring snarls became louder in the backdrop of the city and the compound. It made my heart pump and my stomach clench.

"I'm scared sis," Candance whispered.

"Me, too, but we have to hide. I'm sorry sis," I said regretfully. "I should have left the Demented alone, but I was hungry."

"Don't do that. You couldn't help it…"

Stopping her mid-sentence, I pulled my baby sis to my side. We pressed our backs against the wall to the point where it felt as if we were trying to fuse with it. Again, my heart started to race. The sound of metal dragging against what I thought was pavement hurt my ears. They were here.

Nothing but the uneasy sound of feet shu ing against pavement and the outline of snarling silhouettes filled the compound we were in. From where we hid, I could see, and hear the mucous dripping liquid splatter o their bodies.

"I'm getting hungry sis," Alisha whispered. Raising a finger to my lips, I felt my sister hold my arm tighter.

Growls and zombie-like shu ing, grew closer. We were watching the hatch door which protected us from those things when it bowed forward. Then it flew o its hinges with a supernatural force making us cover our mouths so not to scream.

"They got in!" I hissed low.

Each of the dark, ink splotched things crept our way. They moved slowly in a lethargic manner to sni us out. Many were dressed in work clothes, or casual street attire. Some wore hospital scrubs with badges pinned to their chest. Some were in business suits and dresses. While others were kids with bookbags.

These were normal people once, but not anymore. Unfallen tears glazed the rims of my eyes. It was only a year ago, when we all were normal. Everyone in the U.S. had survived the great change in our nation that caused us to fall into an economic and international downwind that once used to be secure. With it came the creation of the 'Demented,' human things I couldn't even begin to try to explain what they were.

With her back to me, Alisha watched on and asked, "Can we stay hidden longer?"

"Sis. I'll need more blood soon. But...but I can protect us for now," I said. "Please we have to go before the crave hits you harder."

Alisha's usually russet brown skin was now a paling yellow. She was awakening like I had, earlier. Being one of the creeping hunters we are, caused three dots to appear in her golden irises. I knew outside of that obvious change, that she needed to get out of here because of the way she kept licking her cracked lips. She watched the essence fall from my fingers, then down on the chest of the lifeless body under me.

Yes, I had killed. We dragged the body into our hiding spot.

"It's already hitting me. Feed me please," she pleaded with me. My sister kneeled at my side on her haunches, rocking. Currents of dark energy wrapped around her fingers, and wrists, turning her nails black. She needed a charge, fast.

Panicking, I touched the chest of the Demented under me. "There's a little heat left. Eat.

I'll be fine sis."

"Really?" She asked. It was like she needed my approval first, so I gave it.

"Hurry," I urged with a motion of my hand.

I pushed o the body, walked around my now crouching sister in a protective pace, while looking for anything that I could use as a weapon. Shifting on my feed, my hand to my wrist and ran over where my sister had dug her nails into my flesh. She has broken skin. If she had been lost to her craving as I had been earlier, then the act would have made her feed from me by drawing out my heat.

It was a scary thought and I was glad that I didn't have to fight my own sister today.

"You can't hold yourself back if you go into the craving sis. Okay?" I lectured. There was a pipe sticking out from a radiator. Snatching at it, the strength from my feeding helped me yank it out and break it from the radiator.

"Umph!" I grunted, then stepped back with it in my hand. "I know you couldn't hurt me but, we have to be careful."

The sloppy sucking from my sister's feeding was getting to me, triggering me. When she abruptly turned, her glowing golden hue eyes on me, she said "Never. I love you sis and you're all I have now..."

Alisha paused to look away in sadness.

"Since they killed Mama and Dad," she muttered.

Tears lined my eyes. The sharp memory of our parents screaming filled my mind as I tried forgetting that reality.

"Still..." I started then stopped. The snarling was closer.

"We need some more." Alisha interrupted as her long bloody nails scraped over the top of the dead thing's body.

"I need some more," she whimpered.

"Hurry and come here." I coaxed. "Give me your hands."

Only five years younger than me, my sis stopped right at

the top of my nose. I was five-eight and she was five-seven. I was twenty-one, and she was seventeen. I had coiled, natural hair held back by a white scarf in a kinky fro. My sister had her long hair braided in two twisted buns.

We looked like twins in a sense, reflecting the blend of both our parents. My mother would say that I was dark brown like flawless shard. While my little sister had the color of warm brown polished topaz. Neither of us looked or were biracial.

Palms stretched out, we sat lotus style. Knee-to-knee. Eyes locked on each other as the menacing sound of beasties roared around us, I quickly laid my palms on top of hers, then gasped. The beat of our hearts synchronized. Those dark currents appeared around our hands locking us together in a gentle swirl of magic that cloaked us.

Our nostrils flared, and our foreheads bowed forward to touch each other as a powerful means of connecting. Something in our spirits felt like a dam breaking open. If we opened our eyes, we would see our aura dancing around us like magical balls healing us. My sis and I called it magic. Feeding from each other's energy, we learned that this was the best way for us to help each other during cravings. That way neither of us could turn crazy on the other. We had seen it happen before to others like us.

I guess we were lucky in that it hadn't happened for us. I guess it was because we were sisters and could easily feed from each other in this way. Doing this form of feeding was risky though. Our bodies lifted from the floor. Our power gave us supernatural currency to float as we were.

"Don't get tired okay," I softly said. "Is this enough?"

My sister shifted her hand, then made it where our hands laced together.

"Just a little more," she said.

The dull pain in our stomachs stopped. I could feel it because we were one mind right now. Her rapid beating pulse had stalled to normal and a gentle look of peace was on her face. Yes, our craving was done for now. We could go.

A hissing sound near us made me jump. I hopped up to grab the metal tube then ran with my sister behind me. I shield her from any threats. The Demented had broken in through our barricade.

"How many do you see sis?" I asked rushing through the shipping hanger. There was a door ahead of us. We just needed to get to it.

"I see five," Alisha quickly shared.

"Five? That's it? We can take them." I said with a smile on my face.

As I looked her way, I frowned. I didn't feel my sister's presence behind me. She wasn't here. I quickly turned then ran. She was ahead of me moving like a jaguar who turned into the shadows being reckless.

"Alisha!" I yelled.

My sis was in her hunting mode. She flew through the air by leaping then landed animal-style against one of the Demented. That meant that she was hunkered over them, palms against the floor, on her knees using her strong nails as knives. Being reckless like this could have had her dead within seconds. So, I rushed forward to have her back going back and forth with her to take down those that hunted us.

Charging at the creepy, slimy things that snarled at us, I focused on a tall nasty monster in a business suit. My pole slammed against the pavement and slid up in my hand. I projected it forward, gripped it with all my might, then cracked it against the side of the ashen monstrous face of the thing that tried to reach for my sister. A loud, cracking noise made me grit my teeth.

"Bust his head sis!" Alisha encouraged.

The Demented had bones like brittle wood. Easily able to break, but only with enough force to cause it to shatter. Pieces of black teeth went flying. I watched that supple washed out gray face bunch and pucker due to the force of the hit. The things red eyes focused its hatred on me.

Its short golden hair flew out like a fan. Black ooze sputtered everywhere, and its gnarled fingers reached out to grab at my pole. The thing made a loud animalistic snarl like a dog hit's a car. A jagged bone appeared in its hand and tried to swipe at me. That makeshift blade protruded from its palm.

I knew not to let it get me. That's how our parents died. So, I jumped back trying to avoid it. Panic raged through me. I then felt a familiar scary coldness awaken within.

"Vampire trash!" It snarled at me.

"Please stop," I screamed.

Aimlessly pleading I tried to reason with insanity which was dumb in and of itself. "I'm…I'm not a vampire."

Eyes rolling in its skull the thing shouted, "Demon! Let me purify you."

The semblance of rationalization was nowhere to be found in the monster. I knew that, but I couldn't help myself in trying to trigger any piece of humanity in the thing. All I knew was that we had to survive this. We had to get to safety. I mean at least to sleep and wait for the sun to come out.

"Man, screw you. Leave me alone." I yelled. "You don't want this battle!"

Tears fell. I didn't want to kill her. I really didn't. I still had hope that maybe they could be stopped, or cured. But here I was, hunching over him, ready to eat him like a Big Mac. An itching at my throat started.

I didn't want this, but I had to do this. I had felt tired from feeding my sister, yet I was hungry all over again. I needed him. I needed to feel that sweet burst of sublime pleasure hazed out the painful sensory overload that I was experiencing right now. My own mental capacity was changing. The hunter in me was coming out. The thing I had turned into was coming out and there was no return.

"Disgusting animal!" The Demented snarled at me as I leaned back and punched him in the face.

I could hear flesh tearing in the distance and a foul smell that drew my attention. My sister was tearing at a Demented feeding like a crazed thing. She looked blissful. Whereas, I shifted on my feet feeling the rush of blood in my veils signaled that it was time to battle. My nails lengthened then hardened. Amused, I bit my lower lip while a malicious smirk crept across my lips.

"Dude, come purify me then," I said with a swing of my pole again.

An ominous groan came from my enemy. Metal hit bone and flesh. A heated pleasure ran through me causing me to enjoy the cracking sound as an orange oily sludge leaked from the blood. With a quick lunge, I pulled at the guy's tie keeping him from falling back, then I yanked him

towards me so that I could send my nails into the side of his neck. When I felt my nails slice at the jugular, I gave a pleasing sigh of relief.

"Ahh…" I sighed.

My body began to tingle. My eyes rolled against the back of my head. I needed this. I needed all of this and more. This was a dangerous game I played. I knew it left me open for attack, but I didn't care. I sapped at the heat in the body, then crazed currents of

power in the blood while I drank it all.

Head tilting, I smiled at the pleasure that seeped into every molecule in my body. The pleasure was sickening. It made me heady. It brought me euphoria and it brought me the pain of regret. I didn't want this. This wasn't supposed to be my life.

All I knew was, one day I went to sleep human. The next, I woke up in my dorm craving the very life force of the people that were turned into these things. I didn't understand it, nor did my sister. From what we heard, a weird virus had permeated the airways the day the government decided to make us better.

The virus hurt everyone and twisted once normal people into these beings though the television, the Net, and using our smartphones against us. After turned, the Demented continued the infection through their bite or bone penetration. The nation was crazy now because of them, but that wasn't it. When the Demented changed, a lot of us also changed into something else. We learned that this weird mutation happened due to a global mist that was released in response to creating a war against other nations.

Rumor had it our government had turned into Demented and all they could see was war, so they released the mist. Anyway, that insanity, caused a few of us humans to run from the monsters, but at the same time, once turned into what we are, hunters: we ended up craving the energy that came from the infected. Now the world was chaos and we were looking for safe havens to protect ourselves from the things that hunted us.

"*Candace!*" I heard in my mind. Outside of the heightened senses, sometimes, family could connect through telepathy.

"*Sis, it's not clear,*" I had assumed that it was. But it wasn't.

I could smell them. There was one more Demented. One who tried to snatch me from the side.

"Take her down sis!" Candace yelled.

Focused on the fight, I gave a nod, then stopped the female Demented by grabbing her by the throat. Carefully, I stood up, then stepped over the dead Demented under me. I turned and ended up staring into the milky-red eyes of the monster I held by the throat.

"Oh, snap! I hate this." I said. The woman looked to be in her sixties and white like milk. She squirmed and hissed trying to fight me. She bared her teeth and tried to bite at me with saliva spewing everywhere.

"She's strong," I yelled. I held the old lady away from me keeping distance between us. I couldn't risk being turned.

Demented bites were painful like the sting of a thousand wasps- so I heard. If they chose to turn you by bite, bone scrape and by releasing their dark mucus into your mouth through regurgitation, then there was nothing that could be done. The best chance to survive it was by isolating the mucus, committing suicide, or be like my sister and me.

"Let me purify you! You foul little monkey," The thing gurgled.

"Monkey? Are you for real? Damn, Susan B. Anthony wants her racism back, 'kay?" I spat back.

The old lady flashed a corrugated looking mouth then tried to lung at me. "You disgusting bloodsucking thug!" She screamed. "This world ain't right with you all in it!"

She swiped her nails at me. Tired, I kicked her away to avoid a swipe. That hit could still a☐ect us by making us sick.

Alisha and I couldn't afford a nick by them. We had nowhere to go to heal up or find medicine if we did.

Panic ate at me. A cool chill still hung in my body. I needed just a little more blood for energy. So, I got it when the old lady hit the floor in a hard thud.

Legs in the air and scrambling on her back like a roach, I rushed the old lady then leaped on her. The look on her face was chilling. There was a mixture of fear and elated malice. Her lips curled back into a snarl and a million of tiny jagged teeth revealed themselves. Damn, I didn't want to be touched by this thing, but the hunger was intense.

I landed on the old hag in a hard-slamming thud. My arms wrapped around her, while she threw her arms around me. The female Demented tried to bite into my neck, but I rammed my pole into her heart. Home run.

Sweet heat eloped me. I lapped at her blood. I sucked at her hand, breaking bones by snapping off her fingers with my teeth. My tongue quickly darted back and forth at her yielding flesh in between my chews.

"Ah..." I moaned.

I was drowning in her essence. It felt so damned good. Drawing my knees to my chest, I gasped, laid my hand against my rapidly beating heart then relaxed. This was delicious. Sometimes I couldn't help but imagine how I could miss out feeling like this. This was better than my first kiss.

Ready for more, something tugged at me, stopping me.

"Mine!" A low growl began in my throat until I recognized the connection. The touch of my sister gripping my arm to pull at me, took me out of my plateau phase.

"Sis, don't. She's gone. The thing is gone," she urged.

Alisha sat in front of me on the side of the dead monster.

She reached to ground me by cupping my face as she stared in my eyes with an urgency.

"We need to go before more come Candance."

"Huh?" I muttered in a daze.

Alisha tugged at me again. She was covered in black wetness. The sticky substance dried to her hair. Her jeans, the graphic tee she wore that said, 'Nerdy and revolutionary', her hoodie, and her kicks.

"It's time to go, sis." she said in a gentleness that reminded me of our mother.

"Mom." I whispered in my dazed confusion.

To my eyes, Alisha looked like my mother laced in draping all-white gossamer. Upon her face were the white painted African marks of the great ancestors of our past. The tribes related to those marks, unknown to me. My mother's protective loving smile filled me with reassurance as she reached out to caress my face.

I could feel her telling me to push on. To survive this and that it wasn't my fault that she and our father was lost in this crazy world.

"Candace. You must go. Break out of the compulsion and go," My mother urged.

Her ethereal appearance changed to that the last image I had of her, covered in her blood. Her hand was holding her side while glass dotted her flesh.

Memories played on rewind as I remembered my mother's other hand pulling me from our flipped car as the Demented rushed her, to chop at her while she screamed, *"Go!"*

The sting of her urgent scream brought me back to reality. I hurried to my feet then glanced around.

"I smell them." I said with a shuttering voice.

"I hear them," Alisha said at my side, breathing hard as her fangs slid over her lips.

We stood shaking in our feet. Then we ran. We ran faster than the average human. Bursting through the door, we left the only place of slight security we had and headed back into the streets of St. Louis. Dark twinkling skies highlighted our way. In the mix, were pink clouds. Eﬀects from the mists.

"We need a car," I heard my sis suggest.

"Or a semi so we can run those mo'fo's over!" I countered.

Both of us made our way from south Broadway to Walnut Street. Bush Stadium and the ballpark village were overrun with the Demented. So that was a no-go. Other buildings were so messed up that knowing us, we'd get trapped and the ghouls would easily find us. So, we couldn't hide there, there were too dangerous.

"Where can we go sis? The surrounding buildings are too clustered together. We needed a place with a little bit of space and easy to barricade," she said matching my speed. She shifted on her feet to use the energy from her feed, and cast it back at the Demented behind us. Sending them flying back-wards to impale them.

Taking her arm, I felt her stumble against me in exhaustion.

"I know, sis. We'll find a spot," I said in worry.

So, we ran while I mentally prayed for a place to lay our head away from the Demented we left behind.

"Sis...do you see that?" I asked pointing at the sky.

Wrecked cars blocked the streets.

"Hold on to me sis," I made Alisha wrap her arms around my neck so that I could carry her. It was my turn to use the magic that came with our curse, so I did. I channeled that power to climbed over a few cars. Pacing myself, I, then slid us on the side of a huge SUV to look up at the sky. Flashes of colorful light broke through the dark skies like firework. One burst behind us, down a block behind us. Another followed a little away.

"Hey, is that a signal?" my sis asked peering over my shoulder.

Sitting her down, I checked the pattern in the sky while frowning. I really didn't know if it was a signal, but I knew that I could assume that it was.

"Yes, and no. I think they are leading the Demented away," I said slowly standing.

"Come on."

T□□ □□□□□□ □□ D□□ □□□□□ □□□□ □□□□ □□□ □□□□□□ us. With it were the jarring sound of flying bullets then a rumbling explosion. A battle was going on somewhere near us. Hope hit me heard. That meant that there were other survivors. Quickening our steps, that battle helped us in trying to get the hell outta there.

"Sis, look!" Alisha said tugging on me while we ran.

M□□□□□ □□□□□□□□□ □□□□□□□ □□ □□□ □□□ beaming our way. As we headed towards the lights, a huge street barricade came in view. We had found a safe haven. So, we hoped. People with flashing golden eyes, with the marks of the Hunters in their pupils, walked around in the distance. Many were dressed in everyday clothes. The rest were soldiers.

"Help us, my sister needs help. I need help!" I desperately yelled.

"State your class!" Some solider yelled in the distance.

I wasn't sure what to say exactly so I yelled, "We're not the Demented! We're human!"

"Human is not a class. State your class!"

The longer we stayed in the open with the Demented around, the quicker we were going to die. So, I held up my hands and let my aura wrap around my palms then yelled, "Civilian! We hunt the Demented! Please, help!"

"DEMENTED!" Someone yelled. Followed by, "Let them in hurry."

The sound of an object being dejected followed by a quaking fiery explosion made me hold my sister close to me and look over my shoulder. Downtown St. Louis was on fire, and heading our way were clusters of Demented with snarling nasty faces. They used whatever they could as weapons, like my sister and I also have done. Many leaped in the air, and other's scaled light poles.

My stomach clenched in fear and I shifted on my feet, "Oh, come the hell on ya'll! We're on your side! Let us in please!"

Soldiers disappeared, and it grew silent.

"Are we safe?" Alisha weakly asked.

"I hope so," I responded.

As I said that, as a large barricaded door opened, and masked soldiers with rifles and blades rushed past us.

"Let's go baby sis," I said helping Alisha stand on her own.

"Good," she said. "I'm hungry and tired."

I laughed. "Me too."

With a sharp tremble the echo of our never-ending hunger danced through our bodies and mind, hands clasped together to keep our balance, we walked ahead, exhausted, and full of hope. Only to have it blasted away at the sound of guns going off aimed at us.

"Alisha!" I hollered as she collapsed to the ground.

Whipping around to cover my sis, my moment of grateful-ness disappeared when I saw my sister hit with what I real-ized were darts. I was so dumb. My dad used to say, 'Not all skin folk are your kinfolk' – in this case, not all hunters could be trusted and suddenly that reality hit me hard.

Furious, I used my last bit of strength to plummet into a solider.

I slammed him to the ground knocking his mask o. His dark eyes with two red dots narrowed in anger. He was a Hunter! Two French braids fell on the guy's chest. They swung out when a blade appeared in his hand.

"We didn't come here to jump stupid dude! But ya'll just had to be bums!" I yelled lashing out.

The Hunter's shimmer of his aura was intense. It rushed at me like a second person. *We can do that?* Momentarily, impressed I punched him. These 'sumabishes' had hurt my sister and this solider was going toe-toe with me, so I had to kick his ass and protect myself. That's karma!

"Yo, get this chomping chick up o me! She's strong and rabid!" The solider yelled. "That's an order!"

As I got ready to use my fangs to rip at his throat, what-ever was in the nasty darts that hit me, made my world tilt and wobble. I felt the hard slam of the ground under me as I stared up at the brotha who had pissed me o. The drum of Demented ghouls rushed through the streets and the scream of soldiers grew closer. Fading to black, I had thought this was a safe place for us. But, man was I wrong.

T E

BLACK AND DEADLY

DICEY GRENOR

O▢▢▢▢ ▢▢▢▢▢▢▢▢▢▢ I ▢▢▢ ▢▢ ▢▢▢▢▢▢▢ ▢▢▢ M▢▢▢▢▢ walked in, slamming the apartment door hard enough to make the floral picture frame shift on the adjoining wall. She either didn't notice or didn't care as she stormed in from the foyer to the living room. She threw her briefcase on the floor next to the couch and tossed her navy suit jacket on the co▢ee table. "Did you hear? I mean, what the ever-living fuck?" Her face had a reddish tint, a color that didn't normally show up well on her dark skin.

And that's how Kabira knew the depth of Maajida's anger.

"Yes, girl, yes. I heard." It just so happened that Kabira also recognized that anger firsthand. She felt it in her soul, and knew the source. In fact, she was watching it unfold on the six o'clock news right now. "I'm so sick of this shit. Something must be done." Kabira lifted Maajida's jacket and grabbed the television remote to turn up the volume, so they could learn more about the latest police o▢cer acquitted of

killing an unarmed black man. It was the sort of thing that
should make any human being angry.

Maajida shook her head in frustration as she smoothed her
matching navy pencil skirt and sat on the arm of the couch
next to Kabira. "I heard it on my car radio on the way home.
It's too unbelievable. Once again, no justice, no
accountability."

Kabira and Maajida grew angrier as they watched the officer's press conference. Kabira's fists clenched when the
unabashed officer strutted over to his family for hugs and his
soulless attorney thanked the jury, the judge, and the police
department for participating in the so-called due process of
law. Meanwhile, the victim's family would never see the
deceased again... all over a busted taillight.

The system had failed.

Again.

Kabira's phone rang on the coffee table, startling them out
of their angry thoughts. Kabira answered, knowing that their
oldest sister would be on the other end filled with her own
outrage. "Hey, sis. Yeah. We're watching too. Uh huh... yeah.
Uh huh. Okay... Okay, bye." Kabira hung up and looked over
at Maajida, now standing in front of the television with her
hands on her hips in her Wonder Woman pose. "Badu's on
the way."

Maajida broke away from the insult-to-her-intelligence
flashing on the screen and side-eyed Kabira. "Badu's coming
here? Now?"

"Yep." Kabira sank deep in the couch pillows and closed
her eyes to calm herself from the images on the screen. "Badu
said it can't wait. That we've been sitting around too long
waiting for things to change, waiting for something to
happen. She said it's time for us to stop waiting. It's time to

do something. And..." Kabira pinched her nose to relieve tension that had started building since her twelve-hour nursing shift ended earlier, "I agree with her. If the courts aren't going to make this stop, we must."

Maajida nodded, because she understood why Badu and Kabira wanted to intervene. Maajida just wasn't certain their method was the best way. So many things could go wrong.

Maajida started pacing.

Kabira noticed Maajida's hesitation. "C'mon. You know she's right. You said the court would get it right this time. It didn't."

Maajida stared at the floor, reflecting on how they had gotten to this point. "I know Badu said if another black man was killed unjustifiably by a cop, without punishment, we would seek balance in the universe and resolve the systemic problem ourselves, but..." Maajida kicked off her heels and paced from the picture window back to the coffee table, "this is a dangerous path. If we're caught, our careers are over. Even if we're not caught, we are responsible for our actions no matter how well-meaning our intentions, meaning our lives could be over. There are real consequences to consider. We're not superheroes in a comic book."

"No, we're not. But maybe we should be." Kabira cracked her knuckles and stuck them back in the pockets of her light blue scrubs. "We don't wear capes, but we're not helpless like the families that keep going without justice, listening to preachers telling them to forgive and wait for vengeance in the afterlife. We can do something about it. We may be the *only* ones who can do something about it." Kabira looked at her gold Eye of Horus ring and twirled it around her middle finger. "We were given these gifts for a reason. I'm willing to risk my life to save others with them. Aren't you?"

Maajida glanced at the identical ring on her middle finger, but didn't answer. The question was rhetorical. Of course, Maajida would do what was necessary to save others if it came to that. The real question was— had modern America reached that point? And if it had— would Maajida and her sisters' combined power bring about salvation, or would it make matters worse?

Maajida stopped pacing and plopped down on the couch next to her younger sister. As she and Kabira continued to stare at the television screen, watching the real-life horror, Maajida felt ashamed that she had held onto hope that this officer would be punished by the court system she had sworn to uphold. She had believed the evidence was more than sufficient for a conviction, and she had believed the jury would see it too. The fact that the jury had decided the officer should not be held responsible, made her more willing to listen to her sisters than ever.

"He looks so smug standing there," Maajida said, shaking her head in dismay, "as if he hadn't taken someone's life, who had been on the way home to three children. Anyone that afraid of the community he's supposed to be serving shouldn't be an officer."

Kabira nodded. "We just want to be treated as equals, and for law enforcement to be held to the same laws they are paid to enforce. They take an oath to protect and serve the community then treat us like we're less than animals. To top it all off, they get paid leave then return to duty like the life they took meant nothing. I'm sick of it."

"You're preaching to the choir." A tear, mixed with anger and sadness, trickled down Maajida's face. She wore her passion on her sleeves when it came to advocating for others, so her emotional reaction wasn't anything new. Though she had not been involved with this officer's case in any way, she'd gone through law school, dedicated her life to standing up for those who could not stand up for themselves, and worked at a legal clinic that provided free legal services to indigent clients. She believed in protecting and serving too, and took each injustice to heart. "I mean, the shooting was on video, Kabira, and it still didn't matter."

"That's because they don't see it as murder. They always find a way to justify the killings, because they don't even see the victims as humans." Kabira gestured towards the television and spoke in a matter-of-fact manner. "Look how they left his body out there on the concrete, without medical attention for seven hours, handcuffed and uncovered, for the media to project that image nonstop. He bled out, because they had no intention of saving his life. Then they used his corpse to induce panic and fear in our community. It was by design." Kabira had been on duty at the hospital that day... treating several gunshot victims, in fact. With all she'd seen over the years, she took an anti-gun stance for civilians and law enforcement alike, especially when the officers had so much authoritarian power and not enough de-escalation training.

"Yes," Maajida sighed, "you're right."

Kabira and Maajida sat on the couch watching the news as the camera panned away from the press conference podium to the courthouse. On one side, people marched with signs, shouting, and protesting the verdict. On the other, people cheered for blue lives as if characters from "Smurf" and "Avatar" existed. The sisters didn't understand what protesting would accomplish any more than they could fathom why people were cheering over another officer joining a long list of officers who had gotten away with murder while on and off duty.

168 BLACK MAGIC WOMEN:

Moments later, a fight broke out and spread so deep between the groups that it was impossible to determine who was on which side. Instead of a commercial break, the news switched from the fight scene to replaying the video that started it all: the officer pulling his gun and unloading on his victim. The visuals were gruesome enough that most of it was blurred.

Though Kabira had seen the footage before, it startled her again once the officer began firing. The victim had declared seconds before that he suffered from anxiety and was unsure of what command the officer had shouted. Though he had not followed the officer's orders to get on the ground, he had begun to raise his hands in surrender, and had not reached for a weapon or moved toward the officer.

"Geez." Kabira used the remote to turn the television off. She'd had enough and knew Maajida had too. "And people have the nerve to call us violent."

"If enough of them feel our wrath, I'll bet this shit will stop," Badu said from the doorway where she stood.

Kabira and Maajida jumped off the couch, screaming in shock. Badu had come in quiet as a mouse.

"Badu! We told you not to do that again." Maajida gripped her chest tight to still her nerves.

"It's time to be proactive, my sisters." Badu walked closer to them with her arms folded, as if Maajida hadn't said anything. "These officers— this system built on violence, supremacy, and hate— wants blood." Badu adjusted the colorful wrap on her head and emptied the contents of her large bag onto the center of the floor. "We're going to give it to them. We will show them violent." She walked over to the blinds to close them, so that the room became dark. "Enough is enough." She moved to the center of the room and sat on the floor. "Come, sisters. Sit with me. It's going to take the three of us. Our combined powers. Our magic is strongest when we touch and agree. We cannot wait. We must call upon the magic of the black goddess, Keondra, and get the vengeance our people deserve."

Kabira and Maajida didn't move. They had not found their nerves yet. Their eyes had not adjusted to the darkness either.

Badu patiently sat, waiting in silence and darkness. She had already said everything she'd planned to say on the matter. She'd wait until her sisters came to grips with it and came to her willingly. Badu was the most knowledgeable, most experienced, and most patient of them all, and it showed. It also came in handy in her teaching profession.

Kabira was the first to move. "They'll never see us coming," she said as she sat at a sixty-degree angle from Badu.

"That's the beauty of it." Badu held Kabira's hand and went back to silence and darkness, waiting for Maajida to join.

After minutes passed without Maajida joining them, Kabira spoke. "Are you with us, Maajida? For a conjuring spell, our triangle of power requires all three of us. Do I need to remind you the courts returned a not guilty—"

"No, you don't." Maajida walked over and sat across from her sisters. "I was just wondering if we should draw the line at o cers... or if Neighborhood Watch trigger-happy wannabe cops should be added as well. Either way, I'm in." Maajida gripped her sisters' hands to complete their black magic triangle of power. "No one gets to be judge, jury, and executioner anymore. Not without consequences. Not on our watch. Time to call out to the goddess of our ancestors. She'll show us the way."

"Very good." Badu nodded her approval. "So, here's what

we're going to do." Badu began lighting three black candles on a dish in the center of their triangle, which meant the spell had commenced. "We will call upon Keondra. Now. Before another life is lost and justice is eluded."

Each sister stripped off her work clothes and rubbed a poignant herb all over herself, per Badu's instructions. They returned to the triangle around the candles and drew blood from their wrists with the sharp edge of their Eye of Horus rings. Once their blood covered the bottom of the candle dish, they held hands again. Badu chanted the conjuring spell aloud, holding onto her sisters' hands to maintain their magic connection. Once the spell was cast, the sisters sat and waited.

Right when Kabira looked at Badu for assurance that the proper steps for conjuring the black goddess had occurred, wind started blowing in the center of their triangle. The three candles became one as the wind picked up. A low hum began as the dish gradually rose from the floor. It continued to rise as the space where it traveled became filled with the essence of a merging being. First, just the silhouette of a curvy woman appeared then her whole body formed. The third eye in the center of her forehead was the last part of her to become visible.

"I am Keondra, Goddess of Divine Retribution. Who summoned me?" Each of her three eyes focused on a different sister and blinked. Her long, gold gown flowed with the consistent motion of the wind.

The sisters exchanged glances. They all thought the same thing: Keondra was an overwhelming vision of beauty, strength, and wisdom. The epitome of these qualities, in fact. Her voice sounded mellow and soothing, which surprised them, given her commanding presence.

Badu held her chin high, but cast her eyes downward as a show of respect. "We did, Goddess Keondra." Badu held her sisters hands up for Keondra to inspect their rings. Her sisters followed suit. "We are descendants of the Black Magic Women."

Keondra assessed each of them with eyes so dark and intense, she seemed to look deep into their souls. "You seek revenge? Punishment? War? Death?"

The sisters nodded.

"Yes. Revenge... and all that it entails," Badu said.

Goddess Keondra smiled and leaned toward Badu. "State your case for revenge, and I will render my decision forthwith." She brushed Badu's cheek. "Did your lovers cheat on you?" She moved to Maajida's cheek. "Were you abused?" Lastly, Kabira's cheek. "Did someone steal from you?"

"No. This is not for a personal offense against us, but our race of people." Maajida's voice trembled, but now that she had committed to this plan, she would go all in. "We've survived slavery, Jim Crow, mass incarceration... Now, law enforcement officers continuously get away with murder, and we want them to get the justice they deserve."

Goddess Keondra studied them with all three of her eyes. She appeared to be listening to what they had not said aloud. "You want revenge on police officers? For murder?"

The sisters nodded.

"Are they not here to maintain law and order? Are these *murders* just casualties in fighting other murderers?"

"We would not have summoned you, if that were the case. While we respect the ones that do their jobs, there are some bad apples in the bunch, and they are seldom brought to justice." Badu, whose husband was a retired police chief, spoke confidently on the matter. "We need your help to avenge the lives taken by those bad apples, who are usually put back on the force."

Keondra's third eye blinked. "Do you fully understand the consequences of revenge magic? Whatever you send to your target comes back to you tenfold if they are innocent."

The sisters nodded. They'd come this far with confidence. They would not be dissuaded by fear of consequences.

"Though the courts have found them not guilty, these offi - cers are not innocent." Maajida had made her peace with her initial reservations. She had seen black people serve lengthy jail sentences for petty crimes, and watched offi cers get slapped on the wrist for ruining whole families. No, they were far from innocent.

Keondra had not decided yet. "Do you have proof of which offi cers deserve revenge? You stand the risk of dismantling the whole judicial system if you are in error. A lawless society would be more detrimental to your people than a flawed one."

"Goddess Keondra, I implore you— please turn on the news." Still holding tight to her sisters' hands, Badu nodded her head in the direction of the remote on the coffee table. "Just hit the ON button."

The remote lifted from the table and floated in midair over to Keondra's hand. A hand, bedazzled in gold and tattoos, held the remote and turned on the television. Keondra watched a continuation of the coverage from the shooting and subsequent acquittal that the sisters had watched earlier.

"We know which offi cers are guilty." Maajida's voice sounded more confident now. "A life for a life seems reason- able retribution."

"Also..." Kabira waited until she had the attention of one of Keondra's eyes before explaining to the goddess how to pull up old news reports of other officer-sanctioned murders on Kabira's smartphone.

As Goddess Keondra read through headlines and news stories on the mini computer screen, her countenance began to shift to a vicious lion. A literal lion. With sharp teeth and whiskers. Her full, coarse afro became her glorious gold mane. "This is not right."

"That's why we called you," Badu said. "No more protesting. No more legislatures. No more prayers to the God of Light and Love. We want justice, and we want it now."

Keondra held the phone extra tight, shaking her lion head as she continued to read the screen. "A man was shopping in a store for a toy gun when he was gunned down. A young boy was shot within seconds of the police pulling up to the scene. A father of six was choked in broad daylight on the street while complaining that he couldn't breathe." Keondra looked up with bloodshot eyes. "There were really no consequences for the officers?"

"No. Some of the families may have received settlements, but that money's eaten up in legal fees. Plus, no amount of money can make up for the life lost." Maajida's eyes watered. "When there's a black on black civilian killing, the perpetrators are held responsible. That disparity of justice must stop. That's why we've summoned you. We must make a stand that says we will not allow our lives to mean less than others. Neither will we allow law enforcement to act with impunity."

Keondra turned off the devices and released the remote and smartphone to float back to the coffee table. "You are all pure of heart right now. A healer, a counselor, and an educator. I have but one more question." She paused for effect. "Are you prepared for the stains on your souls for being responsible for taking someone else's life?"

They nodded without hesitation.

"We are descendants of the Black Magic Women. It is our duty to do what's necessary to preserve our community." Badu was more than ready to move on to the revenge phase. "Will you help us?"

Keondra turned back into her original woman form and took a deep breath. "Yes, I will help you get revenge."

The sisters sighed in relief.

"Thank you, Goddess," Badu said on their behalf.

Suddenly, Goddess Keondra morphed from a beautiful woman with glowing midnight skin and a satin gold gown to a fierce warrior, holding three sharp spears and a mean mug that would scare the skin o a rattlesnake. "By the time we are finished, the privilege of protecting and serving the community will be honorable again."

The sisters looked at each other like *Oh, shit!* They weren't sure what would happen next.

Keondra set the candle dish down that had been levitating over her head and handed each of them a spear along with detailed instructions. First, they had to create three separate lists of guilty o cers, irrespective of race or gender, who had killed unarmed black men and gotten away with it. The criteria had to be exact to avoid negative energy coming back to the sisters. Next, the sisters had until sunlight to locate each target, go to them, and strike with their spear twenty-six times to coincide with Keondra's divine number of power. They had to leave the same note on every scene: "No justice. No peace. No more police brutality. Signed, Keondra, the Goddess of Divine Retribution."

There could be no deviations from the instructions, so that the following morning, it would be obvious that the mass killings of these o cers were the result of divine intervention.

The message would be clear: no life was precious until all lives were.

Each sister researched targets, and combined the names into one large hitlist then they separated it into three smaller lists, according to regions across America. The idea was that they could do more damage in a shorter amount of time if they separated and went after di⬚erent targets.

Keondra sharpened the spears while the sisters gathered intel.

"One question—" Kabira said once they were done, "are we going to get a special sleigh with reindeer to make it around America overnight or what?"

Keondra laughed, an eerie but comforting sound. "You conjured a goddess to help you kill for revenge, but you doubt the magical method to carry out the plan?" Her laughter ended abruptly. "I will impart my spirit into each of you, and you will go forth like the wind." Without warning, Keondra dispersed into three parts and melted into each sister's body.

In an instant, they felt power like they'd never had before, and hopefully, never would again. The point to the terror they were about to unleash wasn't just vengeance for the lives that had been taken without retribution. They also intended to spread enough fear to stop others from getting away with murdering black men in the future. The sisters were about to put the world on notice that the unjustified, unaccountable killings would not be tolerated. If their plan was successful, they would have no need for revenge magic again.

They had no time to delay.

Armed with spears, a thirst for justice, and black goddess power, the sisters moved like molecules through the air, out into the night... to kill them all.

Keondra's power mixed with their combined power made

their bodies non-corporeal, which ensured there would be no DNA left behind. Metaphysical spears ensured no weapons would be recovered later either. Their spears would return to the spirit world with Keondra once they were done, and that knowledge helped the sisters plunge repeatedly without mercy or hesitation into the bodies of their communities' bullies.

Nothing could be seen with the naked eye. Nothing could be caught on camera. Not even the targets could see the sisters coming like grim reapers in the night. The sisters didn't have to knock on doors or wait until the targets were alone. They only had to make sure they had the right target. Magical power from the black goddess did the rest. To anyone who may have been nearby to witness the o cer's sudden death, it appeared as if the target su ered from cardiac arrest.

The sisters moved with stealth and dangerous grace through the night until they had killed everyone on their lists. Once the sun rose, law enforcement across the nation would remember the night justice was served. Hell, *everyone* would remember. Until the systemic racist system treated everyone fairly, no one would rest easy. No one would feel peace.

They went around like thieves in the night seeking justice and finding it. They didn't even have to leave a trail of blood to get it done. Just death. They delivered death. And notes.

When they were done, they had no time to spare. The sun was on the horizon. They barely made it back in time, slipping through the front door of the apartment just in time to escape the trickle of sunlight that threatened to trap them in their non-corporeal states, as Keondra had warned.

They fell to the floor from exhaustion as Keondra withdrew from their bodies. Though Keondra would never be compensated for her help in restoring justice to a broken judicial system, the sisters thanked and worshipped her. Keondra also thanked them for being brave and risking their own lives. She expressed how proud she was of them, and how proud their ancestors would have been that they had used magic in an unselfish manner. She touched their heads and bestowed a special blessing of wisdom, beauty, and strength upon them and their future offspring.

They watched in awe and reverence as Keondra shifted to the form of a soft, gentle black lamb.

"I will go into a long, deep slumber for generations to come after this revolutionary war you have brought down on America in one night." Keondra touched each of their cheeks and gathered her spears. "But now that you have gotten justice, I believe there will be peace." The candle blew out the same moment she disappeared.

The revolution was not even televised... until the next morning.

The next morning, all the news stations had switched from discussing the officer's acquittal and had shifted to the Angel of Death that had swept through America during the night. Since more officers had fallen dead of cardiac arrest in one night than had died in the last three years combined, the media and all of America took that as a sign. The notes left at the scenes of each death had been a major clue as to the Angel of Death's motivation, and no one wanted to risk a second night like the last.

The president, vice president, national security advisor, cabinet, and all local governments across the country wanted to discuss the same issues: new police department policies and training, new investigation procedures, new gun control legislation, and new diversity and inclusion programs to tackle America's racial problems. Sure, many police officers resigned across the country. The community took that to mean the trash had taken itself out. Good officers rejoiced in the absence of trigger-happy officers too. The officers that remained after that dark and deadly night were truly there to protect and serve. In the meantime, while the departments were rebuilding their forces with competent officers, the community began initiatives to police itself.

The night of the Angel of Death— which only three women knew correctly as the night of the descendants of the Black Magic Women— was a win for everyone, except the guilty officers.

After a shower and a full day of rest, Badu went back to teaching students how to become productive members of society. Kabira went back to treating sick patients at the hospital. And Maajida went back to advocating for indigent clients in a system she believed would maintain justice. Because if it didn't, she and her sisters would call upon the magic of the black goddess, Keondra, again and make sure that it did.

A few days later, as Maajida walked in the apartment, tired after a long day of court, her phone rang. She answered it as she kicked off her heels and plopped down on the couch next to Kabira, who looked worn out after a long shift too. "Hey, Badu." Tension in Badu's voice over the phone immediately put Maajida on red alert. "Uh huh..." Pause. "Uh huh..." Pause. "Uh huh..." There was a long pause as Maajida's eyes widened and stared at Kabira. After listening to Badu for a minute more, Maajida's hand covered her mouth in surprise.

"What is it, Maajida?" Kabira sat up, alarmed. "What's she saying?"

Maajida held up her index finger for Kabira to hold on. "Yeah..." Maajida said into the phone. "Okay. I understand.

Okay. Okay, bye." She hung up, and put the phone down slowly.

Kabira waited for the bomb Maajida was about to drop.

"You know that stain on our souls?" Maajida began, her eyes wide and haunted. "The one that makes us no better than the murdering cops, because we'd become murderers too? Calculated, first-degree murderers, in fact, not just second-degree or manslaughter-type murderers... which technically makes us worse than—"

"Can you just get to it?" Kabira waved her hand to hurry Maajida along. "What did Badu say?"

"She said her husband was really upset. Some of his police buddies from his old precinct had died suddenly of heart attacks the night of the Angel of Death, and he wants revenge. The whole department does. All the departments across the country do. They reasoned that since magic had been used to kill the men in blue, they'd use magic to get revenge." Maajida shook her head with hopelessness. "Badu said she just found out her husband's a descendant of the Greek Magic Gods, and he and his pentagon of brothers are summoning a powerful god to kill whoever used magic to kill those offi-cers." Maajida gave Kabira a meaningful look.

"Okay... that sounds threatening in theory, but really— what can they do?" Kabira began to relax. "They can't find us. They don't know *we* did it."

Maajida sighed. "Turns out we killed an innocent, Kabira, a rookie cop on Badu's husband's old force whose gun had malfunctioned. It fired while it was still holstered, accidentally killing the unarmed suspect when the officer was handcuffing him on the ground."

Kabira pinched her nose and closed her eyes. "Which

means we have blood on our hands that a magical locator spell will be able to track."

"Exactly." Maajida sat deeper on the couch and sighed again. The damage had been done. Now, they had to suffer inescapable consequences. "Nemesis, the Greek Goddess of Justice and Revenge is coming for us. First us, then all black community activist organizations. Black Lives Matter groups, Black Panthers, Black Coalitions, NAACPs... everybody."

Kabira looked defeated. "But they didn't have anything to do with it."

"No, but that's part of the ten-fold consequence." Maajida looked defeated as well, bereft of energy for sadness or anger. "Badu's husband wants the revenge killings to make a bold statement: Greek gods are superior gods." Maajida closed her eyes and rested her head on the couch to await the forthcoming vengeance. "And this time, there's nothing we can do about it."

T E

LEFT HAND TORMENT

R. J. JOSEPH

I ⬚ ⬚⬚ ⬚⬚ ⬚⬚⬚⬚ ⬚⬚⬚⬚ ⬚⬚ ⬚⬚ ⬚⬚⬚⬚⬚⬚⬚⬚⬚⬚⬚⬚⬚⬚⬚ ⬚ ⬚ found we did not really need a protector. Most passersby tended not to notice our nondescript entryway in the worn down building. Even those who did notice it were deterred by the dark cloak of misery in our eyes. Despite my queerness and my race, those doorways to my soul which broadcast unspeakable rot allowed me kinship with the men inside. Her eyes held the same blackness, despite their light gray color, and it announced her as kindred, served as her password into the club. I let her in and followed her up the stairs, as my shift was done.

There was more to her life story than her eyes, apparently. The foulness of whatever tortured her spirit bubbled just underneath the surface of her being. Her dusky colored skin shone with determination and fury. She glided ahead of me up the stairway and into the parlor, removing long white gloves as we walked. Severe burns covered both hands, the puckered skin reflecting in the lantern lights.

Even Whitson, the resident playboy, did not set his flirtations upon her. He simply asked her what she was drinking, the same as he did the rest of us. He often told us that he did not seek companionship with fellow su⬚erers. He said their beds were already too full with them and their demons.

"Bourbon, please." The rich tones slid from her throat and escaped into the quiet murmur of the fifteen of us. She accepted her glass gracefully and settled herself into a chair close to the fireplace.

Not forgetting our Texas manners, we quieted down and allowed the lady the floor. I watched her take a sip from her glass.

"Merci." She accented the appreciation with a brisk nod to the side. When she gazed back at us, the flames from the fire flickered around the shadows resting beneath the smoky orbs of her haunted eyes. She pulled her bonnet o⬚ and placed it on the table next to the chair. Kinky curly strands spilled down to her shoulders and the room gave a collective gasp as the flames caught the sandy tresses. This was the only acknowledgement we gave to her beauty that night.

Without preamble, she spoke, in accented tones. "My name is Dominique Aimee Beaulieu and I was born and reared in New Orleans. I had an ordinary childhood, if that as the daughter of a placee` on Rampart street could be called such. Papa and Maman loved me very much and I was a rather spoilt child. They loved each other, as well. I know Papa loved her more than he loved his wife. But he could not stay with us all the time. I once asked Maman why he had to leave and stay away so often and she explained to me that we could not be selfish and keep him all to ourselves. He had another family with whom he had to stay most of the time, but he was always thinking of us.

"Maman had a picture of a beautiful woman with blond hair and she often gazed wistfully at it when she thought Papa and I weren't looking. I would ask her about the woman, whose features I saw staring back at me in the mirror, albeit through darker skin. Maman would evade the answer until I turned sixteen. When I finally got my answer, I also got the explanation for our way of life.

"'This is my sister, your aunt. Papa's other wife. He met me as he courted her and wanted me for his left hand wife. She knows about us but cannot acknowledge us publicly. But she must accept our existence. You are of courting age now. Papa will arrange for you to attend The Quadroon Ball next year, to find you a wealthy, white husband. Do not waste yourself frivolously on any colored man. Even if he has money, he can't elevate your status or guarantee that your children will be free men.'

"She grabbed my hand. 'Just take care to always respect your husband and do his bidding. Love and honor him despite the feelings of jealousy that will come when he takes another to wife. We are the wives they choose, when their other will be chosen for them through making familial alliances. These arrangements are our only way to freedom.'

"I didn't understand why she beseeched me so dramatically on these points. Our system of placage was shocking enough to discover without her telling me I had to accept it, that I had few other choices. I knew nothing of love between a man and woman, but I could see the love between Maman and Papa. If it meant she had to share him with her sister, did that make it of any less value? Did that make me, the product of their left hand union, any less valuable? Of course, I would love my husband, legally bound or not, because of all the things I did not understand, there was one thing I knew and never wanted to change: my freedom.

She paused her story here, seeming to look at us for the first time. She turned her fierce gaze on each of us, one at a time, her fellow beasts of demonic burdens. She settled her gaze finally on me, the lone other woman in the group. I did not know how I understood that she knew my secret. My fellow club members knew and did not care. "You understand when I say fighting for one's freedom is a frantic battle when losing means losing your personhood and often, your very life."

I nodded in acquiescence. I did know what a constant fight for freedom to simply exist required. Dying was preferable to giving in to bondage of any kind, hence my membership there. These, my brothers in terror, did not make anything big over my masculine clothes and obviously feminine body. My haunted heart bore witness to more important things to them. The rest of the world did have problems with me, as soon as my "charade" was discovered. Explaining that this was who I am did nothing but result in a trail of bodies. Thus far, my own body did not increase those numbers.

"I was excited about my first ball. Maman fussed over my dress and hair and Papa fussed about the shortage of eligible men he deemed worthy of his daughter. He finally settled on two men from prominent families who would arrive at the hall under the cover of night, just as the other attendees would.

"It is di cult to gain full understanding of a person through a portrait and word of mouth about his family, but I felt an attraction to the first man before I met him in person. I told Papa I wanted to meet and dance with him first, and as much as indulgence was against the proceedings, my Papa gave in.

"His name was Alesandre Pasquet. He nodded to Papa to request permission to dance with me. From the moment his hand touched mine, I felt panicked. Strange and uncomfortable feelings bubbled up inside me. They were frightening and unsettling in a way I was not prepared for. The closer Alesandre moved against my body, the more I wanted to pull away from him. The way my womb ached and my nether regions melted created an imbalance inside me. Maman had told me nothing of this. I could not catch Papa's eye for guidance. I thought I would swoon.

"And then Rene was there. He looked like a fallen angel with his dark hair worn just a bit longer than was fashionable, one curly lock falling over his eye. I felt an immediate sense of calm, discomfort gone in an instant. I looked into his dark eyes and found nothing there that explained...anything. 'May I, Pasquet?'

"I was grateful for the rescue but did not overlook the fact that the question was not a question at all. Alesandre put up no fight and simply left me standing in the middle of the floor with Rene, as he fled. Sweat broke out onto his forehead and he stumbled backwards, eyes opened wide. I felt no pity towards him, nor any curiosity over the dealings between love rivals.

"'Please do not think me forward', my rescuer began, 'but you look quite terrified. Would you like to sit and have a drink?'

"I fell into his eyes, those bottomless brown pools of serenity. He placed his hand on my bare arm and led me back to where Papa sat. My sire was apoplectic. 'Who are you and what are you doing with my daughter?'

"'I am Rene Fanchon Villemont Duplanchier. I am pleased to make your acquaintance.' Papa had no further fight, returning to his seat next to me. Trickles of sweat ran down his neck, and I had not seen them before I had left him moments before. He struggled with something, barely restrained. I had seen this expression before when workmen sought to cheat him when doing home repairs, or when passersby subjected Maman to insults as they walked on the streets. In those instances, he confronted the o☐enders. At that time, I was left to question what had engaged his ire.

"Rene returned with a glass of punch. 'Mr. Beaulieu, may I walk with your beautiful daughter on the balustrade?' Papa barely nodded without speaking or moving otherwise. The sweat flowed faster. His eyes communicated something... sadness, maybe...and I thought him lost in reverie over my imminent engagement, as it was. It was clear at that point that I would become Rene's left hand wife.

"My savior took me for a round in the cool night air. No words passed between us, and that comforted me. There were no terrible feelings bubbling up inside me, threatening to break out of my skin. He did not try to touch me, which was good, because my skin still ached deliciously from where he had touched my arm earlier. At the end of the stroll, he returned me to Papa and stated that he would call for me and make the final arrangements for our alliance.

"I went to bed that night with dreams of my own household and a calm, beautiful husband. I was awakened by Maman and Papa's argument.

"'You cannot let her go to that...that...demon!' Maman never raised her voice at Papa and she never went against his wishes.

"'We cannot stop it. He has placed his mark upon her. He

will let no one else have her.' Papa sounded defeated, smaller than I had ever imagined. I tiptoed from my room to eavesdrop with a visual advantage.

"'I will place this gris-gris upon her. It will work. I know a woman in the Quarter who can help.' Maman spoke mostly to herself. Papa rocked ceaselessly in his chair, his despondent façade placing an ache in my heart that rivaled that of my arm.

"'We won't deal with that slave magic. She must go. To try to prevent him will being the sure destruction of...all of us.'

"Maman exploded. 'So it is your other children you are fearful for? You worry for your other wife, the one who does not love you as I do? The one who has your legal heirs?' Her mane of curly, ebony hair flared around her head like a crown of fury, unleashed from her headscarf.

"She dropped down next to his chair, unwilling to be defeated. 'Please, Dominique is all I have. You cannot sacrifice her. You cannot.'

"Papa remained silent, stroking her back as she sobbed loudly. I went back to my room, confused about their talk of sacrifices. I fell into a fitful slumber, dreaming with no remembrance.

"As promised, Rene called at the townhouse the next day. 'Mr. Beaulieu, Mrs. Beaulieu. I have come to make arrangements for Dominique's hand.' He stood on the townhome stoop, hat in hand.

"'No.' Maman whispered the word so that I had to come further down the hallway to hear her.

"Rene tilted his head, the expression on his face never changing.

"'If we do not invite you in, you cannot cross over our threshold. Papa stood behind her, his hands on her shoulders. He restrained her as she moved in the direction of the door.'

"'I will get the invitation I need. Dominique?'

"I had thought myself nearly invisible around the door, standing deep in the bowels of our house. I moved to the door in slippered feet, forgetting the decorum of receiving male guests only at the permission of Papa and Maman.

"' Dominique! No!' Maman moved towards me and halted, mid-step. Papa, drenched in sweat, also froze. Tears welled in Maman's eyes. 'Where is your gris-gris, beloved?'

"I had removed the pouch from my neck at the end of the hallway. I arrived at the door and stretched my hand out to Rene. He smiled and walked into the living room.

"'We will not be staying. Tell your parents goodbye. We will be married at once and will retire in our own home tonight.'

"'Goodbye, Maman and Papa.' Rene did not release my hand, but I was not returning to my parents. I belonged to Rene. I spared one glance behind us as we departed, barely a fleeting thought given to the tears that flowed down my parents faces as they stood in the same places.

"True to his word, Rene and I went directly to the church and were married. I hardly remember the ceremony, thinking only of being with Rene. I napped as the carriage rode across New Orleans to my new home.

Dominique paused again, here, to sip her bourbon. She must have intuited the rules of our club and that we would wait patiently until she resumed her story. She took long moments, lost in her reverie. When she spoke again, her voice lowered.

"Rene did not come to me in the bedroom I occupied alone until after I had been there for three weeks. Then, he sent a note to request permission to come one night. In the three weeks' time, I had become acquainted with the servants, learning as much as I could from them about my new home. My husband had informed me that I could have the run of the house and that once I decided on décor items, he would send into town for them.

"The servants tried to prepare me for my imminent marital bed duties. I explained that my Maman had already done her job, but one woman, Nan, insisted.

"'You do not understand, Mistress. You must be ready when he comes to you. I can help you.' Her eyes begged me to give permission.

"Instead, I laughed. 'I will be fine, Nan. This is what wives have done since the beginning of time.'

"She nodded, sadness overtaking her eyes. I felt bad about hurting her feelings, but I wanted everything to start on a positive note with my new husband. I already held some trepidation at the fact he had waited so long. I wanted everything to go naturally so we could start our intimate journey with no obstacles.

"I did allow her to help me bathe and rub scented oil over my body. I sat up in the bed to await his visit. My heart pounded when I bid him to enter the room. Under the candle light, his beauty took my breath away. The same giddiness that had overtaken me at the ball almost a month earlier with Alesandre bubbled up in my womb.

"My husband floated with the shadows in the flames and slid under the coverlets I clutched in my hands.

"'Are you afraid?' He cupped my chin in his hands, and my body heated up. I had a hard time breathing.

"Becoming frantic, I nodded. I tried to scoot away from him, but he held my face in place.

"'Do you wish me to make you comfortable?'

"I nodded again.

"'I have to hear the words,' he prompted.

"'Yes, please. I wish for comfort.'

"Rene held my gaze and calm washed over me. My languid body slid down flat on the bed. He rose above me and without warning, pressed himself into my body. I felt the pain Maman and Nan had warned be about, but I could not react to it. My body would not move, even as my mind willed it to do so. But that was nothing compared to what was to come.

"Suddenly, my body was punctured by spikes that assaulted my canal as Rene moved in a rhythm inside of me. His member grew larger and the spikes stabbed me from within. I screamed inside my head and felt the blood rush through my veins as fear pumped through me just as Rene pumped. He did not require any movement from me as he took his pleasure.

"The torment I felt reflected from my eyes into his, as I tried to understand what was happening. My womb burned and wept, tissue tearing and trying, but failing, to accommodate the assault. He tilted my hips upward, because I could not move them, and he plundered my depths with searing strokes. I knew I would pass out from the pain.

"But then Rene spoke. 'No. Stay here. You must receive me. You will bear my spawn.' Despite the overwhelming pain, my eyes remained open. Tears rolled down the sides of my head, my mouth silent as my brain sought refuge in delusion.

"All I could feel underneath my buttocks was warm, thick wetness. My blood bathed us in the virginal bed, marking the loss of my innocence. And my sanity.

"At the end of his attack, I felt something further up inside my body split. Rene held his position and his eyes changed. I felt movement that was not him. It felt like thousands of tiny feet trampling through my birth canal, upwards to my womb, to the very core of my body. From a mental distance, I worried that ants had become attracted to the blood Rene had drawn from me and had made their way into the bed.

"Those were not ants. They were his seeds, marching from his body, into mine, seeking fertile grounds in which to implant themselves. Up and up and up into my canal, they moved, relentless in their quest. My stomach heaved with nausea, and Rene focused his gaze on me, once again. The convulsions stopped, but the marching went on and on.

"They invaded the end of my opening, and swarmed outward, beyond just the area they were supposed to inhabit. I felt them marching through the tears in my tissues, gnawing their way through veins and muscles, planting themselves wherever they could.

"I had almost succeeded in leaving my body when Rene withdrew from me. Wetness flowed and flowed from the wound he left and did not say anything. I still could not move my body or scream, and fresh tears joined the fluids down below.

"Nan appeared at the bedside and she propped my legs up on extra pillows she must have brought into the room with her. I wanted to scream, but I could not even move my head to beg her to help me. The despair in her eyes as she tried to position me told me more than I wanted to know about my condition.

"She crossed herself and scurried about the room. She left and came back with an arm full of things. No longer able to stand the pain, I passed out.

"My own screams brought me to consciousness. Nan was there, shaking her head as she pressed warm cloths between my legs. I screamed again as the fabric barely grazed raw tissue. She murmured and took something from around her neck and pressed it into the cloth. All the pain did not go away, but I was able to elevate my thoughts above the pain. My body was a mangled mess I sought to escape.

"I did not see Rene again for another month. In that time, my wounds healed superficially, but my mind had grown further damaged. I did not understand as Nan tended to me and clucked, 'He must be stopped'. I agreed, but I did not know how to stop him. He was my husband. I was unable to leave the room, much less, the house. I was a prisoner.

"When Rene came again, I trembled in fear against the headboard. 'Please. I cannot. I am still in great pain.'

"Rene did not heed my pleas. The torture began anew, ripping tender tissue that had barely begun to fuse together. Again, I was paralyzed on the surface. Whenever he closed his eyes, I began to feel the paralysis wear thin. That next assault was physically unbearable. I learned to look into his eyes without looking. My spirit left my body until he was done. Sometimes I did not allow it to return until weeks after the assault.

"The pain took on a different aspect after that second attack. Pain inflamed my body, around the clock, and I became bloated. I thrashed around in the bed, screaming, for many hours out of a day's time. Nan still tended to me, and I could see her sometimes, shaking her head and wringing her hands, consulting with other servants in hushed tones.

"One night, she awakened me and whispered fervently, 'You carry his spawn. Those creatures cannot be borne.' I had no reason to question her. I knew she was right. I felt the creatures gnawing on the internal structures of my body. The constant pain made me delirious and I stayed away from my physical prison more often than I remained conscious.

"But Nan's observation pushed me to action. I begged her

to help me move around the bulk of my belly and get to the hallway. Once I reached the top of the stairway, I waved her away. That action would be mine, alone. I threw my body down the stairs, the bumps and collisions mild compared to what I had already endured. I prayed that I would die along with the monsters that my body hosted.

"I was not so lucky. I survived the fall. I was no longer pregnant. This meant that Rene visited me again for the following two months, shredding my body in his quest to procreate. He succeeded again.

"That time, I was leaving nothing to chance. Nan had disappeared after my fall, so I no longer had a confidante willing to help. I was on my own.

"I threw myself down the stairs a second time. I bumped my head and passed out. When I came to, I dragged my swollen body down to the kitchen and found matches. I did not care if I burned with the house. I wanted to die. I wanted to be sure to destroy the lives that burrowed inside of me.

"Once everything was engulfed in flames, I lay on the floor and allowed my spirit to escape my earthly bonds for what I planned to be a final time. I watched, detached, as Rene came riding up on a horse, truly embodying the fiend he was, screeching as he saw his legacy, his home, ablaze with the host for his monstrous offspring trapped inside. He burst into the house, his clothing already on fire, rushing from room to room.

"When he found my body in the foyer, he first checked on his progeny. A hoarse bellow of rage billowed from his chest. He picked up my body and walked towards the door. He took a step, and suddenly stopped. A mirror positioned by the door, where it shone directly in front of his face captured his gaze and he became as if paralyzed, and dropped me outside the door, onto the porch.

"I listened as he howled impotently, and the house began to fall down around him. I wavered in and out of consciousness. Blessedly, I do not know what happened after that point, because I succumbed to unconsciousness yet again.

She set her glass down on the table next to her and slid her gloves back onto her scarred hands.

"'I thank you all for bidding me an audience. I had no one else in which to confide, as my parents died as soon as Rene took me from our townhome. I could not remain in New Orleans after his death, so I will continue on my journey. Maybe I will end up back there when everything dies down; maybe I will not. I wish you Godspeed in your adventures, as well.'

She then spoke directly to me. "Perhaps you and I will meet again. I pray it is so."

Dominique walked, alone, to the stairway and left the club. None of us spoke after she left, out of reverence for the trust she had bestowed upon us. We never betrayed the confidence of another club member, and her secret would ride with our own to our graves.

———

T□□ □□□□□ □□ □□□□ □□□□ □□□□□ □□□□□□□□□ □□ □□□ not. Try as I might, I could not keep Dominique from invading my thoughts. When I was trying to be honest with myself, I said I thought of her because I wondered if there could possibly be anything romantic between us if I sought her out. We had made a connection that night at the club, and my heart wanted to pursue it.

When I was actually honest, I admitted that she simply haunted me and I would never rest until I had seen her again.

Years later, I travelled east to New Orleans to see if I could find any clues to where she might have gone. Inquiries on her name concluded with many widened stares, and more than a few crossing of the bodies and grasping of artifacts. I was finally led outside of town, to a burned structure.

Though few details remained, and the smoke had long burned away, my heart knew this to be Rene's original home. In the distance, another house peered through the trees. I rode in closer, following the sounds of children playing. My first glance of the yard's inhabitants was of four toddlers, sandy haired and dusky skinned, running around the side of the house.

Closer inspection revealed two servants, each with baby carriages made in fours in front of them, rocking the structures with bundles inside. One of the servants grasped her gris-gris in her hand as she performed her duties, fear etched on her face, arm extended as far as possible away from her body.

Standing on the furthest side of the house, I finally saw her, head tilted in the same way as she had held it that night. Her kinky curly hair was shorter than before, laying close to her head. She was still beautiful, from what I could see. I slowed my horse, still quite a distance away from her. She turned in profile, and I saw her extended belly, full of life. Even from my post several feet away, I could see frantic movement from her body, in varied directions.

She raised her gaze to look in my direction. I would have sworn I was too far away for her to see me, but her look was only for me. As she turned to more fully face me, I saw the exposed skull and tissue that should have been covered by skin. Skeletal hands and arms appeared from frock pockets. She moved in a stilted manner, haltingly, towards me. She raised one bony finger and pressed it to half lips, extending the kiss into the air between us. Dominique then raised her head towards the house.

In an upstairs window stood a man of dark visage, peering down onto the women and children in the yard. He then raised his head and looked towards the fields surrounding the house. I followed his attention. And there I found my true Dominique. She floated through the fields, unencumbered, untouchable by her tormenter.

T□□ E□□

TRISHA AND PETER

KAMIKA AZIZA

Trisha

T□□□□ □□□ □ □□ 'R□□ □□□ □□□ □□□□ □□□□' □□□□□□ to herself as she combed her dolls' hair in the sparsely furnished living room. Sunlight peeked through the boarded windows shining on her brown Afro like fire surrounding the crown of her head. Trisha spun her 'new' Molly doll in the air to check the fit of the tattered dress she'd made from old rags. Jackie slowly walked into the house, dragging a canvas bag filled with cans and other things she found during her search.

"Mommy!" Trisha jumped up quickly, throwing her dolls to the floor as she ran over to her mother, snatched the bag from her and then carried it carefully to the kitchen.

"I got it mama. Did you have a good run? Did you get any peaches? It's been a while since we had peaches."

"Trish..." Jackie's voice was weak. She stumbled as she

walked behind the upbeat ten-year-old, trying her best to keep up but standing was getting near impossible.

" Is there still cans over at the Mitchel's' place?"

"Honey..."

"Or even just cherries, I like their cherries, they're sweet. Or does that tree down the road have oranges? Is it even orange season yet? I can't wait for orange season," Trisha began placing the cans on the kitchen counter and separating the other little treasures into their piles.

Jackie leaned against the counter top for balance and took deep breaths. She slowly lifted her bleeding hand and tried her best not to fall over.

"If you teach me how to shoot the guns better I can help you fight the bodies, then we can go out together instead of being by ourselves all day, because I always feel scared alone without you, and it must be scary out there too right mama?" Trisha looked up at her mom with a huge smile which disappeared as she saw the blood dripping down her mother's arm. Without a moment's hesitation, she was ready to leap into action.

"Mama you're bleeding, did you get cut? I'll go get the kit."

Jackie grabbed Trisha by the shoulder with the strength she had left. "No honey I don't need the kit. Sit down for a second, I need you to listen to me."

"But your hand mama? You need a bandage!" Trisha turned to get the first aid kit but her mother's voice stopped her.

"Honey, don't worry about that, just listen, okay?"

"Okay." She stared at her mother's hand, focusing on what she would need to wrap everything properly.

"Mommy needs to leave."

"Another food run?"

"No honey, I need to say goodbye. I need to leave."

Trisha touched her mother's bleeding hand and as reality set in, she began to cry, "You got bit, just like grandpa."

"Yes." Jackie saw the world falling from under her daughter's feet. She had contemplated just dropping the food in the hall and running but she had to see her baby one last time.

"Are you leaving so that I won't see you die, too?" Trisha stared up at her mother with tears trickling down her face as she bit her lip, trying not to lose the little control she had left.

"Do you remember how to take the safety o☐ the gun?"

Trisha nodded her head and wiped away tears.

"Where should you aim?"

"For the head."

"Good girl," Jackie brushed her unbitten hand across Trisha's cheek and smiled as she fought within herself to keep her composure. "Now you don't want to waste bullets so use your knives, but remember run if you can."

"Yes mommy."

"Only go out if you need to, don't wait till you are out of food just go when you are running low so that you can stock up."

Trisha nodded slowly and wiped away her never-ending tears.

"And honey, stay away from Oak Brook, they have a large swarm down there. Always aim towards the train tracks, if you get cornered anywhere just climb whatever you see, or run uphill it makes it harder for them so they will lose interest. OK."

"OK. OK. I promise mommy, I will be OK."

Trisha woke up in her corner in the living room. Her black hair was matted down and her eyes were sunken with circles around them. She looked around the dark room and hugged her blanket as she listened to the faint groans outside her window. She was still alone in the darkness, so she rolled over and went back to sleep.

The next morning the sun barely shined through the window which left the house with little visibility. Trisha stood at the kitchen counter and ate an orange while spinning her knife. The groaning outside began to get louder, which made her look around in fear but she was just as alone as she had been for the past five months. Trisha looked upstairs and took a deep breath as she walked slowly up the creaky boards fearing what she might see. As she entered the hallway she ducked into a dusty bedroom and walked cautiously to the window. She stared outside with her eyes widening in fear then as if she was pulled by some unknown force. She instantly dropped to the floor, breathing heavily.

"Shit!" she exclaimed in her loudest whisper as her heart began to beat out of her chest. She slowly peeked up again and saw a swarm of twenty to thirty 'Bodies' walking past the house slowly. One stopped and looked directly at the window as if it saw Trisha, but once another 'Body' bumped him he just continued with the group.

Trisha crouched on the floor with her back against the wall and head leaning against the window sill. As the groaning subsided, her breathing relaxed, then slowly she looked through the window, and the swarm was gone.

She slowly made her way downstairs and began packing her backpack with as many extra shirts and as much supplies as she could carry. She picked up Molly and inspected her carefully before throwing her to the ground. She continued to pack her knives by wrapping the bigger ones in cloth, then stu ed them into the side pockets, then placed the bag by the door and sat on her blanket and stared at the stripping wallpaper. She looked over at her Molly Dolly in the tattered dress she had made for it with the needle and thread her mom had found and smiled. She crawled over and grabbed the doll, then curled up with it in her blanket and hummed quietly to herself.

The next morning she woke up as early as she could will herself to, but every time she stretched her hands up she couldn't feel the sunbeams. She looked at what she had left on her kitchen counter, two cans of fruit and five cans of beans, and contemplated finding ways for them to fit into her bag, Then she decided to leave them so that if her five-day trip failed at least she would have something to come home to. Trisha opened her pineapple slices and began drinking the juice as she ate in between. As she reached the bottom of the can she could see the sunlight as it peeked through and hit Molly. She began to get ready for her journey.

She cautiously stepped through the door with her large knife on her hip and throwing axe hanging o□ her backpack. She looked down the street with her hand against the door, parting it just enough for her to make a quick retreat before closing it, then running towards the community gate.

She walked down abandoned streets and hid quietly whenever she spotted roaming Bodies strolling by. She knew every hiding place and every trick to getting out of harm's way. As the sun went down, Trisha skillfully climbed a tall tree then locked her bag to one limb and tied herself to another. She pulled a piece of fruit out of her jacket pocket and ate it while surveying her surroundings. Sometimes she watched as a few lonely roaming Bodies walked by without noticing her. Other times she wondered if she would ever see her mom again and what would she have to do. Trisha then leaned back against the coarse bark and closed her eyes.

Trisha woke up to the sunlight shining on her skin and

smiled at the warmth. She could feel herself becoming happy again and shook herself from the thought. Out here she had to fight the joy; it was no time for her to be weak. She untied herself from the tree and unlocked her bag and began her descent. A growling sound came from below. When she looked there was a Body walking over to the tree and trying its best to reach for her. Trisha pulled herself back onto the branch and looked down at the decaying corpse.

"God Damn it." Trisha looked around to see how screwed she was, then let out a relieved sigh. "At least it's not a swarm."

She pulled a small, wrapped knife from her bag and put it in her pocket; she unhooked her knife on her hip and took three deep breaths as she looked around one last time. She pulled her bag on her back and began climbing down the tree, looking down occasionally at the Body reaching up the tree still trying to grab her. Once she got as close as possible, she used her legs and one arm to keep her grip, then took the knife out her pocket and stabbed the zombie in the hand, making him stick to the tree. As she moved out of his free arm's reach, she grabbed her bigger knife and pushed it through his temple. His body slumped over, hanging from the tree. She pulled the knife from his hand, then jumped down and removed the other from his temple then crouched and ran towards the street, stopping to look for any more trouble.

Trisha reached a safer distance and continued her journey, staying even more alert as the adrenaline rushed through her veins. She stopped abruptly as she heard a strange sound behind her and stared as a red pickup truck came closer and closer, then passed her, screeched to a stop, then reversed. The door creaked open, and a middle-aged man with red hair and full beard stepped out and stared at Trisha with the same look of confusion as her.

"Hi, I'm Peter."

Trisha just stared at him in awe. The only white people she had seen in the past year were either all dead and trying to kill her or trying to steal from her, so she couldn't figure out if she was safe.

"Little girl, please tell me you're not alone."

Trisha looked down at the ground shaking; she thought of ways she could escape, but this man could probably catch her. She wanted to reach for her knife, but she had never killed anyone who wasn't already dead, so her hand froze, leaving her completely defenseless.

"You're alone, aren't you?"

Trisha looked up at the man with tears in her eyes, "Are you going to hurt me?"

"No, sweetheart, I promise, I am never gonna hurt you. You real close to Charleston, and over there ain't safe no mo', especially for a little girl on her own. I can take you down to Georgia to somewhere real safe; they got families there with kids, some even smaller than you. You can play; you will have enough food. Can I please take you there, to that safe place?"

Trisha continued to cry as Peter smiled kindly at her with a worried look in his eyes. Groans came from the bushes behind her and a small swarm unfolded reaching for the girl. Peter grabbed Trisha, then jumped into the truck and closed the door as she screamed and kicked in fear.

"It's okay, honey, it's okay; they are not gonna hurt us, I promise; no one's ever going to hurt you."

Peter

T⬚⬚ ⬚⬚⬚⬚ ⬚⬚⬚ ⬚⬚⬚⬚⬚⬚⬚ ⬚⬚⬚ ⬚⬚ ⬚⬚⬚⬚⬚ ⬚⬚⬚⬚⬚⬚⬚⬚⬚⬚ any attention as a group of disheveled people sat around it. Peter placed his hand around a small framed young woman and kissed her on the temple as she snuggled into his chest. Everyone around the campfire had some form of a makeshift weapon and an injury to match the mood. Smoke from the flames hazed everyone's vision of the woods, but no one cared. This was not camp, just a rest stop to get some food and get back on the road as there was no time to waste. A figure stumbled out from behind the trees. Peter noticed it, and stood while passing his revolver to grab his knife. Another figure crept from the woods and soon more stumbled out following the smoke.

"It's a swarm!" Peter's shout brought everyone to their feet, ready to fight.

Carol, the young woman Peter held, used a makeshift crutch to stand up and began hobbling towards the cars. Others followed her as they screamed in fear while some stayed fighting back the dead Bodies.

Peter led the attempt to hold back the enemy, but the swarm continued to grow as they revealed themselves. As he began to give orders to his troops, he became distracted by a hair-raising scream. He looked back to see Carol using her crutch as a weapon, hitting a Body whose attack had left her laying on the ground.

"No, Carol!" Peter shouted as he ran to her aid. Once he had a closer range he shot the Body on top of her, but it was too late. Carol was bleeding profusely; she was bit. Peter held her close as she cried.

"How bad is it, Daddy?"

"Not too bad. Let me get you to the truck."

"No, Daddy! Let 'em finish me; I can distract 'em and y'all can get outta here."

Peter shook his head relentlessly and wiped the tears away from his little girl's face. "No, baby girl; Imma find a way to get you outta this mess."

"Please, Daddy, just go." Carol pushed Peter with all her strength, but she could hardly move him. "Go now before it's too late, please."

Jason, a tall dark-skinned man with a pick axe in hand, grabbed Peter right before a Body lunged forward. At first it tried to adjust for Peter and Jason but then it noticed Carol just lying there and began to dig in.

As Carol screamed in pain, Peter reached out for his little girl, trying to break Jason's grip and save her, but with ease Jason dragged Peter towards the cars as he swung his axe, taking down all the Bodies that blocked their path.

Peter regained his composure and raised his revolver. Jason looked back at him and released the grieving man, guarding him from any of the monsters that tried to attack.

"Bye, baby girl." Peter pulled the trigger, and a bullet pierced through Carol's temple. He quickly wiped away the tears that had flowed down his cheeks before they ran into his beard.

With that cue Jason tapped Peter on the shoulder and pointed to the red truck. They ran to the vehicle and jumped inside, and in silence they took one last look at the devastation before leading the caravan to safety.

Peter drove down the quiet street with his revolver in his lap. On the dashboard sat the letter Jason had carefully placed there. It read:

'We are gonna keep heading to Savannah, maybe double

back and see if the swarm is gone and we can pass. Peter, I want you to come with us; we are here for you. You have to live for her… we all have to live for the ones we have lost. If you change your mind, please, Peter, please change your mind.'

As Peter drove down the road he saw his daughter, Carol, standing on the side with her long locks flowing through the gentle breeze watching him. Peter slammed on his brakes and in a moment of disbelief and joy he reversed. He finally stopped his truck and realized he was startling a confused little girl standing alone on the side of the street. Her brown Afro glowed in the sun, and her beautiful brown skin, though crusted with dirt, somehow showed that this girl had been through a lot but still managed to remain so pure and innocent.

'Peter please change your mind. I know it feels like the end of the world, but that's why you need to find something else to live for. Just live for her because she wants to see you survive.'

Peter stepped slowly out of his truck, trying his best not to frighten the young child. He saw the fear in her eyes and could tell she was contemplating fight or flight. He could tell she had been on her own for a while, but some part of him just hoped that a girl as small as this was being cared for. He bent over and looked her in the eyes and gave her a kind smile.

"Hi, I'm Peter."

Trisha & Peter

T□□ □□□ □□□□□ □□□ □□ □ □□□□ □□□ □□□□ □□ □□ □□□□ Trisha and her 'Molly' as the young girl brushed the doll's hair down with a singed toy comb. The sunshine filled her with warmth and happiness, and she enjoyed every second of peace that time allowed. She hummed softly to herself as she played, oblivious to the two Bodies that had made their way to the tree. They could not reach her where she was up in the tree, but she was supposed to be the lookout.

"Damn it, Trish; get your brains out the clouds."

Trisha looked down and saw Peter walking over with his revolver raised. She quickly dropped her doll and grabbed her axe and sailed it right into one of the Bodies heads, instantly dropping it to the ground. Peter fired the gun, and just as quickly, the other Body lay there.

"Sorry." Trisha slid down and picked up her doll and then her axe. "It's a good thing it was just two of 'em."

"And if it wasn't, your ass would have been stuck in that tree."

Trisha grabbed her gun from the passenger seat and hooked it to her waist as she mumbled under her breath, "I said sorry." She left her axe and doll on the floor of the truck and began to help Peter finish loading their supplies.

"You gotta be more careful; this ain't no road trip or vaca-tion. I need you to always be focused." Peter had been so 'focused' on scolding Trisha and loading the truck that when the gun went o□ he almost fell face first in the grass. He looked up to see Trisha pointing the gun right over his shoulder then lowering it and put it back in her holster.

"Dad, I said I was sorry."

Trisha spun around and stomped o□ before getting into the truck. Peter turned and saw a decaying Body laying at his feet with its arms outstretched. Peter quickly threw the last of the supplies into the truck and jumped into the driver's seat then exhaled.

"If you want, we can stay here a little longer. Savannah ain't going nowhere."

"No, that's where you were taking Carol; we should finish the journey."

"How about we stay till we can't find any more food?"

"I have a better idea." Trisha turned in her seat and faced her dad, her face lighting up with her bright smile. "We leave after next orange season. I really like oranges."

"From the tree down the road?"

Trisha nodded and began to hum her song as Peter started the engine, and they made their way home. He looked over at his daughter, whose hair burnt like orange flames in the sunlight. He stared at the road ahead of them and joined her softly as they sang,

"Merrily, merrily, merrily, merrily, life is but a dream."

T☐☐ E☐☐

THE KILLER QUEEN

CINSEARAE S.

I □□□□□□□□ □□□ □□□ □□□□□□□ □□□□□ □□□ yellow, but all became clear in a matter of weeks.

The woman was alluring and sensual, but one gaze into her eyes told another story of decadence and malice. She had the body of a goddess—curves that would put Venus to shame. A Creole beauty like no other; a simple wink from her would make a man drop to his knees. Her black, wavy tresses looked as soft as silk. Men flocked to her like flies to honey. She was envied yet respected by the women of town. Everyone looked up to this mysterious woman whom nobody knew much of, and when they saw her, she kept them wrapped around her dainty, gloved finger.

Fluttering in and out of social parties, she'd mingle with strangers, engaging in idle prattle as if she cared, while scoping the ballrooms for her next alleged victim.

I say *alleged* because after some time, the good folk of the town started noticing some of their elite members disappearing without a trace. Despite her happening to be with the victims before they disappeared, no one thought of asking the 'Yellow Dame' about them, *at first*. No one had suspected someone as beautiful as her of any heinous behavior. And with me being part of the police squadron trying to figure out the current goings-on, I was charged with finding out where the Yellow Dame resided and questioning her about these strange dealings.

The first victim, Mr. Stanley Stowe, part owner of a railroad company, vanished after attending a dinner party hosted by the Covingtons, a well-respected couple of society. Many rumors were abounding as to his whereabouts. Several who attended the party were asked about Mr. Stowe's last appearance, hoping something would give some sort of clue.

It wasn't until the next social gathering that she appeared, wearing a pale yellow lace and satin dress with matching wide-brimmed hat. Still, no one suspected her of foul play; her wit, allure, and beauty shielded her from such ugly accusations.

Another gentleman wound up missing, this time at the mayor's own home. Mr. Albius Shrek, oil tycoon. I noticed how much Mr. Shrek was enraptured by the Yellow Dame's charms, although she seemed aloof to his witty banter. As she drank and made merry with the partygoers, gliding through the ballroom as if walking on air, Mr. Shrek followed her like a lovesick puppy. Although he didn't leave with her that night, he still vanished without a trace. Social gatherings were a huge part of this town, and now, many were becoming reluctant to host parties of their own for fear of something terrible happening on their estates. Discussions of the mysterious Yellow Dame were prominent among gossiping women in the streets. Every now and again, I'd follow some of them, hoping to hear anything useful.

"Ms. Viola wants to throw a party, but this latest incident has her in a tizzy. She's so afraid someone will vanish on her watch!" said one that resembled a scrawny bird.

"I bet if the Yellow Dame shows up, *someone* will," said a second who looked panicky.

"Oh come now, how can you accuse that young lady of anything treacherous? There's no way someone of her stature--nor *any* woman for that matter--could do anything harmful to a man. It's just not feasible!" the eldest of the group said.

"Someone could be *helping* her," one with cold eyes and an upturned nose suggested.

"And what would be her motive?" the eldest continued.

"Why, money, of course! For all we know, she could be poor as a church mouse, dressing in her finest, hoping to snag an old, eligible bachelor." She leaned into the group, lowering her voice. "Mr. Stowe was a widower, and Mr. Shrek was never married at all."

Their conversation could wind up being poisonous to the Yellow Dame if they buzzed such rumors in more women's ears. Just as I was about to turn and leave--

"Has anyone found out where she lives?" asked the scrawny one.

"I was told she took a hackney home one time, heading out towards Addondale," the eldest one concluded.

Ah-ha. Addondale was on the outskirts of town. Beautiful place. Lots of land, not many residents. Those who lived there *had* to come into town for provisions. I approached the women head-on this time.

"Good afternoon, ladies. Detective Hart," I said, showing them my badge. "I couldn't help but overhear your conversation about the Yellow Dame. You've heard word about her possible place of residence?"

"Yes, Addondale; that's what Mrs. Browne said," the eldest one answered.

I took out a pencil and notepad, jotting this new information down along with the name of the woman whom I spoke to. She also gave me Mrs. Browne's place of residence, in case I needed to question her as well.

"Thank you very much for your help." I tipped my hat to them. "Good day. Oh, and--" I turned on my heels to look back at them. "It's best not to spread rumors--only speak of the *facts*." I eyed the snobbish one, her face having turned a shade of puce.

––––––––

A□□□□□□□□ □ □□□ □□ □□□□□□ □□□ □□ □ □□□□□ □□□□□ take time to locate her without an address.

I had met her once, when she first moved into this vicinity. She bought some meats and cheeses from the butcher, passing me by on the way out. Our conversation was very brief, as I nearly knocked her over. I apologized for my actions, o□ering to help pick up her groceries, but she politely refused, thanking me for being so chivalrous.

As she left, I couldn't help but catch the heavenly, sweet scent of honeysuckles that surrounded her. It pulled me towards her, making me want to follow her. It was as if I was acting without any conscience. She turned and smiled at me... and my heart froze. Not out of my fascination with her, but out of--dare I say it--*fear*. Her look was a combination of seductiveness and *deadliness*. That's what kept my feet firmly planted on the ground as she walked away. About a month later, I'd see her at nearly all the social gatherings going on around town. I figured she was trying to socialize, as she'd flit from one group to another. If by chance she stood alone for a moment, someone would always come up to her. She'd speak very briefly before they would eventually drift away, leaving her disappointed. Over a short time, her demeanor changed from being more 'open' to being more enigmatic. She'd do no more than wave or say hello, listening to them, yet not listening, blending in with the crowds, becoming a chameleon of sorts. Other times I'd notice her simply watching everyone, observing them like they were prey. *Her* prey.

When Mr. Shrek disappeared, so did Yellow Dame's presence. The usual folks continued showing up, but after three consecutive parties and no Yellow Dame, I wondered what had happened to that mysterious, dark-haired beauty. The lack of her presence hadn't gone unnoticed, and talk of her possible whereabouts could be heard among the din of the music that played.

Finally, she returned when the Wellingtons--another well-respected couple--decided to throw a huge gala. It was October, the party a masquerade ball. I grunted in annoyance. Masquerade balls seemed frivolous. Actually, *all* the parties in town were, but this place wouldn't thrive without them.

I walked through the Wellington's courtyard, watching everyone in their outlandish costumes and gaudy jewelry, traipsing around the grounds, glasses of champagne or wine in hand. A full moon hovered overhead against an indigo sky.

I strolled around the courtyard, taking in a breath of the crisp, night air. I hadn't made any e ort to play dress-up, but I did carry around a large-beaked bird mask so I wouldn't be chastised by Mrs. Wellington if she spotted me.

Someone caught my attention, making me think of the Yellow Dame.

Wearing a form-fitting, silk dress, a train of ru ed lace

trailed down from her shapely hips all the way to the ground. The train was layered in two colors--black and yellow like a bee---and I caught the scent of honeysuckles. I followed after her as discreetly as possible, so not to rattle the partygoers. Her dark hair was pinned up with a silver comb dotted with matching yellow and black rhinestones, exposing an elegant neck. *If I could only see her face...*

She drifted over to the punch bowl, got a drink, and continued moving through the crowd. I lost her in the melee of drunken, heavily made-up, costumed bu oons as music played, drowning out any normal-toned conversation. Frustrated, I made my way back to the front door. The 'bee lady' would have to emerge from that place at some point in time.

I stood on the steps, folding my arms in boredom, watching folks come and go. I made my way back down to the Wellington's rockery. The moon's light reflected o of the pond, as a couple of large fish swam around.

I didn't notice the bee lady's reflection behind me at first. Startled, I turned around, facing her. Her face was covered by her black half-mask, edged in matching fringe, accented with yellow sequins and glitter. She gave a soft chuckle, those golden-brown eyes looking at me in pure amusement, a flute of champagne in hand.

"You're back," I blurted out, standing up.

She blinked, seeming surprised. "I didn't think you cared," she answered facetiously.

"Well, I---" I stopped short, suddenly at a loss for words in front of this woman.

She stepped closer, observing me closely. "I've noticed you at every party I've been to lately."

I grinned. "Are you watching me watching you?"

"I was about to ask *you* the same thing." She extended her drink to me. "Care for some?"

"No, thank you. I'm on duty."

She tilted her head to the side, nodding in understanding.

"Ah. The disappearances." A curious twinkle was in her eye. "I remember you. We've met before."

"At the butcher's...when you first moved here."

She gave a more genuine smile, taking a sip from her glass. "You can call me Miss D."

"Detective Hart," I replied. "Actually, Miss D, I'd like to ask you a couple of questions about the last party you attended...the one Mr. Shrek disappeared from."

She raised an eyebrow, taking another sip from her glass, giving me a seductive stare, like she wanted to eat me alive. I felt myself getting hot, losing focus.

"What would you like to know, detective?"

An ear-piercing laugh sounded from behind her as three young ladies came stumbling towards Miss D. "There you are!" someone in a pink, ru ed, sequined dress and butterfly mask exclaimed, putting an arm around her shoulder. "There's a gentleman in the ballroom looking for you!" They dragged Miss D away, disappearing into a group of people heading back into the mansion. Sighing, I followed after them.

Entering the mansion, I couldn't find Miss D anywhere. I strode the ballroom and halls with no luck before deciding to go back outside again. This gala was getting overbearing, and it had barely hit midnight. Then, in the distance, I saw her with a gentleman, arm in arm. From his hunched-over stature, I knew he was much older than the majority of the partygoers, but I couldn't tell who he was from so far away. They disappeared before I had a clue to their whereabouts.

I didn't see either of them for the rest of the evening. I

surveyed the mansion one last time before heading out, Miss D's alluring eyes the last thing I thought of as my head hit my pillow that night.

The following morning, I awoke to the ringing of the telephone, my sergeant telling me to get to the Wellington's estate ASAP. Once there, I met with three of my squad members standing around the rockery; Mr. and Mrs. Wellington looking as if they'd seen a ghost. She grabbed my hands in earnest, her eyes wide, pointing to the pond. "It's horrible…just horrible!"

A black pant leg was hanging out of the pond. As I peered into it, an elderly gentleman immersed in the cold water stared back at me with dead, milky-white, soulless eyes. A tiny fish swam past his face, grazing his nose.

"He was with a young lady earlier last night, dressed like a bee," said Mr. Wellington, his expression grim.

"And who is this gentleman?" I inquired.

"That's Mr. Foggarty," Mrs. Wellington answered. "Owner of Foggarty Funeral Home."

I wondered who would be *his* undertaker, as I sni□ed at the cruel irony of it all.

"*Find* that woman, Hart, and bring her in," my sergeant told me.

I nodded, leaving the scene. The rest of my team stayed behind to case the estate for more clues.

———

I □□□□ □□ □□□□□□□□ □□□ □□ □□ A□□□□□□□□ instead of a squad car; it felt better going incognito.

Things weren't looking good for Miss D, but for some

reason I tried not to look at her as a suspect. She may have appeared sinful, but looks were deceiving...

I saw those big, beautiful eyes of hers in my mind's eye, those pouty lips I longed to kiss, that body I wanted to caress...

Taking a deep breath, I shook those thoughts away. I stopped in an area that faintly smelled of honeysuckle. I got out of my car and looked around for a moment.

Perhaps the scent was caught in the wind. I saw a few homes in the distance, nothing out of the norm. Stopping at one house, I inquired about Miss D's whereabouts. The elderly gentleman had no idea who she was. It took two more times before I got some sort of lead, taking me further down the road. I smelled honeysuckles again, getting hopeful.

I came to a quaint house surrounded by white picket fencing; every type of flower imaginable sprawled everywhere. Several bees hummed as they flew by. I parked alongside her gate and opened it, going up the walkway. I knocked on her door, waited, and then knocked again.

Miss D popped up from behind her house. "Detective?" she asked, surprised at my presence.

I tipped my hat to her. "Good afternoon, Miss D," I replied. "You're a hard woman to find."

"Not my fault," she answered. I thought that was a strange thing to say.

She waved me over to where she was. "I'm out back, enjoying the weather."

I followed, noticing ivy hanging from the windows' awnings. In the back was a porch area, painted bluish-gray, a table and two chairs sitting in the center, shaded by another awning as wide and long as the porch.

"Lovely place you have here," I began, starting with some friendly conversation first. "It feels very private."

"I prefer the term *cozy*." She pulled out a chair for me, extending her hand to it. "Make yourself at home. Would you care for some tea?"

"Yes, ma'am, thank you," I said, sitting down.

Entering her kitchen through the porch door, she returned five minutes later with a large silver tray; teapot, cups, spoons and honey awaiting our disposal. She set the tray on the table, preparing my tea as I watched.

"So, what brings you down here to my neck of the woods, Mr. Hart?"

I listened to the sound of her voice; a deep, sultry tone that would have been perfect for a film noir. Not wanting to jump in with the interrogations, I kept things friendly a little longer.

"Pretty interesting costume you had on last night," I gave a playful smile.

She laughed. "I made it myself. You didn't put any e□ort into yours at all." She poured the tea and put a few spoonsful of honey into it, stirring it slowly before handing it to me. The color reminded me of dark amber.

"I'm not much of a party-person." I took a sip, noting the hearty, robust flavor that intermingled with a hint of mint underneath the dominating honey taste. I watched her make herself a cup of tea as well. She had thin, dainty fingers that I envisioned myself kissing. "Do you take up a job outside of town? Seamstress, perhaps?"

She shook her head, sitting down. "I'm a beekeeper," she stated plainly. "Surprised?"

I nodded. Surprised was an understatement.

"I sell honey to the local bakeries and sweet shops around

town. Bees are so industrious and *very* intelligent...and have the most adorable little faces."

I grinned, sipping my tea again. How an insect's face could be considered *adorable* was well beyond my comprehension. Most women I knew shrieked at the mere sight of an ant.

"How did you acquire such a profession?"

"I inherited it from my father, who inherited it from *his*." Taking a sip of tea herself, she stared at me intently. My pants were beginning to tighten in the crotch, my face feeling flush.

"There's no real mystery to me," she continued, sounding befuddled. "I can't understand why people are suddenly so interested in me."

"A mystery indeed," I replied, shifting in my chair, waiting for my problem to calm itself, but my wandering eyes couldn't help but linger on her cleavage. "You've lived in this town for barely a year, and still no one knows a thing about you."

"Except for *you*, now," she replied, never letting up on her gaze. I caught the heavy scent of honeysuckles on the wind, getting the strongest urge to kiss this raving beauty. "Besides, no one bothers to ask me anything, so why o er any information?"

I put my cup down. "I've seen you mingle with nearly everyone at every social gathering I've attended!"

"Mingle yes. *Talk*, no. People are too self-absorbed to listen to what others have to say. I can't even count how many times I've wanted to start a conversation, but became lost in everyone else's. The art of *listening* has long died." She sighed, and I stole another glimpse of her heaving bosom as she leaned over to take my empty cup and carried everything into the kitchen. Checking my pants, it was safe enough to stand up and follow her inside, despite fighting the rising urge to just take this woman upstairs and do unspeakable things to her...

For crying out loud, where was my head?

She was at the sink, washing the dishes. I stood o to the side.

"People these days seem very superficial. There's so much more to life than worrying about what the neighbors down the road are doing."

I blinked. "You do have a point there, Miss D."

"I'm a simple girl, Detective Hart," she continued, her voice having a hint of hardness to it. "I live for a simple, quiet life. I'm fond of this place; I can enjoy nature in the aesthetic, unbothered by the busyness of town."

"I understand," I said, getting the feeling she knew where I was headed with my 'gentle' interrogation.

"And now, after socializing with everyone, I find them uninteresting, which explains my dwindling presence."

"So...you're bored of this place already?"

"Not with this place, the *people*. As I've said, I'm fond of where I live. The folks, not so much."

I decided to cut to the chase. "You were the last person to see Mr. Foggarty alive, Miss D," I began. "Two witnesses claimed to have seen you with him. This morning, his corpse was found in the Wellington's rockery, in their pond."

She wiped a saucer with a small towel, firmly placing it on the counter. A loud 'clink' sounded. The look in her eyes was steely and cold.

"What are you getting at, detective? That *I'm* responsible for his murder?" She gave a condescending laugh. "I regret to inform you that you have the wrong person." She put her hands on her hips, the honeysuckle scent getting stronger.

Some of the bees from the rookery were buzzing outside of her kitchen window.

I had a sudden urge to get on one knee and beg for her forgiveness but fought the urge. Still, I felt like an idiot for accusing her. "Miss D, I'm not trying to blame you; I want to clear you of suspicion, prove to everyone you're innocent."

She eased up somewhat. "You might want to check with the Wellington's caretaker." She raised her eyebrow, her tone of voice stoic. "Mr. Foggarty was complaining of head pains, so I escorted him to the groundskeeper's carriage house, hoping he'd have some aspirin to oer the poor man. It was already late, so I left that hoary, old coot in his care." She chuckled and smirked, looking o to the side, remembering that night's events. "A charming person, but old enough to be my grandfather. For all I know, he could have had a heart-attack and fell into the pond long after I departed."

I jotted down what she said, putting the notepad back in my coat pocket. "I'm sorry if I've oended you in any way, Miss D, but you know how folks can get."

She stepped up to me, tilting her chin up to my face, as if challenging me. "And how *is* that, Mr. Hart?"

I swallowed. "Well, you know...sometimes folks are quick to condemn without knowing all the facts. They'd rather kill what they fear instead of trying to understand it."

She laughed, sounding more contemptuous than anything else. "What is this, a witch hunt?" She snied. "Why do the quiet ones always get harassed?"

"I'm not trying to harass you, ma'am," I said quickly. "And I sure as hell don't want them judging you."

She pressed her chest to mine, the honeysuckle scent enveloping us, the bees outside her window growing by the minute. I couldn't help but stare down at her ample cleavage again, those soft, caramel-colored globes pleading to be suck-led. More sinful thoughts entered my mind that I was less inclined to push away.

"Is that so, detective?" She lowered her gaze to the buttons on my shirt, her dark lashes brushing the apples of her cheeks. Her slender fingers ran up my shirt, undoing one button, and then another. My cock had a mind of its own as it began to swell, pushing against her thigh. She must have noticed; her other hand cupped my heaving balls.

"Yes, ma'am," I said, claiming her lips with mine.

———

N☐☐☐☐ ☐☐☐ I ☐☐☐☐ ☐☐ ☐☐☐☐☐☐☐☐☐☐☐☐☐☐☐☐ ☐☐☐☐☐ then, I was with the woman of my dreams, an angel that fell from heaven…and she was *mine*.

I scooped her up, carrying her upstairs. I entered the first room I saw, placing her on the bed, then took o☐ my coat, tossing it to the floor. I crawled over to her, our lips locked in another deep kiss. I felt her fingers running through my silvery hair; surprised she wanted me as much as I wanted her. I was already in my mid-forties, but my hair made me look older. Blame it on the job. Miss D was still rosy and youthful, probably in her early thirties.

Our hands rushed over each other's bodies, taking o☐ one another's clothing. I undid her low-cut blouse, burying my face between her breasts, kissing every inch of them. Her head dropped back, into the moment. I pulled her skirt o☐, admiring her firm legs, running my hands up the lines of her thighs before parting them. As I tasted her womanhood, I caught the scent of vanilla mixed with her own muskiness. She gripped the sheets as my hands groped her curvy hips, holding her firmly in place as she tried squirming away from me.

That honeysuckle scent was becoming su⬜ocating. Where was it coming from? Her? Losing control, she went completely spread-eagle, crying out in bliss as her thighs trembled. That's when I knew she was ready for me.

My cock was throbbing. I stood up, never getting my pants o⬜ so fast before. Pulling her by her legs towards me, she gasped as I thrust into her with a heated urgency, wanting to feel every inch of her. She moaned and gripped the headboard as I fell on top of her, not missing a beat. Wrapping her legs around my back, she held on tight as I pumped harder and deeper, giving her my all. I watched her breasts bounce and sway in rhythm to my motions.

I wanted this to last. I wanted to make her my wife. All sorts of crazy thoughts ran through my mind as we continued having unbridled, passionate sex.

Her raven hair splayed across the pillow, I couldn't help but cradle her head as I kissed her hard. To my surprise, she rolled me onto my back, the sheets damp under my buttocks. My dark-haired goddess impaled herself on me, riding me like there was no tomorrow.

Letting the lady do all the work was a di⬜erent experience for me; much more intense. She moved to her own pace; tightening her walls around my aching member. She grabbed my biceps, her nails digging in deep as she continued riding me, her breasts bouncing in front of my face. Man, how I wanted to suck on those perky, caramel nipples. I felt her muscles spasm with her orgasm while I watched our sexes still in action, sweat running down my forehead as I reached my climax, my load filling her. This time, she fell forward, rolling onto her back beside me.

"How long has it been for you, Mr. Hart?" she asked, barely out of breath. "I've never known a man to last as long as you have."

I rolled onto my side and caressed her face. "You made me want to make it last."

She looked incredulous to the notion. "Hm...I've never heard that before."

"I hope you don't find this too forward of me to say, but..."

She put a finger to my lips. "Please don't. I can imagine how scandalous we'd look if you decided to proclaim to the town of our romantic ties."

Was she a mind reader too?

"Besides," she continued. "I wouldn't want you to risk losing your job over this."

Those words shattered the little world I had created for us just then. I had forgotten all about her being a suspect in the murders. I had been enraptured by her beauty, drawn in by some sort of magic she possessed.

Again, she read my mind. "I'm quite fond of more...distinguished gentlemen." Miss D grinned, tousling my now-damp hair. "It always takes longer for the boys to mature. Personally, I find it very attractive."

Although I felt privileged, the words of that snotty woman came back to haunt me. She had mentioned Miss D's possibility of wanting of an older, eligible bachelor, and Miss D said she preferred distinguished guys.

"I think we both need a shower," she said, sliding off the bed as I admired her full-blown nudity. "Care to join me? There's room enough for two."

I got up, following her. Why pass up an opportunity like that?

A□□□□□ □□□□□ □ □ □□□ □□□□□□□ □□ □□□ □□ □□□□□ loveseat. Before we knew it, we had dozed o□. It wasn't like either of us had anywhere to go, and I was growing fond of being around her.

I tried focusing on the case again. Miss D *couldn't* be a murderer. She was a demure, passionate, misunderstood woman, longing for someone as much as I was. As soon as I cleared her name, I'd ask for her hand in marriage. That would shock the beejesus out of the townsfolk, but right then, I didn't care.

The sun was setting as I woke up. I eased her out of my embrace, laying her down on the loveseat. Getting a good stretch in, I walked around the grounds, taking in the rest of the scenery.

About twenty yards away from her home was a small gray shed. Approaching it, the humming of bees became prevalent. There were several openings that the bees flew in and out of; I deduced it was probably where she kept them. There were so many honeysuckle bushes overgrowing the shed that the scent was sickly sweet---but there was an underlying scent that did not mix well with it. Sort of a meaty, rawhide stink.

When I opened the rookery door and peered inside, I couldn't help but notice a large, long lump in the corner. It felt like a chunk of ice formed in the pit of my stomach as I approached it. It was shaped like a human body, completely unrecognizable. The skeletal carcass was covered head to toe with insects--a skin-suit made of writhing bees. A humongous honeycomb was present in another corner, hanging from ceiling to floor, pregnant with golden yellow liquid dripping into awaiting collection jars—and not too far away was another corpse completely cleaned of flesh and tissue. A few remnants of muscle was left on the skull, two bees crawling in and out of the empty eye sockets, making sure nothing was left behind. I spotted a monocle laying a few feet from it---a possession that I knew belonged to Mr. Stowe.

I slapped a hand over my mouth, too mortified for words. I backed away towards the rookery entrance.

"Honey is nothing but the regurgitations of what bees eat. So while I provide them with plenty of honeysuckle, human flesh helps to add an earthier, heady taste to the sweetness, don't you agree?"

I whipped around, surprised to see Miss D standing in the doorway. I never heard her walk up. She gave me a wicked grin with a hint of sardonic calm. Replaying what she said to me, I felt my stomach lurch.

She had put honey in my tea. Honey that was made by her *flesh-eating bees*. Honey that was made with *Mr. Shrek and Mr. Stowe*.

Watching her little workers finish o Mr. Shrek, my stomach lurched again, emptying itself of the tea I had earlier. It had an acrid taste, but I surmised it was the bile from my stomach combined with that wretched drink.

"You're crazy!" I spat, incredulous to the fact that she *was* a murderer. "Why?"

"Why does anyone do the things they do? I told you my reason. *It makes the honey taste better.*" She took a step towards me, and I tried holding her back at arm's length.

"Stay away from me," I said, but she ignored me, going towards the huge honeycomb. Holding her index finger under a golden colored drop of the liquid, the honey dribbled onto it. She raised it to her lips, her pink tongue extending to slowly lick at her fingertip. She gave me a seductive glance.

My God, this woman made me feel like a quivering pile of jelly, even though she was a homicidal lunatic.

"Mm. They really do make the best honey around, don't they?"

"M-Miss D, I-I'm afraid you're under arrest." My cop-side was trying to emerge, but with alarming di￼culty.

She tilted her head to the side like a curious bird. "Are you sure you want to do that?"

"Killing two men to make your honey doesn't justify your murderous actions."

Giving me a disappointed glance, she sighed, looking at the swarm of bees in the rookery for a moment. Within seconds, they migrated away from the corpse and moved in *my* direction. What trickery was this?

Not trickery at all, but a dark magic of sorts. The same magic she enraptured everyone--including *me*--with.

"After what we shared. So intimate, so close..." she lowered her head and clicked her tongue. "Why did you have to go nosing around here? I was falling so hard for you, Mr. Hart."

I heard what she was saying, but my eyes were fixated on those damned bees. "Call them o￼!" I yelled while staring at them.

"And what would you tell your sergeant?"

My lovesick side wanted to say "nothing," but my cop-side kicked in again, saying what we both didn't want to hear. "The truth," I blurted out.

She folded her arms, her warm, loving disposition icing over into one that was hard, unyielding. She blinked, and in that second, her beautiful eyes disappeared, replaced by solid black orbs. *Black like a bee's.* My jaw dropped. Were my eyes playing tricks on me? What I saw didn't make sense, but--

"You leave me no choice, Detective Hart." She glanced at her swarm, silently commanding them to do her bidding. They began surrounding me in a dotted mass of darkness.

I took o, running from her property, down to the hills and vales beyond, her passionless laughter trailing far behind.

Even so, this wasn't good. Why didn't I take o in the *other* direction, toward the front of her house... *to my car?!* Panicking makes you do stupid things.

What the hell was she? Those horrifying, solid, bug eyes...I'd never forget them.

The bees were still chasing after me, a buzzing, black cloud of death. There was nothing I could do to shake them, nowhere to hide.

I was no track-star, either. Youth had long since left me, and I was losing wind fast.

I was done for. Completely taken by her beauty, I'd be killed by the same--and not even by her actual hand, but by her little brood of winged followers. Her *colony*.

As I lost my footing, twisting my ankle and falling to the ground, I watched as her swarm of bees hovered over me for a moment, as if deciding where to start in on me. Then they descended their painful, fiery-hot stings unbearable as I screamed in agony...

...And all the while, I couldn't help but wonder if Miss D would still love me enough to have me in her next cup of tea.

T E

ALTERNATIVE ™

TABITHA THOMPSON

Prologue: Just One Drop

A ☐ ☐☐☐ ☐☐☐☐☐☐ ☐☐ ☐ ☐☐☐☐ ☐ ☐☐☐☐ ☐ ☐☐☐☐☐ ☐☐ ☐ ☐☐☐☐☐☐ did. She sat in her bathtub, trying to suck in air as if there was a sudden lack of oxygen, but concentrating on the warm water bath or breathing became the last thing on her mind. The only thing on Michelle's mind was soothing her painful cramps. She couldn't remember the last time she had cramps that severe; maybe the very first time she had her period at age 12, but otherwise nothing drastic. Her body was growing, but she wasn't pregnant.

It had been several months since she had gotten her period, but the symptoms were there. Chocolate cravings and mood swings were mild, but the bloating and back pain were the worst. Michelle was starting to resemble a pregnant woman of seven months, leading her family and friends to believe that the pill wasn't working after all and that she was pregnant. But numerous pregnancy tests came back negative. Last week, she had made a visit to her doctor, who assured her that the bloating was just a temporary side e☐ect. Similar for all oral contraceptives, and that it should be gone sooner rather than later. With a weak smile Michelle left, but her mind was still haunted by "what-ifs" and self-doubt.

Shooting pain from her lower back and stomach almost made Michelle scream in agony. This agony was something she had never felt before during her experience in taking birth control. As she ran her hand across her swollen belly, it no longer resembled a stomach to her, but more as if she swallowed a bag of hot rocks and her insides were burning.

Please just one drop, that's all I ask for. Just one drop. She begged and pleaded that something would happen, anything. But now, as her breathing slowed and the room felt less closed in, the pain still lingered. If she didn't know better, she could've sworn that her stomach was forming a life of its own. *It can't be…there's no way, it's just my eyes. Nothing more.*

Since the age of 19, Michelle had been on birth control. She decided to get on it when she became serious with her boyfriend, Richard. After three years, she decided to get o☐ birth control in order to have her body go back to normal. That all changed when Richard got tired of using condoms and stumbled upon a new birth control pill that doctors said prevented pregnancy with an oral dose only once a month.

No more daily pills or being inserted with an IUD. It would have her hormones in a longer cycle, reducing her periods to only three a year, according to medical reports. Though Michelle wasn't the type to go for certain things a second time, she didn't want her children to become a statistic. It was bad enough the numbers were at now 73% for black babies. She wanted to be part of the solution, and not part of the problem. So without much persuasion, Michelle agreed and got a prescription from her doctor.

At first, everything worked normally, and the couple couldn't have been more excited. But after a few months, Michelle became concerned that her period had not started. However, the symptoms other than bleeding would appear. Her doctor assured her that there was nothing to be concerned about, and a little bloating and water weight were perfectly normal side-effects to the medication, So for months, Michelle didn't really worry.

Until now. Once her stomach started bloating to almost twice the normal size, Michelle immediately stopped taking the medication. She figured maybe if she stopped taking it, the side-effects would go away. Unfortunately, they didn't. The pain was swallowing her whole, clearing her mind of anything and everything. She could only focus on the sharp jolts of pain that awakened with her every move.

By this time, the water was cold because she had lain in it for almost two hours. She could feel her skin getting more wrinkled by the minute. Although Richard was at work, Michelle had errands to run. She knew she couldn't spend all day in the bathtub. She tried her best to walk out carefully to avoid any more pain. When it came to birth control, she was aware of the risks, but was not prepared for what happened once she had stepped out.

Suddenly, trickles of crimson kisses flowed between Michelle's thighs. *Oh thank goodness, I finally have my period.* Except that when she touched the fluid that was flowing and then looked at her fingertips, it wasn't red, or even brown, but black. Waves of cramps and contractions roared through Michelle's lower abdomen, causing her to scream out in pain, as it vomited out whatever discharge that was held in

Michelle's belly. She quickly sat back down in the tub, knowing any other movement would be almost impossible. If she didn't know better, she would've thought she was going into labor. More cramps, and dark fluid shortly followed. Michelle fought back tears as she continued to bellow out in pain, but her cries just turned into echoes throughout the empty apartment.

It has to be a backup of fluids, but why does it hurt so much? The pain confined her whole body, so she couldn't even reach for her phone to call Richard for help. She had to deal with this on her own. As she saw the bath water turn from clear to black, her eyes grew heavy. She was losing too much blood, and was afraid of dying in her bathtub. But there was little she could do.

Another sharp jolt of pain forced Michelle to open her eyes. She used a few fingers to reach down, and feel what was in her body. Before she reached her womb, something touched her fingers. She immediately pulled her hand out of the water.

Was that tentacles or was that a head? Was that something even human? Something was in the tub with her squirming. Something sinister..

Oh my God, do I have some kind of parasite? She looked closer into the water and tried to catch whatever was in the tub and throw it away. After several attempts, she managed to grab what felt like its neck, and lifted it out of the water.

She couldn't believe what was staring at her, dripping wet from water and dark fluid. Her eyes widened, and her scream became piercing, a sound that was completely unrecognizable to her, and caused whatever the thing that she holding to cry.

Immediately, Michelle threw up in the tub in pure disgust and horror. Before she passed out, she heard the unknown parasite utter a word. "Mama."

Experimentation

"Babe, I already told you that I'm not going on birth control." Those two words had started to really bother Victoria, Kyle had been spewing that same line at her for years now. She was growing tired of him asking, as if he had no care for what she wanted to do with her body.

"Why can't we just stick with condoms? We have so far, for the past four years." Victoria replied, trying to bury herself in her schoolwork and ditch the conversation.

Kyle sighed in frustration. "I know. But you know I hate condoms, they're too restricting."

"I understand that, but even in our late twenties, neither of us can afford a child right now. School and saving for a house comes first in my book before anything." She knew he was bothered by her constant refusal, but he had known her long enough to know that she couldn't handle and did not want to have hormones added into her body.

Kyle and Victoria had first laid eyes on each other back in 2006 at J. Andrews High School. They had met through a mutual friend, Although they had some differences, they also had similarities. Kyle was the 6-foot 2 football player who was considered among his friends as "the blackest white guy" they knew. Whereas Victoria was "the whitest black girl" among her friends.

One thing Victoria admired about Kyle was he didn't care what her friends thought about her. He was totally different than the other white guys she'd previously dated. They either had massive egos and were only attractive on the outside or were burnouts with no ambition. To Victoria, Kyle was the perfect balance for her. He gave her the confidence she secretly needed. They both loved scary movies, video games, and traveling. He was a very smart guy who Victoria saw a lot of potential in, even during his thuggish phase.

All the other relationships either of them had prior to each other were just puppy love. Nothing serious, but even though they were both still teenagers, 16 and 17 respectively, it was real. Kyle immediately knew there was something different that he loved about Victoria. She only stood at 5-foot 4 and loved all things punk rock and goth. He loved that she was passionate, kind, easy to talk to, intelligent and well-spoken, and as a bonus, very attractive. Eleven years later, touching her warm chocolate skin as she gazed into his beautiful, mesmerizing blue eyes still set them on fire, as if the passion between them would never die.

"You're right about the kid situation, because I know you want to get married first. However, I did see an ad on TV the other day showing this new contraceptive that apparently you only have to take once a month, no injections, no implants, no daily pills, and it only gives you your period three times a year," Kyle said, walking into the kitchen to grab a cup of coffee.

Victoria's ears perked up with interest as she sat her laptop on the couch. "What do you mean only once a month? That sounds way too good to be true."

"It does, but it's actually real. I did the research online, and so far there have been no real complaints about hormones. Just a little bloating, which they say is a temporary side-effect," Kyle responded eagerly, almost too eagerly for Victoria.

"Great, but you've only done research online. That's not always a reliable source. I can go online and type in reasons for swollen neck glands, and it'll come back to me and say cancer when it's just a simple sore throat."

"I know you're skeptical. I talked to my sister Liz about it, because she was also considering it. According to her doctor, he has had no complaints from his clients. Believe she's going in next week to get herself a prescription," Kyle replied, slowly sipping on the co□ee, in slight hopes that Victoria would agree.

"Yes, I am skeptical. I like to have a more holistic approach to how my body is taken care of." Victoria drew a huge sigh, knowing that her curiosity was getting the better of her. "However, you do make a good point. There's nothing wrong with doing a little research and checking things out. I'll make an appointment to the doctor for tomorrow morning, and I'll let you know what happens."

"Thanks, babe. I'm glad you're giving this a chance. Not just for me. I don't want you to think that way at all. But for you as well, so we can both focus on our careers and still have amazing sex without any worries. I love you." Kyle walked over to Victoria and kissed her so gently, so lovingly, so passionately.

The next morning, against her reluctance, Victoria went to see her doctor. "Okay, Ms. Carter, based on our most recent checkup, everything is normal. We don't have to worry about that, so what can I do for you today?"

"Well, Doctor Harris, my boyfriend had seen the new birth control that has been advertising on TV and online called *Alternative*™. I wanted to get more information on it," Victoria replied. "Well, from what I've personally gathered, it is like most of the birth control contraceptives that prevent pregnancy. But unlike ones such as *Seasonique*™, this one delays your hormones a bit longer so instead of twelve periods a year with *Seasonique*™, with *Alternative*™ you get only three."

Doctor Harris replied, "You take it only once a month, right and that's it?"

"That's it, and you can also take it today instead the Sunday after your last period if you want to. Just make sure it's with a meal."

He said with a slight smile, "Now what about the side-effects?" By this time, Doctor Harris's smile faded, making Victoria a little nervous.

"Well the side-effects include bloating, water weight, irritability, mood swings, slight cramping, and possible constipation. But like I tell my other patients, the side-effects are only temporary, and after three weeks, you should get your period. Now if it's been more than six months and you haven't gotten your menstrual cycle, discontinue the contraceptive and come back to me, okay?"

"Okay." Victoria replied softly.

"Good. Now here's your prescription for *Alternative*™ and enjoy the rest of your day." Doctor Harris smiled, handing Victoria a sheet of paper that unbeknownst to her would change her life.

It was the longest ten minutes of her life as she stood waiting at her local drug store to pick up the prescription. Only forty dollars, and it's much cheaper than a dealing with a child for the moment, Victoria thought.

"Here you go, have a nice day."

"Thanks," Victoria replied as she quickly grabbed the prescription and headed back to her apartment to get ready for school. Once home, she sat on the couch for almost two hours until Kyle arrived, staring at the package of pills, wondering if she was making the right choice for her body.

"Hey babe. How was your day?" Kyle asked, "How was school and the doctor's?"

"Both were fine. I got the pills before I went to class today, I didn't take any yet, though," Victoria responded softly.

"That's fine. Let's look at this together once I'm out of the shower. Work was okay, can't complain really," Kyle said.

"Ok, I'll make us some dinner. Chicken parm?" Victoria asked.

"Sounds perfect." Kyle smiled, causing Victoria to blush. He always had that charm about him that Victoria secretly loved.

9pm. After dinner, Victoria was still staring at the package of pills.

"Babe, you can take them today according to the doctor. So why aren't you taking them yet?" Kyle said, breaking Victoria out of her trance.

"I'm sorry, but I'm still a little bit nervous. What if there are side-effects that are unheard of? What if I can't get my body back to normal after this?"

"Well, you can always stop taking them if you feel that your body's not responding to them properly. And we'll go straight to the hospital if anything were to go extremely wrong. I promise," Kyle replied.

"Ok. You're lucky I love you, otherwise this would never be happening," Victoria laughed, taking her first dose.

"I know. Now come here, I'm actually going to wear a condom tonight to celebrate it being our last."

Three months later, the birth control continued to work well for Victoria with no harsh side-effects, and her period came regularly.

However, after six months, something didn't feel right in Victoria's lower abdomen.

"Are you okay, babe?" Kyle asked.

"I'm okay I guess. It could be just cramps and the bloating like the doctor said, nothing to worry about." Victoria said. Yet, once it became seven months, Victoria hadn't seen her period in almost four months, and her body was starting to bloat a lot more.

"Kyle, I feel like something's wrong. I haven't gotten my period in almost four months, and this bloating with these cramps are starting to become a bit bothersome." Victoria started to rub her swollen belly.

"Four months? That's strange, but I say give it another month or so. Remember, it's just a temporary side-effect." Kyle touched her belly, quickly moving his hand once he felt something poke him back. "What the hell was that?"

"What was what?" Victoria asked.

"Nothing. Thought I felt something could've been shock. Just take it easy, babe. I have to go to work; have a good day at work." Kyle gave her a kiss and walked out the door.

In recent months, Victoria had grown more reclusive and become afraid to leave her house because of the gawking stares she would receive. Often someone asked if she was pregnant, which she constantly denied. At doctor checkups, nothing suggested that Victoria was pregnant. Everything was relatively normal except for the temporary side effects.

One night, as Victoria was drinking chamomile tea, something was poking her in the stomach. Thinking it was just a minor cramp, she ran her hand across her belly and felt something abnormal, something was moving in her stomach.

"What the hell is that?" Victoria continued to poke her stomach to figure out what was it that she had just felt, but there was nothing. Heavy cramps and contractions soon followed, causing Victoria to bellow out in pain.

"Vick, is everything alright?" Kyle shouted, running to her bedside.

"No! These cramps are really painful. They just came out of nowhere, and now it's getting into my lower back. Can you get me a hot compress?" Victoria asked, wincing in pain.

"Of course. I'll be right back." The warm compress seemed to help her cramps subside, and Victoria managed to get a decent amount of sleep. But by the next morning, her body suddenly changed.

Her belly had grown almost twice as large. She resembled a woman who was six months pregnant, and was barely able to bend or see her feet. "What the fuck is going on? I thought the compress worked. Why is this happening?"

"Oh my God..." Kyle stared in shock, horrified at what had become of his girlfriend's body. "Vick, are you still using the birth control pills?"

"No. I stopped using them almost a month ago because of the bloating. That's why I didn't want to have sex; I'm so sorry." Tears began to flood Victoria's eyes.

"It's okay, don't apologize for that. I completely understand. Right now, all we need to care about is your health. We should make a trip to see Doctor Harris again," Kyle said.

"I've seen him already, last week, and all he would say is the same thing that he's said before. The side-eꞏects are only temporary and everything should get back to normal soon," Victoria said as she sat back on the bed, already winded and tired.

"Well I think we need a second opinion because this isn't looking right. Not at all. It's really freaking me out."

They headed over to Kyle's doctor to see if they could get a second opinion on Victoria's condition. Unfortunately, the response was the same. Everything is temporary. She was prescribed to take a couple of days o☐ of work and school if possible, and keep her body rested with a warm bath instead of a compress. Victoria had no choice but to agree. Her fingertips ran across a stomach that felt like droplets of lava were swirling into her stomach. Although there she had no problem eating or drinking, each time she did it almost felt like there was something in there, feeding o☐ of her.

Once home, Kyle tried his best to make Victoria comfortable, starting with the hot bath. She called her school and work to tell them she wasn't feeling too well.

"Thank you, Kyle. You're amazing," Victoria said as she placed herself in the soothing warm water, planting a kiss on Kyle's soft lips.

"Anything for you, babe. I'm going to grab a sandwich for us, and I'll be right back. Call me if you need anything else."

"Ok, I will."

To Victoria's surprise, the warm bath was working. No cramps, no painful contractions, no back pain, and it even looked like the swelling was starting to go down. Breathing in the scent of lavender, Victoria forced herself to clear her mind and just focus on her breathing, like she used to do in yoga. "That's it, Vicky, just relax. Your period will come really soon, and you won't have to deal with this anymore. Just stay positive."

Kyle walked in with the sandwiches, breaking Victoria's meditation. "Did I come at a bad time?"

"No love, I was just practicing my breathing and reminding myself to stay positive about my body returning to normal," Victoria responded with a smile "Also I have to admit, the warm bath is actually working. Since I've been in here I've felt no pain."

"That's great Vick. I made you a sandwich and tea for your stomach."

Five bites in, and Victoria's stomach started to quickly churn in disgust. "Oh no. I don't feel so good." Shortly after, Victoria vomited onto the bathroom floor, missing Kyle by mere inches.

"Holy shit! It's okay, babe, I'll clean it up." Kyle quickly grabbed a spare towel to clean up the mess.

Victoria was writhing in pain. "I'm so sorry, hun...my stomach...it hurts so bad. These cramps are so...brutal."

"Don't worry about me, babe, just worry about your breathing." Suddenly, the hot droplets in her stomach we re starting to feel more like stones that were swirling around, causing extreme heat and discomfort. She tried to get herself out of the tub and lie on her bed, but her body wouldn't allow her to; it was if she was paralyzed. After what seemed like forever, Kyle finally returned after several minutes of cleaning.

"Can you move at all?"

"No, I can't. My body can not move; I literally feel para-lyzed, and my body feels so heavy," Victoria replied in tears.

"Don't cry, love. I'll call the doctor, don't worry." Kyle's blue eyes softened, feeling so bad about what Victoria was going through. "I'm so sorry Vick. This is all my fault; I should've never pressured you into getting this birth control knowing that it's something that you're completely against."

"I accept your apology, love. It's okay; I forgive you." Victoria could barely form a smile through the unbearable pain, but Kyle understood.

Before Kyle could leave the room, Victoria screamed, "Kyle!" She felt a gush of fluid flow through her legs and quickly became relieved. "I felt something drop between my legs; I think it's my period. Thank God."

"I agree." Kyle replied. It wasn't long before immense pain, cramps, and screams soon followed. "It's just the side-effects. Focus on your breathing; I'm with you every step of the way." As Kyle stared at Victoria's belly, his eyes started to widen in fear as he noticed something sinister. He thought it was his eyes playing tricks, but he could've sworn that something was moving in her stomach.

The bath water quickly turned from clear to almost black, and as Victoria reached between her legs to observe the color, she became speechless.

"Kyle...something is inside of me. It doesn't feel right." With every push Victoria made, the mysterious creature was beginning to leave her body, as if she were having a water birth. As Kyle reached down in the water to pull the plug, something gelatinous ran across his hand, and he screamed. "What the hell is that?"

"I don't know..." Victoria could barely muster a whisper as she felt her body weaken due to a lack of blood and intense pain. Gathering up the courage, Kyle reached down into the tub and pulled the plug, releasing all fluids and whatever else was lurking in the murky water. The creature that remained in the tub almost resembled an abnormal tapeworm with human features such as a face and eyes and greyish skin. It gave Kyle and Victoria a creepy, sinister stare. Kyle quickly dropped the creature and vomited in the toilet in pure disgust as Victoria lay in the tub limp and barely coherent. Then it made a sound; it cried. But then another sound came quickly after that stunned both Kyle and Victoria: a voice. "Mama."

Unknown

D□□□□□ □ □□□ □□□ □□ □□ □□□□□□□ □□□ □□□□□□□□□□ To this day, no one could figure out the reason the results of *Alternative*™ were so gruesome. After doing a study on the thirty women who'd taken the drug, they found twenty-eight of them bled to death due to hemorrhaging. Whatever was in those pills they have discovered was a parasite, treating the women's bodies like a host and developing a life of its own.

The first two patients who died, Michelle Barker and Victoria Carter respectively, were both healthy Black American women who wanted an alternative to birth control. Sadly, they weren't the only victims to fall prey to the mysterious parasite, which lurked in their bodies for up to seven months. Scientists are still trying to figure out what went wrong as more young women are at their doctors', filling out a prescription to receive an alternative.

T□□ E□□

BLOOD MAGNOLIA

NICOLE GIVENS KURTZ

M☐☐☐☐☐☐ B☐☐☐☐☐☐ ☐☐☐☐☐ ☐☐☐ ☐☐☐ ☐☐☐☐☐☐ blossoms bloomed in the spring. They fluttered like snowflakes, but bigger, more vibrant, softer. Wind kisses. She strolled along the illuminated path that cut through Arbor High School's spacious grounds. Her thoughts had finally settled into a cloud of calm, perfect musings. Tranquil. Life should always be so sincere. The tiny wiggle of worry had been held at bay by the lush, warm sunlight, and the scent of Japan, falling at the gentle pu☐ of the wind's breath.

Beside her, Cree Carnie practiced levitation. Arbor encouraged all its students to embrace their magic. Cree's brunette hair lay flat despite the breezes' attempts to muss it up. As if. Cree's ironclad focus earned her a perfect score. Meditation strengthened her—in every way.

Pure magic lit the area around her. The way light attached to her gave Magnolia goosebumps. The good kind of chills. Every time she looked at Cree, her stomach flip-flopped. No potion or spell could dissolve it.

Believe that.

Magnolia's thick afro caught petals in an eager, haphazard manner. When she brushed a hand across them, soft petals rained down across her shoulders and torso. Drowning in their scent, she allowed joy to spill out of her in raw laughter.

Cree peeked open a pretty brown eye and shushed her.

"My fault, baby." Magnolia blew her a kiss.

She smiled. That quiet grin spoke volumes. Love. Friendship. Commitment.

They came to a series of benches along the path. Magnolia sat with her legs crossed at the ankles. She nibbled on slices of mango. Fresh, sweet, and succulent, they swished around her bowl until she fished a slice out with her fingers.

The wind switched direction; whether by chance or by choice, she didn't know.

Across the courtyard, other students played futbol, clumped together in packs, or disappeared into their portable electronic devices, bubbled spheres encasing them in complete isolation from their peers. Saturation of stimuli started. Learning to control the Earth's power and their connection to it kept them all busy.

Magnolia smirked but tried to stay quiet so as to not a ect Cree's concentration. Unlike the other students, Magnolia didn't get trapped seeking that ever-elusive faster fix. No one wanted to fool with practicing. Downloads must be better, quicker, and more vibrant. Any breaks or lulls could let in the real world. Or time to train or cast. They sought out artificial emotions conjured by technology, not the planet.

Magnolia shook her head. They had no connections to true emotion. Real air. Authentic interaction.

"Maggie." The nickname indicated friend or family, but the tone implied fear. Few called her by that name, for it had been given to her by her grandmother. None of her classmates would dare truncate her name.

Not ever. Not even Cree.

Not if they valued their devices.

Or their body parts.

"Maggie. I know you hear me."

"But I wish I didn't." She put her fruit down. "Lunch has only ten more minutes."

The last taste of fruit vanished under the rise of concern. Shivers raced along her spine. His shadow fell over her and blocked her sunny bit and its warmth. If only the day could keep being bright and brimming with happiness. But it wouldn't now.

Cree's eyes opened. With a gasp, she crashed to the ground.

Claude.

He had no last name.

This could not be good at all. Claude rarely left their home for this one. He complained about the food, the air, and the noise on this side of the Divide.

Magnolia'd done all she could to blend. She and Cree had enough issues. The Transformation course was killing their overall G.P.A.s. One visit from Claude, and now she stood out like an outdated computer.

"Warmth becomes you, Cree."

"Thank you." Cree uncrossed her ankles.

Magnolia stood and turned her dark brown eyes to his.

Tall, thick, and brooding, Claude wore the dark gown of her clan. It brushed the tops of his boots. Long sleeves hugged his arms. His customary smile had gone, and his lips downturned in a scowl. He bowed. A thin sheen of sweat glistened on his smooth, cinnamon-brushed skin. Round, marble dark eyes gazed down a sloping nose. His high cheekbones and wide forehead crinkled in his distress.

"Forgive me for bothering you at University." His lack of inflection indicated he felt nothing at all about the action, let alone sorry.

"Sorry?" Magnolia set the bowl down beside her. The wiggle of worry danced inside her belly once more.

Cree came closer and took her hand in hers.

She stilled.

"For what?" Magnolia asked.

It came out as a whisper. Nothing good ever came after *I'm sorry*. In the same way nothing good ever came from a trip down to the corner store. Only booze, cigarettes, and sugar. Heartache, guilt, and shame.

Those feelings rose after impulse actions, and the indulgence in purchasing all those overpriced items because you were too lazy to drive to the grocer. Nothing good ever came of lazy. She could hear her momma's voice declaring those words.

Claude ran a quick hand over his shoulder length dreadlocks, sighed, and grimaced. The thick hair held power. Cords of magic. Ropes of righteousness.

All of them had been crafted from stars, and their power resonated in their blood.

"Answer me, Claude. Sorry for what? Why are you here?" Her heart increased its pace as if in anticipation of the response.

Cree squeezed. Released.

"Your mother died. This morning."

Her momma had died.

The words sounded strange coming from his lips.

Magnolia's wiggling worry won free, graduating to full blown denial.

"No!" Her legs would not move. She demanded they lift her from her seated position, from despair, but they didn't heed her commands. Numb.

Cree gasped. "Magnolia. Oh my goddess."

Magnolia yanked her hand away and pulled her legs up to her chest. None of it made any sense. She had to get out of here. Away from the words.

"It's impossible."

"The magi have found no evil intent. Her death was a natural exit from the realm."

"Natural? Nothing natural could kill my momma."

"Life is a great illusion."

Claude reached for her hand. His face grim, he patted her knee. His people had done this for centuries. Before leaving for Arbor High, Magnolia's constant companion had been Claude. Despite his immense dislike for this side of the Divide, he would have faithfully followed her had she but asked.

"Come! I'll escort you to your room to get your things."

"Let's go." Cree tugged on her tee-shirt. "I'm so sorry."

The softness of her hands as they hugged at her felt surreal.

"Maggie."

"No!"

The initial shock still hummed inside her, but she growled as Claude extended his hand to her. With renewed strength, Magnolia again tried to stand, this time using her arms to propel her body upward from the bench. She managed it, but the clear wobbling of her ankles and knocking knees warned that they weren't fully vested in the endeavor.

Cree grabbed her hand, and she steadied. With her other, she picked up the empty bowl. Magnolia slung her backpack over her shoulder, opposite the hand holding Cree's.

Maggie blew out a long sigh.

"Thanks."

Pushing past his still outstretched hand, Magnolia and Cree started down the campus's primary path toward the sophomore dorms, Claude falling in behind them. For now, the wind had stopped, and the cherry blossoms refused to fall. They clutched tightly to the trees, to *life*.

Life stolen from her momma.

Once they broke away, they could never return home again.

"I dunno what to say." Cree wiped tears from her cheeks. "Death sucks."

"It doesn't follow. Nothing in this world could kill her."

"Everything transforms back to the Great Mother…"

Magnolia clenched her teeth. Nothing else mattered. She couldn't tell her girlfriend that her momma *was* the Great Goddess. There had never been time to talk about the things Magnolia could not say aloud. Blood sworn to hide. Things that could only be told in low voices.

Or that three of her four classes bored her to puddles of tears.

"…The instructors aren't there to entertain us. My mother told me that the first year. So don't worry about course work," Cree finished with a sad smile.

"Thanks." Magnolia had missed much of what Cree had just said.

"She will return to school." Claude didn't smile or try to sugarcoat stu□. His honesty blunted the sharpest retorts.

"Right." Magnolia snapped.

After a few tense moments, Claude's voice rumbled from behind her. "You seem well."

"Looks are deceiving." Magnolia hadn't meant for it to sound angry, but it did anyway.

In fact, she'd been super until he arrived.

"He's just trying to help. You want more mangos?"

For half a breath, Magnolia waited to hear her momma's sharp rebuke, followed by the warm salve of wise advice. Always an attempt to guide and control.

How could she be gone?

"No, thanks."

"Stay in my arms, if you dare," Cree sang, linking her fingers through Magnolia's.

"I can't."

Cree looked back at Claude. "She has to go now?"

Claude nodded. His profile silhouetted against the sunlight cast certain parts in shadow.

"Yeah. She gonna be all alone tonight in somebody's bed," Cree teased.

"Magnolia sleeps alone, now. Tonight will be no di□erent," Claude retorted.

Cree winked. "Oh, absolutely."

Despite her heavy heart, Magnolia smiled. School wouldn't have been the same without Cree. Too late for her momma to meet her now.

Too damn late.

They fell into a hushed, uncomfortable silence. The paved trail snaked around the school, and the soft bends drifted over rolling hills until it forked. Left returned her to the school's primary building and dorms. Right, to the portals. The portals launched them to other places. Often, she and Cree would ditch conjuring class to skip out to the beach, where the salt would saturate the air and sting their auras.

Magnolia stopped.

To the left, her life in the urban city with its tall skyscrapers, concrete and neon seductions. Its techno treats and addicting isolation. Its tasty lure of fast food and seclusion. To the right, her old life with its natural allure of forest, oceans, and unspoiled fields awaited. There the city finger of responsibility beckoned.

"Your things first. Then home." Claude stopped beside her and gazed at the glowing golden circle of the portal. Sunlight poured out of its opening.

"Home."

That sounded nice. *Home*. The woods that marched toward the beaches. Oceans with their scores of waves that had given a soundtrack to her youth. The forest that bled into other realms. Doors which opened to other places, like this one. She hailed from that other place. It thrived with life.

"You miss it?" Cree draped an arm around her shoulders.

Yes.

The rousing glow of the fire pits. It all sang of love, unity, and family. Her momma's melody-rich humming and her daddy's clove pipe-smoke mixed in a tonic of love around the big pit. Starry skies lined the heavens. These memories fueled her passions and repealed her grief. The anguish and the warmth squeezed her heart.

Temporarily.

"The grief..." Claude started with his dark eyes flashing in the sunlight.

"...and glee." Magnolia added. The bitterness made her voice hard. "How many of Dad's other wives waited with baited breath for this day? Now both parents are all gone."

Claude didn't answer, but then he didn't need to speak about the backstabbing, betrayals, and jealousy that saturated the wives' rooms at the palace. None of this would do. The familiar rush of discontent that had originally sent Magnolia to this other realm resurfaced.

Good. The cold anger drove back the wash of grief.

"Do not judge without first seeing."

She cut a quick glance at Claude. "Don't advise me about my family."

"This is hard on everyone."

"Screw it. Blood will have blood." Magnolia spat. Cree gasped at her, but what did any of them know of it? After her daddy's death, all she had was her momma and Claude.

The momma of all, Queen Oya had given birth to People, but in her human form, she only had Magnolia.

As the sole heir of Queen Oya, Magnolia would answer.

And they would be sorry.

She adjusted her backpack, and started toward the path leading to the dorms.

———

T☐☐ ☐☐☐☐ ☐☐☐☐☐ ☐☐☐☐ ☐☐☐☐ ☐☐☐☐☐☐☐ ☐☐☐☐ ☐☐☐ clearing's bright green grass where Queen Oya rested. A formal pyre had been erected. Across from Magnolia and Claude, in the circle, her momma lay on a bed of orchids and the ashes of their ancestors mixed with cherry blossoms. Torches flickered in impatience, mimicking Magnolia's own emotions. The queen's regal hair shot out in a gray halo of curls. Full-bodied and powerful even in death, her momma presented an imposing force.

Empty. Carved out and hollow, Magnolia's blood ran cold.

The village had arrived to witness the queen's return to the Earth. Torches flickered as the roseate flush of twilight deepened to dark. Several of her momma's priestesses dropped lavender in a circle surrounding the pyre.

Priestess Onkya stood and cleared her throat.

"I've known rivers. I've known rivers ancient as the world and older than the flow of human blood in human veins. My soul has grown deep like the rivers..."

A tiny wedge of grief relaxed in Magnolia's chest. Her momma loved Langston Hughes and "A Negro Speaks of Rivers" had always meant a lot to her. The connection to the magic of her people and the Earth resonated with through her.

Already the woody scent of crackling pine needles rose from the flames. The torches burned, belching the queen's smoky essence into the gaping mouth of the night. All around her, cheek to jowl, the people wept. Anguish. Wails. All bled into minutes and hours of mourning.

The agony wore on her. Everyone acted so normal. Like they didn't care at all. Oh sure, they cried. Pretend. All fakers.

As the last flicker of flame escaped, Magnolia stood at the pile of smoldering ash. Behind her, at her momma's home, dancing commenced in celebration of Queen Oya's life.

"Queen Oya—the mother of us all." She blew a kiss.

Claude stood like a sentinel beside her. "Throughout most of my life, the urge to risk all I held dear resided in the winds of disobedience. My head is hard. The queen softened not only it, but my heart."

"Lot of good that did you, huh?"

"The grief blackens your aura. Darkness drips from you, Maggie. The cold evening of loss owns you."

"If you stay, the night will give you up." Claude spoke in low tones.

"The night does not own me." As soon as the words left her lips, she cringed.

"No?" Claude's eyebrow quirked.

"No."

"Whatever."

She didn't expect him to understand. Flag and faith had shaped Claude's beliefs and loyalty. He couldn't understand the crushing anguish that threatened to rend her. She'd appease her bloodlust. But damn if she wasn't tempted to tear through those who failed her momma. Her power itched to be used.

With a steel resolve, she ignored the clamoring inside her which screamed for her to toss herself on the still-hot fire. Unless the seal broke, her *other* wouldn't be free to sate her thirst for revenge. From within, a cackle echoed. Fury and frustration made her blood thick.

"You mustn't leave your naked soul exposed to the sharp, brutal weapons of blind, pointless rage."

Claude folded his arms across his chest.

Oh boy. More sagely advice from Claude. Yippee.

"Blood protects me. Her blood. The blood of my momma."

"Yes."

Claude grunted his disapproval. "That is not the inner life you had. The blood will consume you. You're not done with school or your trainings."

"Don't matter. Blood cleanses and absolves."

"Maggie..."

"Don't worry about it. Before the frost, all will be well."

Magnolia snatched away from him, her fury aflame. Not even the icy fingers of grief could extinguish it. Around her the faces of elders and advisers, servants and priestesses all looked on. How many of them wore masks? None truly ached as she did.

"Ah, you've changed, young Maggie," Cronin remarked, gliding out of the pool of people. He gave her a grin. He must've thought it would comfort her.

It didn't.

One of her momma's three advisors, Cronin had so much arrogance that he was vulnerable in ways he couldn't see. Good. Pride blinded.

"How long have you been eavesdropping?" Magnolia cut through all flu□.

Right to the bone. No bullshit.

He scowled. "Your tongue has changed, too."

"While my momma died, you and Quist feasted. Right? The fun lasted well into the night. In fact, it spilled out to this morn. Or so I heard. The village has mouths but few ears."

"So the old saying goes," Claude interjected.

Stoic and thin, Cronin crossed his arms. Narrow eyes peered down a nose that flared with indignation. A quick glance at Claude and he relaxed. A greasy grin smeared across his face.

"There are few secrets here. The truth runs free." Cronin adjusted his ceremonial robe and cast a side glance at Quist. "We adored her."

Quist, her momma's second magi, saluted her with palms touching. Like always, he jumped into the conversation. Magnolia couldn't figure out if Quist had been confused, because he always wore that expression. She recoiled from the harsh burnt odor that clung to him. Purifying incense.

"Whatever has struck you so aflame?" Quist inquired.

"The death of the queen should inflame everyone," Magnolia snapped.

"Did you not see the village come to watch her ascend?" Quist sipped a liquid from glass. Stony-gazed Quist was mean.

That was then.

"Who killed my momma?"

Claude sti☐ened. "Maggie."

She could feel their eyes as they crawled over her—a thousand ants. Murmurs pushed by her ears, annoyed. It mattered very little.

"No one," Quist retorted.

"We explained to Claude. Queen Oya died of ordinary old age."

Magnolia laughed. "Old age doesn't a☐ect the ageless. One of you killed her."

"Your loss a☐ects your mind." Cronin shook his head.

"And your aura," Quist added.

"The murder of my momma will not be atoned by the shedding of blood!" Magnolia roared. Damn her aura.

"Calm down!" Quist thundered in turn.

People stopped talking, and the singing faltered. He searched the faces of others around him before looking back at Magnolia. "Grief! Her grief befuddles the child!"

I'm no child!

Pinpricks burned in her eyes. White-hot, blood boiling, her vision became scarlet.

Quist flinched, screamed, and wind-milled backwards, away from her. The seal inside her cracked, causing a stitch of misery to rip through her chest.

Oh no!

She clutched at the pain, but it didn't fade. Her blood raced. Faster. And it hurt.

"Breathe, Maggie!"

Through slit eyes, she peered at Quist.

Crimson streams trickled out of his ears, his mouth, and his agonizing screams tore through the tension and talk. Music ceased. Quist clawed at his throat.

"Maggie! No one harmed your momma."

"Yes!" Magnolia roared. They would all pay for this loss.

"No, Maggie!"

Claude enveloped her in his cloak. The hint of musk and magic tickled her nose. Instincts and anger made her want to flee. When she fought to free herself, he held her more tightly.

"Don't let it flow. Stop the blood. You're *killing* him."

She growled. Let him die! Her momma died. Fair.

Then Claude's words of guidance penetrated her anger. "Blood is life, not death."

Her blood began to slow from its accelerated speed. Calmed by Claude's soft words. Her pounding heart, pressed close to his, obeyed her mentor's and slowed as well.

"Practice your meditation! Think of your training!" He turned her away from Quist's collapsed body on the floor.

At last his shrieks stopped.

Magnolia pushed Claude away and turned to Cronin. Her throat was on fire, but she managed to croak out. "The world must be ruled by blood."

The suspicion loomed in his face. Magnolia could see it in his eyes.

Unable—or unwilling—to answer, he fled.

———

"Long ago, before time, our ancestor spoke of the stars. When those glowing bodies died, their last gasps birthed the goddess. From those came magic and of course, the elements. Iron being one of them. Iron is abundant in blood."

"So? Why the science lesson?"

Claude sighed. "Because you must learn to control your blood powers. You almost killed Quist."

"Bleed, bleed, poor village." Magnolia shrugged and gazed outside to the fields. "Besides, I did control it."

"Barely."

A group of people worked to plant a tree, a living monument to her momma's life. They did so in hushed silence, so serious was the work. Either that, or they feared Magnolia would go nuts again. Probably the latter. They kept looking back at her over their shoulders, but none of them would say anything.

She rolled her eyes. Not that she didn't feel bad. She did. Sort of.

"Pay attention! Now, the core of it is, our blood sickles."

"Sickles?"

Claude nodded and created an image in the fire's smoke with the wave of his hand. A circle but bent.

"Yes. It is our gift—and our curse if we don't learn how to control it. The sickles in our blood can change, inside the arteries, so you can manipulate them for our benefit—or detriment. Yesterday, you forced all of Quist's blood cells to bend and block his arteries. You know what happens when you dam up a river?"

"It keeps the river from flowing."

Claude smiled. "And what happens when blood doesn't flow?"

She glared at him.

"Answer me." His face grew determined, as he crossed his arms.

She rolled her eyes again. "People die. Duh."

"It's serious."

"Yeah. Yeah, but Quist got what he had comin'." Maggie didn't want to talk about the mage anymore.

A sickening feeling made her feel nauseous. She sat down and rubbed her bare feet across the grass. When she closed her eyes, flashes of Quist's scarlet-stained face made her shudder. And the screaming. That had kept her awake all last night.

"No, he didn't. The queen died of natural causes. We've all told you." Claude looked down at her. "You must believe it."

Unable to hold his gaze, she looked away. Someone had robbed her of a momma. They had it comin'.

"Some people are afraid of blood's power. You see, it signifies war, death, and injury. It's also a sign of life, such as births, or a successful hunt. What you did yesterday was try to extinguish that life. All life is precious, even those not quite like ours."

She closed her eyes and inhaled the scent of burnt pine needles. On days like today, her momma would sing as Magnolia laid her head on her lap, listening to the words and the lyrical cadence in her voice.

"Now, get up," Claude commanded. "Stand up. Stand firm. Feet flat. Let the balls of your feet anchor your magic. Breathe deeply. Exhale, and focus!"

The burn of her blood rushing at a frenzied pace through her seemed to sear her insides. She focused on the center point of the target Claude had erected about 20 feet in front of her.

"This is stupid." She ran her hands across her hair in frustration.

"No. It isn't."

"I know what would cheer you up." Claude stood. He raised his open palm toward the field. With a fast spell and a hand movement, a portal burst into being and elongated in front of them.

"Well, not what, but who," Claude added with a smile.

Out stepped Cree. The breeze ru□ed her hair, and she wore her school uniform. An ivory polo shirt and dark navy pleated skirt, complete with matching knee-high navy socks, told Magnolia that Cree had been summoned directly from school.

"What's up?" With a wide, toothy grin she leapt into Magnolia's arms, hugging her close and giggling. "I missed you."

Magnolia chuckled. "It's been one day."

She smelled like cherry blossoms.

When she released her, Cree held out a plastic container. "I brought you some mango slices."

"Thanks, baby." She leaned in and kissed Cree's lips. They tasted like cherry balm.

Yummy. Cherry and mangos.

Magnolia turned to Claude. "Thank you.

He nodded, turned on his sandaled heels, and marched across the field.

"It feels like it's been weeks since I saw you." Cree crossed her legs and sat in the air, using her levitation powers. She bowed her head. "I'm really sorry about your mum."

"You been using the language charm again?" Magnolia sat down on the grass beneath her. Cree's accent when she said the word 'mum' sounded perfectly British. The last time Cree had sounded like she'd stepped out of a *Harry Potter* movie, she'd been playing around with a language charm. One she got from Alexander. A poor student, but one who had a crush on Cree.

Cree blushed. "Uh, yeah."

Magnolia froze. Her palms itched as her blood pressure rose. "Did Alexander give you that charm?"

Cree dropped her head. "Yeah. But Magnolia..."

"I thought you said you weren't gonna talk to him again."

"You left, and I needed a study partner for the Charms--"

"My momma died!"

"Magnolia!" Cree crashed to the ground with an *oomph*.

Fury. Betrayal. "You promised!"

At that moment, the seal inside melted beneath Magnolia's roaring grief and anger. Liars! All of them liars! Couldn't trust any of them. Not even Cree.

"Magnolia!" Cree shrieked before she collapsed in a heap.

Ashen, with thin rivulets of blood coursing from her ears, her mouth, and her nose, Cree clawed at her throat. Gurgling sounds escaped between her cherry lips. Magnolia's fury unfurled, but the anguish-laced sounds Cree made pinched her heart.

Oh no! Goddess, no! Momma, help me!

"Cree!"

Panic crept up her throat and pressed impatiently. She fought to keep it at bay because once she gave in her blood magic might kill Cree. Damn it! She had to settle down.

What did Claude say? Meditation! Breathing! Sickles. Right! Sickles. Unblock the dam. She shut her eyes and tried to calm down.

Cree's cries had waned to whimpering. It sounded like an injured animal.

Please be okay. Please be okay. I'm sorry, baby. I'm sorry. Momma, please help!

With that small prayer to the goddess, Magnolia focused on forcing the blood to flow inside Cree. Minutes felt like years, and soon she lost track of everything except Cree.

Until the darkness claimed her.

———

⬜M⬜⬜⬜S⬜ ⬜⬜C⬜⬜ ⬜ ⬜⬜ ⬜⬜⬜ ⬜⬜⬜ ⬜⬜S⬜ ⬜⬜⬜

The voice plowed through the thick fog around Magnola's brain. It hurt, too. She tried to open her eyes, but the agony flashed. Groaning she tried to get enough spit to talk, but she had full on cottonmouth. She tried to hold up her head, to sit up, but none of her body would cooperate.

"Let me."

Claude had spoken just before she felt his hands on her wrists. Warm tickles sprouted across her skin, but those tickles pushed the fog back. The pain receded to a low ache behind her eyes, but she could see. Well, sort of.

"Be gentle." The female voice spoke again. Soft, but firm.

"Momma?" Her voice sounded like she hadn't used it in months.

The blurry image wore the strapless purple gown of royalty and stood at the foot of the bed.

"No, young Maggie."

Magnolia rubbed her eyes hard until they cleared. Priestess Onkya saluted her.

"You."

"Drink." Priestess Onkya handed her a glass of water.

What am I doing here? In the temple?

All around the thick hint of incense clung to the air,

weighing it down from the impurities of others' transgressions. In golden bowls, herbs burned, and further up, closer to the altar, the young priestesses appeared to be preparing for blood sacrifices. Several chickens had been tethered to the stone slab. Nightlights cast eerie arcs of light against the walls.

"How did I get here?" Magnolia tried to recall, but thinking hurt.

Claude stood beside her. "You don't remember?"

"Duh. I wouldn't be askin' if I knew."

"Well, Cree..."

"Cree! I've gotta get to her!"

"Stop! She's in the hands of the healers. "

It all came back, smashing hard against the headache and amplifying the throbbing pangs. Healers?

"I'm sorry, Claude."

He nodded. "Your training must commence as soon as you're well."

"What? But I've gotta get back to school."

"And you will. You must control your anger, or you will murder someone," Claude explained and refilled her water glass. "That is not our way. Our powers aren't to be perverted in this manner."

Magnolia couldn't stand it. She pushed herself forward. "I'm outta here."

Her mind was willing, but her body flopped back against the bed.

"No. You're not." Claude's stern scowl made her pause.

"What?"

"You're going on about this like some spoilt child. We all lost your momma, and the village adored her. Perhaps you should hear from her, eh? She will tell you herself if anyone killed her. Would that sate your angry heart?"

"My momma is dead."

"Yes, but, Priestesses Onkya is a medium."

"I can converse with the queen."

"Can you?"

Mediums could connect with the spirts of the dead. Another form of magic, it tended to run through bloodlines—genetic deposition. Would her momma chastise her?

The woman came to stand beside her, across from Claude.

"I will call forth the queen."

"Just like that?"

"Just like that." She winked.

Onkya closed her eyes and began to chant. Lifting her arms to the ceiling, she chanted louder. A couple of priestesses joined her and fell into the calling with flawless pitch and rhythm.

An otherworldly wind rushed in, and silenced everyone as it if had snatched the words from their mouths.

Magnolia steeled her nerves. "Momma?"

"Yes, baby girl." Priestess Onkya spoke, but the words sounded like her momma.

"Oh, Momma! How come you left me like this? Who—who did this to you?"

So many questions, she couldn't get them out fast enough. Magnolia pushed herself to a sitting position. She reached out to touch Onkya, but Claude grabbed her hand.

"Don't touch her! It siphons the reserves."

"No one did this to me, my child. It was my time to be reincarnated. All must cycle through the planes."

"So...you're alive?"

"Yes. Blood is life."

"Will you remember me when you come back?"

Her eyes saddened. "I live in you, Maggie."

A tight stitch took up residence in Magnolia's chest. Yet as her momma's words sank in, it relaxed.

Her momma would live again. No one had killed her. Claude, Quist, and the others had all been telling the truth.

Tears spilled over and splashed down her face. "Oh, Momma. Cree. Quist…"

"Shush, my pretty flower. I love you and the woman you're blossoming into. Continue your training. All will be well."

Her momma smiled fleetingly in the contours of Priestess Onkya's face, before the priestess slumped over.

"Onkya?" Claude scurried around the bed. "Onkya!"

The priestesses, who'd fallen silent up to that point, rushed forward and lifted Onkya. They carried her without a word into the further reaches of the temple.

"The queen is gone." Claude's words hung heavy with sorrow.

Magnolia smiled. "And yet, she's not."

Claude laughed. "Indeed."

———

THREE WEEKS LATER

Summer had arrived, and the students at Arbor High enjoyed the beautiful weather the way they always did with futbol, teleportation, and soda-spiked love potions. Cree lay on the grass beside Magnolia, a bowl of mangos by her knee.

"So, Duke or Chapel Hill?" Cree asked, reading the tablet's screen over Magnolia's shoulder.

"Duke maybe." Magnolia smiled as Cree kissed her cheek. "Two more years and then after graduation from here, I will go to Duke and get my degree and work towards becoming a doctor of hematology."

"I think it's neat you're going to be healer." Cree touched her shoulder.

"Yeah. I'm going to heal blood diseases. After all, blood is life."

T☐☐ E☐☐

THE PRIZEWINNER

ALLEDRIA HURT

I ☐☐☐ ☐☐☐☐ ☐☐ M☐☐☐ C☐☐☐☐☐☐☐ ☐☐ ☐☐☐☐ ☐☐☐ ☐☐☐ ☐ time, but I had never seen this lady come to tea at the house before. In fact, I had never even heard her mentioned before today. That afternoon, Miss Claudia decided she would take tea in the drawing room upstairs. I liked that room, dark and cozy. A picture-window made of deep purple glass dominated one wall. This was also the room in which Miss Claudia grew her beautiful flowers, those that were not in the greenhouse, tall ones with long white flowers that looked like an instrument only a fairy could play.

I'd begun cataloguing what I would need in order to make the sandwiches the Miss likes when she said, "Oh and Rina?"

"Yes, ma'am," I replied, turning to meet her eyes.

"We'll be having a guest for tea. Be sure to make the tea nice and strong."

"Yes, ma'am." I started out of the room again, fiddling with those cu☐ inks the Miss insists I wear. I never liked the silly things, but the Miss said they made me look like such a gentleman, something a butler is supposed to be, and she paid my portion so I guessed complaining was pointless.

Tea occurred right on time; lateness is never fashionable, but this guest had not appeared. Miss Claudia did not seem the least bit upset, so I kept my mouth firmly shut.

"Rina, get me another plate of sandwiches, please."

"Yes, ma'am." I picked up the small empty plate before I stepped out to head for the kitchen downstairs. Coming back up the stairs, I heard,

"Claudia, it has been quite some time."

Reentering with the plate held before me like a shield, I surveyed the situation. A tall, slender woman with white hair sat across from my petite, brunette lady. Her garments were simple, black and white, to go with her pallor. But what most drew my attention was the flower, set next to her right ear. The flower had wide petals and seemed to be in full bloom. It looked like a flower from an exotic locale, but whereas my mind screamed it should have been scarlet, it was stark white. A white so severe it made her hair look dingy where it hung over her shoulders and down her back. She greeted me with a smile and a low voice reminiscent of a throaty singer.

"Hello."

Miss Claudia interrupted then, gesturing for me to put the plate down next to the teapot.

"Valesha, this is Rina, my sole domestic. Tony doesn't count since he really doesn't set foot in the house."

"I see. A pleasure to make your acquaintance, Rina." She was studying me with eyes that reflected the deep purple hue of the room's glass. She did not extend her hand to me, not that I expected her to.

"It is a pleasure to meet you as well, Miss Valesha. May I fix you some tea?"

"Thank you, Rina. Two sugars and a squeeze of lemon."

"As you like it."

"So, Valesha, have you brought me more flowers?" asked Miss Claudia, deftly moving on from the pleasantries.

"Of course, Claudia, you don't think I would travel all this way without bringing you something, do you?"

The Miss smiled at her guest then, a thin lipped smile out of place in a meeting of friends. I had seen that look enough to know it well. This meeting was upsetting. Miss Claudia picked up her teacup then and asked if Miss Valesha was aware that Mistress Betian had recently passed. This turned the conversation to things I see no need to recount. Anyone can pick up an issue of the local society press and find out about these happenings. The usual falls from grace, divorces, death, and other such hogwash as makes the world of the rich go round.

Rain intruded on the conversation, knocking against the glass of the windows like a di dent visitor seeking entrance.

"How are my babies in the greenhouse doing?" asked Miss Valesha as she nibbled around the edges of a crustless sandwich. She hadn't bitten into anything at all.

"Quite well, considering how unused to the conditions they are. Tony has done such an admirable job with them."

Anthony is the gardener, a morose and silent man whom I only see if there is something here at the house for him to pick up. A much older gentleman, he is always polite, but never talkative. If he has family, they don't visit, and if he ever leaves the premises, it isn't through the front gate.

"Oh, good." Miss Valesha smiled at the information. "I was reluctant to bring more. After all, I don't want to be party to making them su er."

"Of course, but feel free to bring more. They are doing wonderfully."

Something made Miss Valesha check her watch. It was a slim silver affair with a silent mechanism. Somehow I got the feeling she didn't much enjoy the sound of the ticking away of life. As she turned her head again, I noticed something stranger than just her watch. The flower in her hair, I could have sworn it breathed as she turned to look out the window at the indigo-hued rain.

"I've got to dash, Claudia."

"So soon?" The Miss's arch tone was enough to make me wonder as to the true nature of her friendship with our strange guest.

"Yes, unfortunately. You *will* forgive my late arrival and all too hasty departure?"

"Of course, we've been friends far too long for me to take offense at your eccentric behavior." Miss Claudia paused then, setting down her cup with a clink onto its china saucer. "You will send me a few cuttings for Tony to work with?"

"Some seedlings surely, nothing is grown enough for me to cut at the moment. I'll have them sent up by the end of the week."

"Splendid." There was that thin, dissatisfied smile again. "Rina, be so kind as to see Miss Valesha to her car."

"Yes, ma'am." I led Miss Valesha down the stars and into the front hallway where, much to my surprise, she had a long black velvet swing coat hanging in the foyer. I had stepped out to go to the kitchen for no more than two minutes. I had not heard Miss Claudia come down from the drawing room to answer the door. So how on earth had this strange woman come to be in the house? Had Miss Claudia given her a key?

And if so, why hadn't I heard the door while I stood in the kitchen?

I held her coat for her as she put her arms in, and something hissed at me.

"Don't mind him," she murmured to me in an almost sleepy fashion. "He doesn't like for me to be around beautiful people, it makes him insecure."

I stood dumbfounded for a moment before asking,

"Who?"

"Don't worry about that, Aria. I have not been by to visit Claudia much since our falling out, but I think I shall make more time to visit her now that I know you are here." She fixed those eyes on me. They e[]ortlessly drew me into their depths. "You don't mind if I come to visit you, do you?"

She did not wait for my answer, but stepped out the door I do not remember opening into the rain. Crouched at the base of the manor steps was a black car, unknown model, but I will never forget how hungry it seemed to me. She stopped again at the driver's side door to look at me, standing as though the rain meant nothing at all.

My brown eyes stared into her eyes of nameless color for a short eternity before I snatched the door shut between us with a slam. My heart was skipping, and the collar of my pressed linen shirt felt noose tight, as if extra buttons had been added to shrink the neck hole. For a moment, I gasped, praying Miss Claudia didn't come down the stairs and see me with this appalling lack of composure. Several breaths later, I had recovered myself enough to return upstairs. I could only hope the Miss would overlook my lapse.

"Shall I take the tea things away?"

"Yes, Rina, please do. And then would you light the sconces in my studio, I'll be right down."

"Yes, ma'am." I picked up the pieces of the silver tea service, carefully arranging them on their platter to take them down to the kitchen. As I reached the door of the drawing room, she spoke again.

"Rina, stay away from Valesha."

At first, I thought perhaps I hadn't heard her right. Then panic passed under my skin. Had she seen my reaction to Miss Valesha from the staircase? I held the tray balanced in front of me so as not to upset the tea pot.

"Ma'am?"

"She inspires a☐ection in people, Rina. However, she can never fulfill the promises of those eyes. I don't want to see her do to you what she has done to so many others."

I nodded my understanding of her warning and walked out of the room.

———

T☐☐ ☐☐☐☐ ☐☐☐☐☐☐ ☐☐ ☐☐☐☐☐☐☐ ☐☐☐☐☐☐☐ ☐☐☐☐☐☐☐ with the markings: **FRAGILE LIVE SPECIMEN** on three of its sides. These were most likely the seedlings Miss Valesha had promised. I did the usual, called Tony's cottage and left him a message to pick up the package from the back porch when he had time. Then I took the package and left it on the back porch. There was an inordinate amount of shifting going on inside that box, nothing else could explain the hissing sound as I brought it through the house other than pots being slid and jostled. I was happy to leave it on the porch. I didn't want it in the house with me.

———

T☐☐☐☐ ☐☐☐☐ ☐☐☐☐☐☐☐ ☐☐☐ I ☐☐☐ ☐☐☐ ☐☐☐☐☐ incident out of my mind. I assisted Miss Claudia in preparing for a trip. She was to be gone for two weeks with a client to seal some kind of deal. I make it my business to have nothing whatsoever to say about what Miss Claudia does. I am not entirely sure it is legal. I do, however, know that it is lucrative, and any servant, no matter the post, should be glad for an occupation where the checks do not bounce like rubber.

Finally, just like that, Miss Claudia was gone on her business trip, and I was left with the house to myself for two whole weeks. I thought for a moment about going home to Merrybridge on holiday, but I hadn't spoken to my mother in over a year. I doubted she would be all that happy to see me unannounced.

Instead, I stayed on at the estate and enjoyed the relative solitude it allowed. Still, some part of me wanted to know what had become of Miss Valesha. She hadn't come to call again since her tea invitation. Perhaps she was merely having a joke at my expense. I stood divided on the issue. Did I wish it to be some badly out of taste joke, or some true interest in me?

Three days into the Miss being gone, the doorbell rang. It was about the time Je☐ery, the postman, would stop by for some tea and chatter before completing his rounds. I was happy for the distraction from my reading. I understood it to some degree, but not nearly a high enough degree. I wished to continue onward with it. I would choose something more palatable after tea.

I opened the front door wide without checking and was given a rather pleasant surprise. Miss Valesha stood in the doorway, clad once more in her black swing coat, flower tucked neatly behind her right ear. Lovely as ever.

The hand that grabbed my shirt collar was only slightly redder than the shirt itself.

"I've been thinking of you."

Pop went the top button of my shirt, loosening my collar. Then the whisper of manicured nails down the flesh of my throat. "Have you been thinking of me, Aria?"

I started at the use of my middle name, a name only my mother used. I hadn't noticed it the first time she said it. Now I remembered her calling me that in the foyer as she left the last time. I frowned, pulling away.

"Miss Claudia is not here," I said pulling the door to shut it. "She won't be back for at least another ten days."

"Always so proper, Aria, the perfect little servant. I know Claudia's not here. I didn't come to see her. I came to see you, as I promised." She reached for me again, laying her hand against my collar this time. The brush of her hand across my shoulder wasn't unpleasant. "I want to see you lying on a bed of roses, Aria."

My good sense roused again at the sound of the name.

"Miss Valesha, I'm sorry, but Miss Claudia did not leave any orders or provisions for the care of a guest in her absence. You will simply have to call upon her again when she returns." I drew the iron curtain of servant formality against her invasion with success. She removed her hand from my person and brought it to her face, as if to hide it from my gaze.

"I see." I heard a pout in those words. "So this is what is to be. Claudia has told you to have nothing to do with me, and you being who you are will not disobey her. I shall have to take that up with my old friend when she returns. I have a favor to ask of you, Rina."

"Ma'am?" I responded automatically.

"Point me in the direction of the greenhouse. I want to check on the new flowers."

"Go around the house to my left and follow the path into the stand of trees. The path goes straight to the greenhouse."

"Thank you. Are you sure you won't accompany me?" She tried to hook me with her eyes, but I looked away.

"No, ma'am. Miss Claudia forbids me to enter Anthony's domain. He's very particular."

"Oh, I see." She was disappointed. "Thank you for your help, Rina. I will be calling on Claudia again when she returns."

She left me standing in the doorway and I was struck by two things. First, where was her car? I was looking at the driveway and there was no vehicle parked anywhere along its length. Second, what had happened to the flower in her hair? It seemed to have tripled in size. I was leaning against the doorjamb, trying to make sense of it all, when Je□rey drove up in his little car.

———

O□ □□□ □□□ M□□□ C□□□□□□ □ □□ □□□ □□ □□□□□□□ home, she was set to arrive on the 2:45 train. The train was late by twenty minutes. After collecting her luggage, I dutifully inquired about her trip. She chuckled. I made no further attempts at conversation, as she did not seem to be in a talkative mood.

Pulling into the driveway, I noticed Miss Valesha's car, still, dark, and predatory, parked in front of the stairs. Its owner was standing on the front porch, her back to one of the pillars with her arms crossed over her chest and a scowl on her fragile face. I let Miss Claudia out at the front door and drove the car around the house into the garage. After that, I removed her luggage to her bedroom so she could unpack it at her leisure. Finally, I went down into the kitchen to make tea, as the Miss had just returned from quite a trip, and began the preparations for dinner.

Opening the kitchen windows for the afternoon breeze, I was startled to hear, "You are simply jealous you cannot command my a☐ections for yourself. It upsets you to see me in love with someone else because you wish we were…"

"It is nothing of the kind, Valesha, and it is foolish for you to even insinuate such a thing. I just don't want to see you hurt Rina--."

"Like I hurt you? Was that what you meant to say? Claudia, you are transparent. You always have been. Why I put up with you this long…"

"Because you need me, Valesha, that's why. Leave Rina alone."

"Do you realize how much she hates it when you call her that? She prefers the name 'Aria'."

How had she known that?

"Regardless of her personal preferences," I could hear a chill creeping into my Mistress's voice. "She is in my employ and thus, paid to follow orders. I have told her to stay the bloody hell away from you."

"So I understand." Then there was a long pause. "Shall we go see how the babies in the greenhouse are doing?"

The change in conversation was so sudden I thought for a moment I had misheard. Then I heard retreating footsteps.

The clock struck 4 p.m., time for tea, and I was not prepared. Half an hour later, I finally had things ready and set out on the dining room table where Miss Claudia generally takes her tea. Yet, no one reappeared at the house. In fact, the hall clock struck 6 p.m., and I still had not heard anything as simple as the opening of the door to announce the Miss's return.

At 6:15 p.m., I heard the door open. I was busy working on the gravy for the beef at the time, and only saw the shadow of someone running up the stairs from where I stood in the kitchen. I continued my work, keeping one ear open for the sound of the upstairs summoning bell. What I heard was not the light silver tinkle of the summons bell, but the ear-splitting sound of the hall telephone ringing, interrupting my thickening the gravy. I have never known a sound more annoying than that telephone. I stepped out in the hallway to answer it, despite the urge to throw it through a wall.

"Good evening. You've reached the Singular Estate."

"Hello and good day."

"I apologize, my lady is indisposed at the moment."

"Fortunately, we are not looking for Miss Claudia Singular. We'd like to speak with a young lady in her employ, A Rina Danvers. Would she happen to be about?"

"Speaking. May I ask the nature of your business?"

"Silas Cherry, Merrybridge Undertaker, at your service, Miss Danvers. I'm afraid I must be the bearer of some powerful bad news. Your mother, Mrs. Operetta Danvers, has just recently passed away. The Merrybridge Parsonage has set her funeral for a few days from now, seeing as they weren't sure how to contact you. I wanted to be sure myself you were notified. Will you be attending?"

"I cannot say for certain, Mr. Cherry." I felt as though the wind had been knocked out of me. Mother, dead. How, when, why? "I will make every attempt."

"Very good then, ma'am. We'll be looking for you. I

assume you will be putting your mother's affairs in order when you come?"

"Sir, I don't know if I will be attending, much less in any state to care for my mother's affairs should I be able to come." I pressed my knuckles to my forehand and half-turned to look at the clock on the kitchen wall. Instead of seeing the moon-faced clock with large black numbers, what I saw was a spout of flame with sooty smoke.

The gravy was burning.

All in one moment, I cried out, dropped the receiver, and covered the distance to the stove. Snatching up the small bag of flour I had been thickening with, I dumped it liberally all over the blaze. Thankfully, so smothered, the fire went out quickly, leaving behind a white wonderland of flour all over the stove, countertop, and floor of the kitchen.

"Aria, my goodness, what in the world is going on?" The shocked question came from the hallway arch. Miss Claudia was there when I turned, looking quite splendid. She wore an ankle length velvet cape, high heels, and a lace hat covering her long ringlets, forcing them to frame her heart shaped face. Tucked near her right ear was a white flower, quite a contrast to the smooth darkness of her ensemble. On her hands, she wore lace gloves to match her hat and carried her slim cigarette holder.

"Forgive me, Miss. I was distracted by a phone call and the gravy started to burn." I could feel the color creeping into my cheeks as I looked away.

"Oh, don't worry about it. Valesha and I will be dining in town anyway. There is a new club opening, and she insists we attend. You won't wait up, will you?"

"No, ma'am. Are you sure you do not want me to escort you?"

"That really won't be necessary, Rina. I'm sure there will be quite a few young men looking to play escort this evening, and you look as though you have your hands full with this mess." She gestured at the flour-covered kitchen, using her cigarette holder as a baton.

"Yes, ma'am."

The busy signal from the telephone started stridently crying for attention.

"Ma'am?" I began to ask even, though part of me hoped she would say no.

"Yes, Rina?" Miss Claudia made no attempt to hang up the phone. It probably would have been quite a feat for her to bend to pick it up in her present attire.

"May I take a few days off? My mother has passed away, and I'd like to go home to Merrybridge to bury her."

She stopped, looking at me appraisingly as she considered my request. Then she waved me off dismissively.

"You may go. I suppose I shall just have to get along without you for a few days. I assume you will find your own way to town?"

"Yes, ma'am."

"Well then, I expect this mess to be cleaned up before you go and may you have a safe trip." She walked away then, leaving me standing in a drift of flour. I noted the sound of the heavy door opening and closing. Faintly, I heard a car start and then drive away.

She was gone. I breathed out.

With her gone, I took out the broom to start cleaning up. It was whilst slowly sweeping up the mess I remembered Miss Claudia never wore flowers in her hair. A slight smile tugged at the edge of my lips. Perhaps Miss Valesha had been successful in charming my Mistress over to her side of thinking. With that light thought for company, I hurried in cleaning so I could pack. Though I knew I would not leave, officially, until the next morning, some time off would not go amiss to get my thoughts in order.

———

I □□□□□□ □□ □□□ □□□□ □□□□□ □□□□□□□ □□□ command not to, listening for the sound of the Miss's return. She didn't. Nor did she phone to announce she would be returning with the sun. I had begun to worry some by the time Jeffrey came with the morning post. Still, I did not choose not to go, simply because something did not feel right. Miss Valesha's car was in the driveway when I walked down the stairs to leave. They must have taken Miss Claudia's car into the city. I lightly ran my fingers across the hood feeling a slight shudder run down my back. I would be a liar if I said it was from utter revulsion.

———

I □□□□□□□□ □□ □□□ □□□□ □□□□□ □ □□□ J□□□□□□□□ □□ offered me a ride in from town. Miss Valesha's car was exactly where it had been when I left. Did that mean she had never left? The postbox was crammed full of letters and the papers of the past days. It spilled out onto the drive. I grabbed up the pieces off the ground, as well as the newest additions given to me by Jeffrey in lieu of adding them to the pile and held them awkwardly under my arm as I walked up the drive to the front door. The door opened, needing some unusual coaxing, and I dropped everything on the threshold, along with my jaw, at the sight of the front hallway.

It was a shambles.

The small side table, usually found near the front door where the lady was accustomed to leaving her keys, was now firmly embedded in the wall just to the left of the kitchen archway. The wall along the staircase had a gouge in it where the molding had been, as if someone had ripped the molding out in one long strip. Every third step was crushed while the second and fourth had moon-shaped indentions in them as if something with huge feet had come stomping down the staircase. The pattern continued down the stairs and then turned to my right to head into the parlor. The other furnishings of the hallway itself were strewn about and broken as if someone had intentionally tried to make them into firewood.

Leaving my things and the mail where I dropped them, I gingerly stepped into the house. I hopped, skipped, and outright jumped my way up the stairs to investigate the rest of the house as a sick feeling grew in the pit of my stomach.

The second floor was in little better shape.

The footprints continued. Lamps lay half-shattered and twisted. Furniture was indi⬚erently tossed in every direction, some of it embedded like the downstairs table in the wall from the force. Portraits and landscapes done by Miss Claudia hung ripped as though by claws. Sections of the floor were punched through, and walking near them made me feel as if the house were swaying under my weight despite my certainty only I was moving. Before I reached the purple drawing room, I heard a floor-shaking crash. Then there was a crack, as the floor gave way beneath me, and I hung suspended in air before landing, painfully, in the rubble of the lower staircase.

"Welcome back."

I coughed and moved to stand, feeling a touch of warm wetness against my leg where I was pierced. Wiping the dust from my eyes, I found myself staring at Valesha standing in the ruins of the hallway with her back to the front door. She was still the lady carved of crystal I remembered. She was still dressed in black as I remembered. What was beside her, however, was something I could hardly believe.

My eyes moved up from muddy brown writhing tentacles to a flower so vibrantly beautiful it gave color to the destroyed walls around it. The flower itself was stark white at the tips of its petals but bloody crimson at the base. The stem was thick, tree thick, and greener than the grass of the front lawn.

"The baby thinks you're pretty too." Valesha's voice drew my attention back to her. I took her in all over again, certain something was di erent. Then it struck me; the flower in her hair was di erent. That flower, once white as disease, was now red like just kissed lips. I remembered vividly thinking it should have been that color all along.

"You like it?" She turned her head so I could see it better. "You can have one just like it, if you want, to go in your lapel. You do, after all, want to be my gentleman, don't you?"

She reached for me. I stared at her hand as though it were something alien. I reminded myself she was still Miss Claudia's guest and a certain amount of decorum was thus expected. I denied the urge to hold her to my heart.

"Claudia's gone."

She interrupted my thoughts with her statement.

"Huh?"

"She's gone. I've done away with her, Aria. She was standing in my way. I got rid of her."

"You killed her?" I could feel a horror creeping in my mind, threatening to overtake my sense.

"No." There was a smile in that word. "I've done much better. She was just what the baby needed to grow big and strong and be the prize winner I want him to be." The flower ducked its head to her level and she absently stroked its petals as one would a precious pet. "Do you want to see?"

The horror was still there, circling, just waiting to snap up what sanity I had left. A giant human eating flower cared for by a woman who was reading my mind...who undoubtedly knew I was wondering if I would be next to be fed to her creature.

"I suppose."

Valesha held out her hand to me again. This time, I took it. Her fingers closed, cold, around my wrist, and I realized she was never going to let me go again. The horror snapped its jaws. I was going to become plant food.

"Only if you do as she did and upset me." Her eyes were as alien as the rest of her.

The walk to the greenhouse was short. Though I knew it was noon, the shadows in the greenhouse made it seem like night.

The flower opened the door for us and held it as we entered. I passed so close to it I could have sworn I heard it actually breathing. Looking around, I tried to understand what I was seeing. I had never been in the greenhouse. It felt like a jungle dominated by trumpet flowers. Valesha stopped at a fountain settled in the exact center and sat down on the granite lip. With a broad sweep of her hand, she beckoned me to take it all in.

"Look in the water, Aria."

I stepped close enough to look into the water, but not close enough to fall in without being pulled. There were forms in the water. Two of them I recognized: Tony and Miss Claudia. They both seemed to be peacefully sleeping, underwater.

Panicked, I reached for them, but Valesha's cold grip halted my movement.

"Don't worry about them, Aria. They can't drown. The magic will keep them alive forever and while they sleep, they'll feed my babies."

"Babies like him?" I asked, pointing at the giant which had replanted itself in the soft soil not far away.

"Oh yes, like him, though not so big. He's for a show back home."

"Back home?"

"Yes, back home, where I will take you when you realize there is nothing left for you here and say yes. Your mother is dead; Claudia is gone; the manor is destroyed. Why remain?"

I sat down at the edge of the fountain, numb. When she curled up close to me, I thought nothing of wrapping my arm around her and letting her press her head to my neck. I hardly felt her fingers as they played with my carefully pressed curls.

"Come with me and be my gentleman, Aria. I can help you be happy." Something hissed. "Oh hush," she chided. "Just because you cannot hold me, you do not wish me to be held."

The hissing stopped. I thought it sounded a trifle guilty.

"Answer me, Aria. Won't you come?"

"Yes, Miss Valesha, I'll come." Where else would I go? After all this I would be branded mad if I ever spoke of it, and how could I possibly live the rest of my life without speaking of this?

"Not so formal, Aria." She was smiling as she looked up at me. "Valesha will do." She pressed a kiss to my cheek. "You'll love your new home."

Darkness consumed me and I swore I smelled a perfume laced delicately with decay.

———

I □ □□□□ □□□□□□□□□□ □□□ □ □ □□□ □ □□□□□ □ □□□ my suit jacket, neatly folded, thrown over the back. Valesha stood not far away with others sharing a similar pallor, all female. Their color was crystal clear white like an elegantly bleached and starched dress shirt. When she realized I was awake, Valesha came to me and sat down in my lap.

"You missed the show."

"What show?"

"The Garden Show, silly. I won this year. My Soul Stealers' Trumpet was the biggest they had ever seen. Did you sleep well?"

"I suppose." The perfume smell was there again as she breathed. Cloyingly sweet and decadent to death. "I wasn't expecting to sleep."

"I thought you might need a nap after the stressful day you've had. Come, let's go home." Vales slipped out of my grip and began to walk away. I grabbed up my suit jacket and hurried after her. I had no wish for her to become upset at me.

T□□ E□□

SWEET JUSTICE

KENESHA WILLIAMS

H□□ □□□□ □□□□ □□□□ □□ □□ □□□□ □□□□□ □□□□□□ girl that writes all of those bad boyfriend songs, oh yeah. *I knew you were trouble when you walked in.* That's the thought that entered my mind as soon as Detective Nelson walked into my o□ ce. Actually, it was a garage I turned into an o□ ce, but dammit you get the point.

I really wasn't surprised that he walked into my o□ ce; I knew sooner or later the PD would get their heads out their ass and come inquiring about my assistance on their latest spate of murders. I should have known they wouldn't come kowtowing until they absolutely had to, though. Especially since the last time we'd worked together I'd thoroughly showed them up after countless excuses why they couldn't get results. But I knew they'd come knocking soon, and I should have known that they'd use one of my biggest weaknesses against me, Detective Nelson.

Nelson had the swagger of Idris, the face of Morris, and the body of...well the body of Morris Chestnut, too. He was six foot three of delicious, dangerous, and dirty manhood, and the last time I saw him was when I threw my mom's favorite vase at his head as he was buck naked and coming out of my shower. Luckily it wasn't my favorite vase because that bad boy cracked into at least a million tiny pieces. Unfortunately, it narrowly missed connecting to Detective Adam Nelson's handsome block head. He knew how I felt about commitment, and his fool ass asked me for the key to my house. He was lucky I gave him time to get dressed before I threw him out.

Understandably, he hadn't come by since then, but now here he was looking just as fine as he did that morning that he narrowly escaped a busted head. He came hat in hand and inquiring about my help. The body count had been adding up for at least six months, but the deaths were swept under the rug until the Assistant D.A. was one of those bodies. First pimps started disappearing, and when they reappeared, it was as gnarled and dried corpses in back alleys that no one should have been down anyway.

No one knew what to make of the disappearances and subsequent almost mummified bodies, but no one really cared. Good riddance was the attitude. Then the Johns started to disappear. A few frantic 911 calls from housewives looking for their husbands, but still little fanfare. To be honest, some of the wives didn't want the husbands found. It seemed like once the detectives started looking hard at the victims, they found that those who were missing were abusive bastards and major assholes and therefore had many known enemies. In fact, it turned out the lot of them had more enemies than friends. And if you asked anyone who knew the A.D.A., they'd count him in with the bastards and assholes, but he was the A.D.A. and therefore people, important people were looking for justice or at the very least a miscreant to pin the charges on.

When they couldn't find a single shred of evidence, and someone on the force with sense looked at the clues they did have, shriveled body, no mortal wounds, unspecified cause of death, they called upon me and my unique gifts.

In plain terms, I was a Supernatural Private Investigator; my business card however just had my name, Maisha Star, PI. I know it sounds like a porn star's name, but it was the one my mother and father gave me. I kept the supernatural part to myself or to those who were on a need to know basis. Still even without spelling out the unique part of my talents, word of mouth always kept me with a steady supply of clients and my mortgage paid on time.

Speaking of mortgages, although I wasn't happy that some weird magical killer was on the loose, it was getting close to bill time, and my last client had flaked on my payment. Actually, I killed him and like they say, dead men tell no tales, but they also pay no invoices. If we're being technical, I didn't kill the client because you can't kill something that's already dead. I guess if we were being spot on, I re-killed the client who was trying to lure me to my death. I'm sure there was still a price on my head since he had failed miserably to carry out his orders, but such is the life of a Supe PI.

"Don't just stand there looking stupid; sit down," I said and waved to the two guest chairs that sat in front of my mid-century modern wood desk. He did as he was told and continued to look everywhere but into my eyes.

He took in a big gulp of air as if he needed more wind in his sails to spit out whatever he had to say before we got down to business. I braced myself for the barrage of words but was surprised when all he said was, "I'm sorry."

I leaned forward on my desk, wondering if I wasn't imagining the words. "Excuse me?"

"I'm sorry. You told me how you felt about rushing into a commitment and then my stupid behind goes and does just that. And for that I'm sorry."

He said it all in one breath like if he didn't say it all at once, he wouldn't be able to say it at all. I sat back in my chair speechless, for once in my life. It took a lot of cojones to admit you made a mistake, and I was honestly surprised at the apology.

"I'm sorry, too. I should have talked to you about it instead of trying to inflict bodily harm," I smiled and then laughed at the joke. Luckily, he laughed too, and all the weird energy in the room dissipated.

"Alright now that that's out of the way, what took y'all so long to contact me? Shouldn't take a big muckety-muck's death for the law to be seeking justice, right? All Lives Matter, huh?" I asked, disdain dripping from each word. Seems like as long as certain folks are victims, the police felt like maybe someone was doing their work for them, but now that the chickens had come home to roost, they wanted my help.

"You know I don't feel that way, Maisha," he said as he looked me in my eyes. I crossed my arms in front of me. Sure, I knew he didn't feel that way, but his brothers in blue were a di erent story. I was going to help out, of course. I was afraid that whoever was doing this was going to start attacking the working girls next, and I knew they'd get no kind of justice from the police.

"I know," I said. "So, what do you think is going on?" I asked. Although Adam didn't have the gift like I did, he had a pretty strong intuition that served him well on the force.

"It seems like someone's getting revenge if you ask me. All

these creeps dying." He leaned closer as if we weren't the only two in the room. "Between you and me, I'd heard that ADA Johansson sometimes let crimes go unnoticed if a pro gave him a little loving on the side. Also heard that he liked to play rough, too rough, and sometimes would push the boundaries of consent."

"So, he was a rapist. Is that what you're telling me?" I shook my head in anger. "That bastard. He deserved what he got."

"I'm not arguing with you. I just need to get this person o☐ the streets; who knows who they'll take next?"

I leaned as far back in my chair as I could without falling. I knew that Adam wasn't like the ADA or those dirty cops in California who'd been passing a teenage prostitute back and forth for years, but seeing what he represented vexed my spirit in ways he just didn't know. I was happy that I knew for myself that there was at least one good cop on the force, but it still didn't make me feel any better when I knew how many bad ones there were. I thought maybe I could beg o☐ on this case and wait for whoever was doing the killings to knock o☐ a few more assholes, but that wouldn't be fair. Assholedom shouldn't be an automatic death sentence.

"So, will you help me?" he asked giving me puppy dog eyes all the while.

"Of course," I said, "but you owe me something."

———

I ☐ ☐☐☐ ☐☐ ☐ ☐☐☐ ☐ ☐☐☐☐☐☐☐☐☐☐☐ ☐ ☐☐☐☐ I ☐☐☐☐☐☐'☐ breathe. I was trapped under something large and immovable and began to panic. Then I heard a loud noise that could only be the sound of Adam's insu☐erable snoring. Realizing that he'd thrown his tree branch-like arm across my chest in the middle of the night and that's why I could barely move or breathe calmed me down. I threw off his arm and slid out of bed.

It was still early, and the alarm clock on my dresser glowed the time of three am in fluorescent green. Seeing the clock's lights reminded me of something I'd noticed in one of the pictures Adam had shown me last night at one of the crime scenes. There was a bright fluorescent orange hoop earring that reminded me of something that Lisa Turtle might have worn on Saved by the Bell near the body. It was far enough away that the police didn't think anything of it, but something about it caught my attention. Had the idiots thought to bag it I might have been able to use it to scry.

I walked to the bathroom and grabbed my fluffy white robe off the back of the door and looked in the mirror. My hair was flying all over the place because I hadn't had time to even grab my hair turban before Adam grabbed me and placed soft kisses all over my throat after I agreed to work on the case. He went straight for my weak spot, so I went straight for his, and after that, there was nothing but the shouting left. I hadn't had a romp like that since I kicked him out my house, so I wasn't complaining about the hair.

I looked around the bathroom trying to remember where my turban would be and remembered that I had placed it in the small shelf above the lavatory. I grabbed my turban, and something fell as if it were placed on top of it. I bent down to look to see what had fallen, grateful that both the seat and the lid were closed or it would have definitely been in the bowl. I reached my hand behind the commode base and closed my hand around something small and circular. When I brought the item to my face, I knew what it would be, but looked anyway; the bright fluorescent orange hoop earring lay in my palm.

I instinctively looked around the bathroom, as if someone might pop out at any moment, but no one did. I padded back to the bedroom and shook Adam awake. He lazily opened his eyes and grinned with a line of dried drool across his cheek, no doubt thinking I was waking him for round two. "No, it's not that," I said before he got any ideas. He frowned but sat up in the bed awaiting my next words.

Seems like the killer might have left us a clue.

———

T☐☐ ☐☐☐ ☐☐ ☐☐☐ ☐☐☐☐☐ ☐☐ ☐☐☐☐☐ ☐☐☐☐ ☐☐☐☐☐☐☐ ☐☐☐ death; even the antiseptic properties of the sun couldn't erase the pulchritude. I thought coming back to the scene of the crime in the day would make the whole thing less grimy, but it had the opposite e☐ect. Women who looked pretty under streetlights in the dark looked decidedly less so in the harsh rays of the sun's light. They looked like what they were, downtrodden women who needed a chance to make it in this world, by hook or by crook. And one of them was making her way through the men in blue on the beat one by one. Not that I could blame them one bit.

"Hey, Miss," I shouted to the youngest looking girl out here. She had her hair dyed an unnatural shade of red and wore a skirt in the same color hitched up to her hoo-ha. She looked young enough to be my daughter if I were able to have one. I could tell she wasn't even nineteen under all the war paint she'd put on, but I understood the need to look fierce when facing an even fiercer opponent, life.

"Yeah," she said swaying towards me on spindly high heels.

In another life, she could have been a runway model. In this one, she was some unkind man's cum receptacle. Life was funny like that.

She was now so close to me that I could see the color of her eyes; they were a light hazel that was striking against her ebony face. Her lips were full, and she turned them up in a way that said, I've seen it all before, but her eyes told another story. I don't know how long she'd been out here, but whatever she'd seen had spooked her. Just not enough for her to give up the corner. She didn't look like a junkie, so I was thinking runaway.

"You see a girl who wears jewelry like this?" I asked holding up the orange hoop that I'd found this morning.

The girl held out her palm and I dropped the earring in her hand. My attempts at scrying with it back at the house had produced nothing. It was odd. Seemed like someone wanted me to find them, but they weren't giving me enough clues.

She looked at the earring and then held it back out to me in between her thumb and pointer finger. I noticed her chipped manicure which told me she still tried to keep herself up. "Nah, don't know anyone who wears stu☐ like that. Looks old."

"Yeah it does," I said mostly to myself. "If you see something can you give me a call?" I held out my card to her, and she pinched it between those same two fingers. I saw her eyes squinch up to read it and could make out her lips moving as she read.

"Maisha Star, PI? What does that mean?"

"Means I investigate stu☐ that others can't."

"Yeah, like what, ghosts and stu☐?"

"And stu☐," I answered back.

"My granma could see stu☐ like that," she tossed out and then closed her mouth tight like she'd said too much.

"Your granma still with us?" I asked as nonchalantly as I could.

The girl ducked her head down and looked at the toes of her shoes as if they held life's mysteries. "Nah, she been long gone. I was ten when she died."

"And your parents?" I knew I was being nosy and was waiting for her to tell me to mind my own damn business, but I needed to know.

"I don't know. Mama left me with her mama, and I never knew who my daddy was. Don't think my mama knew either." She looked around to see if anyone else had heard what she'd said. The streets were pretty empty, it being so early. Just me, her, and some other working girls either leaving to go back home or on their way to set up shop.

"It's pretty early, not too many...customers this early. You want to come with me and get some breakfast?" It was a hunch that I needed to follow up on. If her gran had the sight maybe she did too. And hell, if I was being honest, there was something about the girl that I liked, that I wanted to protect.

Before she could answer a black car pulled up to the curb behind her. "Babydoll," a man's voice called out from the car.

I watched as the girl's face crumpled while she faced me. She then whipped her head around, and I could hear the smile in her voice as she said, "Hey Baby." She had turned from school girl to coquette in a matter of seconds. But the look on her face before she turned told me that the man in the car was nothing but trouble. Trouble she knew, but trouble she needed.

I walked over to the car where she was now leaning

halfway into and cleared my throat. She was so deep in her negotiations she jumped a little.

"So, about that breakfast," I said throwing my arm over her shoulder, all the while peering into the car. There were two men in the car. The man at the wheel had a pockmarked face the color of left out mayonnaise and the man in the passenger seat next to him wasn't winning any beauty contests either. The third man in the back scooted further into the seat as to remain hidden.

She gently shrugged my arm off of her and turned to face me with pleading eyes. I didn't know whether she wanted me to save her or if she wanted me to let her go with the men. But until she told me to shove off I was going to be sticking right by her side.

"I'm good," she said through teeth clamped down so tight the words sounded like the hissing of a snake. I took the hint and backed up a bit. Watching her get into the back seat with the man I couldn't see made my body buzz like an electric current. I got nothing but bad vibes and couldn't do a damn thing about it. I watched helplessly as the car drove off but committed the license plate to memory. If Babydoll didn't come back by tomorrow morning, I was having Adam look up the plates and find out who it was registered to.

It's a shame, I didn't have to wait until the next morning to find Babydoll because the eleven o'clock news had her face plastered on it.

———

Y□□□□ □□□□□□ □□□ □□ F□□□□ D□□□ □□ S□□□ **Alley as District Attorney.**

Those were the words on the bottom of the television

screen. I was in so much shock that I couldn't even make out the words the reporter was saying. I watched the scene unfold on the television; they showed the alley I'd just been earlier in the day and on the ground was a white sheet covering what I could only assume was her body.

Hot tears slid down my face, and I used my balled-up fists to wipe my eyes. If the person who killed the cops killed Babydoll, they were going to have to personally deal with me. I know it was a cliché, but this time it was personal.

I walked like a zombie to my closet and pulled out a pair of shorts that I wore with tights last Halloween dressed as a Soul Train dancer. I carefully made up my face, spritzed on some rosewater perfume, and strapped a sheathed knife to my upper thigh. Mama was going hunting tonight.

———

T□□ □□□□ □□□ □□□ □□□□ □□□ □ □□□□□ □□□□□□□□□ all that remained was the yellow police tape. It still didn't stop the johns and the ladies from doing their business. I craned my neck towards the alley seeing if I could get a glimpse of Babydoll's spirit, but I didn't see a thing.

Seemed like maybe she wanted to move on. I was happy her soul was at rest, but I selfishly wanted to see her one last time. When I turned back towards the street, my eyes fell on a woman about a half a foot taller than me as well as a whole two feet wider. She looked me up and down and then sneered as if what she saw was lacking.

"You new?" she spat at me. I didn't know whether it was a question or a statement, so I just nodded. "Yeah, you look like it. You smell too clean, and you look too eager. Ain't gonna be nobody but the desperate and the depraved out tonight. The cops and the reporters spooked all the regular guys away. Watch out for yourself."

Before I could come up with a response, she swaggered away and melted into the scenery. I took my hands to my hair and pulled it in different directions giving myself a roughed-up look. I didn't want to look like I was an easy mark. I sauntered up and down the street a bit, hoping I wouldn't make any enemies by taking some of the regular girls' customers.

It didn't take long for what I wanted to show up. Criminals are dumb. They always return to the scene of the crime. I don't know why they do, mainly for bragging rights, I guess, but it was a damn risky thing to do. The black car from this morning slowly circled the block. Just when I thought it had disappeared, I saw it round the corner again.

I stepped out from the shadows and made myself seen. I was hoping that pock face had a need for another girl. Hopefully, they didn't just have a taste for young flesh. I was pushing forty, but on a good day could pass for twenty-nine. My legs were good, my ass was round, and my tits hadn't succumbed to gravity. The car stopped in front of me, and the window rolled down.

"You looking for some fun," I sang out to pock face. He looked me up and down like a slave on the auction block, and I held in a shudder as he appraised me from head to toe.

"Yeah, sure am," he said. I leaned into the open window and saw that his partner that rode shotgun was missing, but the man in the back was there.

"Sure am," I repeated.

I grabbed the door handle, but before I could open it a hand touched mine. The hand was cold, dead cold. I turned to see a woman behind me. She was about my height with a mahogany complexion, and her hair was in a roller set shag reminiscent of Claire on the Cosby show. In her ear, the other orange hoop.

"I'll take it from here, sugar," she said in a Southern drawl that I couldn't place. She could have been from anywhere South of the Mason Dixon line.

"Can we talk?" I asked.

"Yeah, y'all fight over who gets to come with us," the driver called out.

She blew him a kiss and then took my elbow in her hand and guided me closer to the alley. "You don't want none of that, sugar. They're into that kinky shit, and they don't believe in safe words," she said in a low voice.

"I think they killed my friend," I said as I ran my hands up and down my bare arms that were now shivering in the frigid air.

"Which is why you need to let me go with them and you stay here." She kept the car in her eyesight, and I looked over at where it idled.

"Your earring?" I asked.

"You got the other one, right?" she countered.

"Ghost?"

She chuckled, and the breath she expelled was icier than the night air. "Something like that," she said with a grin. "Let's just say I'm a worker of justice. Much like you, Maisha. You gone on home. I'll take care of everything."

I wanted to protest but knew that she could give these bastards a better home going than I could with my knife. Plus, it'd be two on one. Not exactly a fair fight for me, but a spirit, well now that would even up the odds a bit.

"Make it hurt," I said and then walked away.

"Oh, I will," I heard her say in the distance.

———

M□□□□ □□□□□ □□□□□ □□ U□□□□ N□□□□-W□□□ Home. Body of Missing Woman, Justice Hawkins, Missing since 1987 Found in Basement.

This time I watched the chyron on the screen and smiled. The picture of the missing woman was the spitting image of the woman I'd met the night before with the icy breath and the Southern drawl. She wore a smile as big as the sun and as bright as the highlighter orange hoops in her ears.

"Hot damn!" I exclaimed waking up my cat at the foot of the bed as well as Adam who was sound asleep on my right side.

"What happened?" he asked as he sprang up from his pillow.

"Justice happened," I said as I laid my head on his chest. I used the remote to turn off the news and then threw it off his side of the bed. "Sweet Justice."

T□□ E□□

ABOUT THE AUTHORS

IN ORDER OF APPEARANCE

Crystal Connor lives in Seattle where she operate her business, Seattle Crystal Concierge. She's a member of the Dark Fiction Guild, and belongs to both the Authors Anonymous and The Seattle Women's writing groups and she's also an active member of The Critters Workshop. The Darkness, is her first full-length novel. It is published by Bennett and Hastings. Her current projects, "...And They All Lived Happily Ever After" and "Artificial Light," the sequel to The Darkness will be released in 2011.

Mina Polina is an author of horror and speculative fiction.

Nuzo Onoh is a British writer of African heritage. Born in Enugu, in the Eastern part of Nigeria (formerly known as The Republic of Biafra), Nuzo has been championing the horror subgenre, African Horror, and has featured on multiple media platforms promoting this unique horror subgenre. She is the first African Horror writer to have featured on Starburst Magazine, the world's longest-running magazine of cult entertainment and science fiction. Nuzo holds a Law Degree and *a Masters Degree in Writing from Warwick University, (England). A keen musician, she plays both the piano and guitar and enjoys writing songs in her spare time when not listening to her playlist of Jazz, Bossa Nova, Soul & Swing. Her book, The Reluctant Dead (2014), introduced modern African Horror into the mainstream Horror genre. Her other books include Unhallowed Graves (2015), The Sleepless (2016) and Dead Corpse (2017). Nuzo lives in West Midlands, England.*

Valjeanne Je☐ers is one of the screenwriters of 7Magpies, a black horror anthology film (in production). She is the author of the Immortal series; The Switch II: Clockwork (includes books I and II); Mona Livelong: Paranormal Detective; and Colony Ascension: An Erotic Space Opera. She was included in 60 Years of Black Women in Horror Fiction. Her writing has also appeared in numerous anthologies including: The City; Steamfunk!; Griots: A Sword and Soul Anthology; PurpleMag; Genesis Science Fiction Magazine; Pembroke Magazine; Possibilities; 31 Days of Steamy Mocha; Griots II: Sisters of the Spear; Drumvoices Revue; Say It Loud: Poems About James Brown; The Ringing Ear: Black Poets Lean South; Liberated Muse: How I Freed My Soul Volume I (also under Valijeanne Je☐ers and Valjeanne Je☐ers-Thompson); and Genesis: An Anthology of Black Science Fiction Volumes I and II. Valjeanne is co-owner of Q & V A☐ordable Editing. Contact her at: www.vje☐ersandqveal.com or sister24moon@gmail.com

Delizhia Jenkins-*I first discovered my love of writing in the third grade, after having to transition to a life living with my grandmother while my mother completed her time in the military. By the end of my fifth- grade year I spent quite a few of my days writing short stories, but never contemplating the idea of becoming a writer. Fast forward to* adulthood, after a series of ups and downs, the desire at Last in 2013. After that, the invisible and incessant Muse kept me awake many a night, propelling me to write my first science fiction fantasy novel, Nubia Rising: The Awakening. And in 2014 I self- published both Love at Last and Nubia Rising: The Awakening. Since then, I have published several additional books: Viper the Vampire Assassin, Sin: Daughter of the Grim Reaper, and Blind Salvation; The Vampire Hunters Academy series, and just recently Into the Shadows.

I currently reside in Southern California with my awesome eleven-year old working on my next line of books.

Sumiko Saulson *is a science-fiction, fantasy and horror writer and graphic novelist. She was the 2016 recipient of the Horror Writer Association's Scholarship from Hell. Her works include the reference guide* 60 Black Women in Horror Fiction, *novels include* Solitude, The Moon Cried Blood, Happiness and Other Diseases, Somnalia, Insatiable *and the Amazon bestselling horror comedy* Warmth. *She has written several short stories for several anthologies, including* Forever Vacancy, Babes and Beasts, Tales from the Lake 3, Clockwork Wonderland, *and* Carry the Light 5 *where she won second place for the science-fiction short story* "Agrippa"; *She writes for* Search Magazine, *and SumikoSaulson.com. The child of African American and Russian-Jewish American parents, she is a native Californian who grew up in Los Angeles and Hawaii. She is an Oakland resident who has spent most of her adult life in the San Francisco Bay Area.*

LH Moore has been published in both fiction and nonfiction publications such as FIYAH Magazine, the upcoming Chiral Mad 4 anthology; Sycorax's Daughters; the Dark Dreams anthology series (Dark Dreams, Voices from the Other Side, and Whispers in the Night); and the African-American National Biography series published by Harvard/Oxford U.

Press. Her poem "Vox" was published in the April 2017 issue of Apex Magazine.IMG_20170630_231902_684. Also an exhibited fiber artist, her art quilt pieces have been seen in galleries and museums across the country. In addition to the textile arts, she is also skilled in watercolor, pencil, and charcoal.

Moore is a historian with a BA in History and Journalism from The George Washington University and a MA in Historic Preservation from Goucher College. She loves history, genealogy, classical guitar, travel, art, architecture, and technology. An avid gamer, you can follow her PS4 craziness on Twitch.

Kenya Moss-Dyme began writing short-form horror in her teens and won several scholastic writing awards for her creative work. Prey for Me - the hard-hitting story of a monstrous child-abusing preacher - was her first published work in early 2014, followed by the Amazon best-selling dark romance, A Good Wife. She has since firmly established her place in the horror genre with the Halloween 2014 release of Daymares, as well as appearances in anthologies and publications.

"The only genres in which I don't feel comfortable writing are comedy and romance. Whenever I try to write a romantic story, it ends up turning dark and the couple will go from taking marriage vows to going on a crime spree! So I tend to stay away from those genres altogether."

USA® Today Bestselling Author Lori Titus is a Californian with an a□nity for speculative fiction. Her work explores mysticism and reality, treading the blurred line between man and monster. She thrives on co□ee and daydreams when she isn't writing or plotting out her next story. Paranormal/Urban Fantasy: The Marradith Ryder Series (Books 1 and 2), and three novellas in the same world: The Culling, Marradith, Darkly, and The Moon Goddess. Horror: The Vampire Diaries (Bennett Witch Chronicles)-- Chrysalis Lights, Blood Relations, The Bell House, Lazarus, and Hailey's Shadow. Post-Apocalyptic: Two books with co-author Crystal Connor under the pen-name Connor Titus: The Guardians of Man and The End is Now.

Kai Leakes- *Dear reader, wish to know about speculative fiction author Kai Leakes? Well, keep all eyes on your surroundings or you might find yourself swallowed by the dark or embraced by loves light. Hailing from the Midwest, St. Louis, Missouri to be exact, author Kai Leakes has had an imaginative mind since childhood. Her world-building gift has led her to dip into her love of romance, and fantasy. It was her love for all-things vampires that also led to honing her pen on dark fantasy and horror in the form of her popular series 'Sin Eaters: Devotion Books 1-2 & Sin Eater Chronicles novellas (Rebel Guardians).'*

Having the goal of adding color to a gray literary world. Kai's unique passion for romance with a touch of darkness has allowed her to be featured in the horror anthology Sycorax's Daughters, and sci-fi anthology The City. So, with fantasy and romance always on her mind, watch out for the darkness and magic that always follows.

Still curious to learn more about author Kai Leakes? Or wish to reach out? Visit her website at: www.kwhp5f.wix.com/kai-leakes *"The Light Always Prevails." - Kai Leakes.*

Dicey Grenor is an African American wife, mother, attorney, and author of racy fiction. She enjoys being analytical and thinking outside-the- box in professional and creative contexts. Before following her passion and writing fiction, she earned a Bachelor of Science, Master of Public Administration, and Juris Doctor degree. In 2011, Dicey published her first novel, which set the tone for her brand of sexy, wild, daring, and risky stories. Fascinated by supernatural creatures and the dark side, Dicey also published Vol. 1 of The Narcoleptic Vampire Series, in 2011. There are currently seven books in this erotic urban fantasy/ horror series, which brings her total to ten self-published books. Dicey is proud of writing multi-cultural characters and mixing genres. As a proponent for diversity and inclusion, Dicey also created and moderated the Multiculturalism and Diversity in Sci-Fi, Fantasy, and Horror literary panel a Comicpalooza: The Texas International Comic Con, in 2014-2017.

When she's not writing multilayered characters in intense, unpredictable plots, Dicey enjoys working out, watching TV/movies, reading, and attending comic cons, porn conventions, and rock concerts. Though her residence is Houston, Texas, Dicey enjoys interacting with people from across the world via social media and traveling.

R. J. Joseph is a Texas based writer and professor who must exorcise the demons of her imagination so they don't haunt her being. A life long horror fan and writer of many things, she has recently discovered the joys of writing in the academic arena about two important aspects of her life: horror and black femininity. When R. J. isn't writing, teaching, or reading voraciously, she can usually be found wrangling one of various sprouts or sproutlings from her blended family of 11...along with one husband and two furry babies.

Kamika Azziza is the published author of such works as *The adventures of Kam Kam and League of Maroons,* but this time her young protagonist is taken out of the fantasy adventure and thrown into a grim world of horror. Growing up as a Jamaican girl with a love for fantasy, sci-fi, Kamika felt like the odd girl out and worked hard to find peers with similar interests until moving to the United States and finding clubs to join and meeting friends with similar tastes. With a unique fascination in the macabre she channeled that love of adventure and drama into her writing creating a bleak and unforgiving world beset upon by the undead.

Cinsearae S. is Editor/Publisher of award-winning Dark Gothic Resurrected Magazine--a top ten finalist in the Preditors & Editors Readers Poll for 2008 and 2009. She also received the Author's Site of Excellence Award in December 2007 from P & E, and is a Cover Artist for Damnation Books.

Born in South Florida, **Tabitha Thompson** always had a love for writing stories and at 16, she began writing horror and hasn't stopped since. Her first short story Heading West, was picked up by Sirens Call Publications in 2013 for their online magazine issue #12 Dead and Dying. West Nile was released in 2014 also with Sirens Call Publications for their issue #16 Apocalyptic Fiction. For the past few years since then, she has released several horror short stories and flash fiction. Her latest release, Decency Defiled, a workplace-based horror short story, was released through J Ellington Ashton Press as her first featured anthology *Titled Rejected For Content 6: Workplace Relations*. As long as she has co□ee, metal, a pencil, and paper, there will always be some new stories to tell.

Nicole Givens Kurtz writes science fiction, fantasy, and horror. Her most popular work, futuristic pulp series, Cybil Lewis blends whodunit mysteries within futuristic, post-apocalyptic world-building. Her novels have been named as finalists in the Fresh Voices in Science Fiction, EPPIE in Science Fiction, and Dream Realm Awards in science fiction. Nicole's short stories have earned an Honorable Mention in L. Ron Hubbard's Writers of the Future contest, and have appeared in such noted publications as Crossed Genres, Tales of the Talisman, and Genesis Magazine as well as numerous anthologies.

Alledria Hurt- I have been writing for a long time. I was born in the 80's. I effectively started writing longform fiction in the 90's. I wrote my first full length novel in 2005 and published (self-published) my first short story collection, Objects: Stories of Things in 2014. My first novel, Chains of Fate, came out in June 2015, followed in close succession by Dark King Rising (Dec. 2015) and Wearing His Ring (Feb. 2016). There is also the short story, October Sky (Dec. 2015), the story of an alchemy student who saves the world. The worlds of Chains of Fate and Wearing His Ring have spawned series which remain unfinished. Working on that.

In between working on various books, I have also participated in 48 Hour Film Project a couple of times, written plays for 24 Hour Playfest, completed NaNoWriMo on a number of occasions, and acted in various stage and film productions.

Kenesha Williams is an independent author, speaker, and Founder/Editor-in-Chief of Black Girl Magic Lit Mag. She took to heart the advice, "If you don't see a clear path for what you want, sometimes you have to make it yourself," and created a Speculative Fiction Literary Magazine featuring characters that were representative of herself and other women she identified with. She has happily parlayed her love for the weird and the macabre into Black Girl Magic Literary Magazine, finding the best in undiscovered talent in Speculative Fiction. Her own works spans many genres from mystery to romance, but always with a dark twist. When she has free time, she spends it reading, writing, or using all her iPhone memory listening to a million podcasts. She currently lives in the DC Metro Area with her husband

THANK YOU!

Thank you for purchasing a Mocha Memoirs Press, LLC title.
Please check our other selections of horror.

Visit our website at
http://mochamemoirspress.com.

CPSIA information can be obtained
at www.ICGtesting.com
Printed in the USA
BVHW03s1709110718
521388BV00004B/130/P